J.MICH...

RIS...

C000218202

"Energy. Earth. Air. Water. Fire," I explained. "We had control over all the things anyone would need to build a perfect world. The power was conscious. The power was directed. The power had a purpose. I know that. I can feel it inside me now. That's why each of us gets stronger when one of us dies. Because the job before us would become harder as there are fewer of us to deal with it. The job is still there, waiting to be done. We have the power. We have the obligation. We should do it now, while we still can."

I paused, waiting. Hoping for a reaction. They all just stared at me as if I'd decided that, from now on, all Specials had to wear their underwear on the outside of their trousers.

Finally, Jerry Montrose asked the question they all must have been thinking: "Do what?"

"Change the world."

J. MICHAEL STRACZYNSKI'S
RISING STARS™

Book 2: TEN YEARS AFTER

ARTHUR BYRON COVER

BASED ON THE SERIES WRITTEN AND CREATED BY
J. MICHAEL STRACZYNSKI

ibooks
new york
www.ibooks.net

DISTRIBUTED BY SIMON & SCHUSTER, INC.

An Original Publication of ibooks, inc.

An ibooks, inc. Book

ibooks, inc.
24 West 25ᵗʰ Street
New York, NY 10010

The ibooks World Wide Web Site Address is:
http://www.ibooks.net

ISBN 0-7434-5276-3
First ibooks, inc. printing December 2002
10 9 8 7 6 5 4 3 2 1

Edited by Karen Haber

Special thanks to Matt Hawkins,
David Wohl, and Frank Mastromauro

Cover art by Christian Zanier
Cover design by Mike Rivilis

Printed in the U.S.A.

ACKNOWLEDGMENTS

I want to once again thank every person and institution I acknowledged in Volume 1: J. Michael Straczynski, the creator of *Rising Stars,* Harlan Ellison, Byron Preiss, Steve Roman, Susan Ellison, Kathryn Drennan, Richard McEnroe, Jonathan Matson, my beloved wife Lydia, and all my friends and acquaintances from the Dangerous Visions Bookstore. And I'd like to add my dogs and cats too; they were jealous last time.

But a double measure of thanks goes to Karen Haber, for keeping me honest.

PART ONE

FIRST ANNIVERSARY

The CNN building was still undergoing reconstruction when I arrived. The armed guard at the surveillance station in the lobby looked surprised to see me. Not that I could blame her. Not a single camera had picked me up on my way in. She was seeing me for the first time.

She scowled and her hand twitched: she was thinking about going for her gun. Not that I blamed her. Atlanta mundanes—or "normals," as they preferred to call themselves—were still smarting over the demolition derby the Specials had performed exactly one year ago. The CNN studios had been especially hard hit. Lives had been lost. Lost accidentally, purely as a by-product of the temporary madness that had gripped a small percentage of the Specials as a direct result of the Surge, but the lack of personal malice didn't change the facts, and made it no easier for the survivors to bear.

I looked the guard in the eye. "I had nothing to do with what happened last year. If I'd known about it in time, I would have stopped it." Of course, the authorities happened to be nagging me at the time, a further distraction, but I'd found mundanes preferred having their rites of sympathy be performed with as little political equivocation as possible.

She nodded. Her eyes ping-ponged between me and the screens. Far as the electronic pictures were concerned, I was still invisible. The guard was a broad, heavyset black woman; the sleeves of her uniform were rolled up— probably not a regulation fashion statement, but it did expose lean, muscular arms. I got the feeling, given half a chance, she could paint a happy face in the middle of my forehead with the bullets from that gun her fingers were twitching over.

"My name is John Simon," I began.

"I know who you are."

Lots of people did, for all the good it did me or them. "I'm a guest on *Crosshairs* today. Could you tell Bill Myers I'm here?"

"Nobody told me they'd invited a Special today."

I shrugged. "They've been promoting it all day."

Her fingers relaxed. "Oh. Did you say Bill Myers?" She delivered the message via the portable microphone she had camouflaged in her hair. "He's coming."

I smiled. "Wait here?"

"Yeah."

An awkward silence passed between us, during which she regarded me severely. "I've never seen a Special in person before. My family and I hid in a storm cellar till all the excitement was over."

"I'm sorry your family had to go through that. I wish things had been different."

"What would you have done? Read 'em a poem?"

"I've closed down a lot of parties that way. Look, there are a lot of Specials I dislike just as much as you do. I

4

just ask you to judge me by who I am, and not by the actions of some people I might have grown up with, but who—let's face it—I ultimately don't understand any better than you do." While she was still thinking about it, I added, "But do let me apologize for sneaking up on you. I have this weakness for making dramatic entrances."

"You just think they're dramatic. Your apology is accepted."

One of the elevators dilated open, and out stepped a young man wearing a loud plaid suit and a screaming bow tie. He had a freckled face, a buzz cut, and a professional smile. "It's so good to meet you, Mr. Simon. Thank you for coming. My name's Bill Myers."

"I know. I monitor CNN quite frequently."

"You do?" he asked. His eyes brightened and he released my hand as if I'd been an electric eel.

"Of course. I like to know what people are saying about me, and what better source is there than CNN?"

"Oh," he said, having a slight conceptual breakthrough; he relaxed.

"I'm also a political junkie. I do watch your show, all the time. It certainly does live up to its reputation as an antidote to the polite debate that had led our political discourse down the tedious path of somnambulism. Frankly, I find it an honor just to be asked to appear."

"He's lying, Billy," said the guard.

"Shut up, Carol. Lying about what?"

"About it being an honor," I said. "But I do find your show delicious theatre." I pointed to the elevator. "Are we going down?"

"Absolutely. This building's only five stories high. There are offices upstairs, but Time Warner's never going to build another major facility above ground for a long, long time."

"Not until all we Specials are dead, eh?"

He cleared his throat nervously. "I'm afraid not. This way," he said with audible relief, as the elevator opened again. The interior had an imitation stone facade, to complement the medieval castle architectural style of the new CNN HG in general. The new network logo—emblazoned on the control panel, the control buttons, and even on the doors—was that of a hawk carrying a shield in his claws. As we stepped into the studio level, I switched off my ability to confound recording and radar devices and permitted their automatic scans to check me for weapons. I had none, of course. But I could have fooled them into registering a bomb powerful enough to reduce their grand new building to rubble.

"So," I began, "You folks gonna help me sell more books?"

Myers came as close to looking me in the eye as he dared. "We do like to believe we have a literate audience."

The walls in the hallway were genuine stone. The low ceiling and evenly spaced lights brought to mind a bunker, as if the architect was trying to say through his work that this is where civilization as we know it today will make its last stand, if need be. A year ago, that would have been a presumptive, self-important attitude. Today, I had to admit, it could very well be the correct one.

The studio was equipped with the latest generation of sound and lighting equipment. Sleek, maneuverable, and energy efficient. Portraits of reporters from all media who'd given their lives trying to cover the events of the past year in Chicago were always within eyesight—against columns, on bulletin boards, hell, even on the sides of cameras. The crew wore black armbands and had tiny American flags pinned on their shirts.

"Guys. Gals," said Bill, "I want you to meet someone."

The guys and gals had already stopped what they were doing, were already looking at me as if I was wearing a black hood and a death's head grin, and carried a scythe.

Bill cleared his throat. "This is John Simon. He's the Special known as Poet. He's going to be on *Crosshairs* today."

"Good afternoon, people," I said in my most assuring voice. "It is a pleasure to be with you today."

They didn't buy it. Their expressions did not change, their eyes did not deviate from me.

"All right," I said with a heavy sigh, "I want you to consider something. If I was here to kill you, then you would be dead already. *Capice*?"

Bill looked at me if I'd just decapitated someone.

"Pretty funny," said a cameraman.

"He was joking?" said an amazed grip.

"Of course, he was joking," said the girl laying some prompt sheets on the round desk standing on a podium before a huge replica of the familiar *Crosshairs* logo: the CNN hawk busting out of a cardboard box with the letters CH written on it.

"He was trying to," said Judy Wetton, a cheerful, fair-faced Asian whom I recognized as the host of *Argument Live*, a town-meeting program broadcast from a shopping mall.

"Hi, Miss Wetton," I said enthusiastically, shaking her hand—I couldn't help myself, I was a fan. "I watch you almost every day."

"Thank you so very much," she said smoothly. "And I know you too, of course. From your jacket covers. I love your *Children's Book of Rap.* I read it to my son every night. He enjoys it immensely."

"That's so flattering."

"Please, I'm the one who should be grateful to you. My boy is autistic, you see. You don't know what a delight it is to find reading material that doesn't get him upset."

"Nice chatting with you." I turned to Bill. "Can I see a make-up person now?"

"He needs to look good for his public," said another cameraman, with a nice I've-seen-it-all-before tone in his voice.

I pointed to the set. "And could I have one of those pieces of paper?"

Twenty minutes later I found myself sitting at the desk with *CH* cohosts Steve Gamble and Cherry Rutlidge. Cherry was an archetypal fire-breathing, blonde conservative, while Steve was the archetypal tepid, moustached liberal. They sat at the ends of the table. I was on the left inside. Beside me, on the right inside, was none other than my favorite fire-breather—period—Reverend William Kane. We both glared at one another. I'd no idea he was going to be my guest opponent, and I had the distinct feeling he'd not been told about me before consenting to coming on.

The director in the booth gave the cue.

"Welcome to *Crosshairs*, gentlemen," said Cherry. She introduced herself and Steve, then went on to say: "Today is the first anniversary of an event that transformed the political and social landscape surrounding the existence of that select group of humans known as the Specials, an event today known simply as the Surge. I think it's safe to say that even at this early date, the day of the Surge represents a historic turning point that would have consequences as profound as those of the assassination of Archduke Franz Ferdinand, the bombing of Pearl Harbor, and the election of Ronald Reagan. We have two distinguished guests to discuss some of the consequences. Joining us on the left, we have with us the very first Special to appear on *Crosshairs* or any other pundit show, a man whose name will be familiar to those who read poetry in coffee houses across the nation: John Simon."

I nodded. I have to confess, I felt nervous, though I tried not show it. You'd think after someone's tried to kill you, which had happened to me several times, appearing on television wouldn't be such a big deal. But it was for me. I'd spent the morning before my mirror practicing a brooding, sensitive, but hopefully not too threatening look. It reminded me about the old radio story about the time Peter Lorre was supposed to parody himself on *The Spike Jones Show*: He was spotted talking to the comedians who did Peter Lorre impersonations, looking for advice on how to be himself. Before sitting down, I'd decided having my collar which I habitually left upturned on my overcoat would probably too be much, particularly since my black shirt already communicated a certain rebelliousness. This was one public forum where it paid to be presentable.

"And joining us on our right," said Steve, "is a man who has spoken out against the potential danger represented by the Specials, indeed, a man who by his own admission was among those who first brought before members of Congress the charge that a secret sect of Specials was conspiring to take over the Federal Government—"

"A charge that remains unproven," I said.

"I was going to say that," replied Steve, meekly.

"Pardon me, sir," said Reverend Kane imperiously, "I permitted your introduction, with its rather questionable assumptions, to proceed without interruption. You might want to give me the same curt—"

"She didn't say anything about me!" I exclaimed, glaring at Cherry. "Did you two rehearse this? I've always tried to be a peacemaker between Special and mundane. This man is a hatemonger!"

"I am a man of the cloth," replied Kane, coolly.

"And as such should be in mothballs."

"Gentlemen, we have a format here, which must be adhered to," said Steve, slightly more forcefully. Meanwhile, Cherry gazed at Kane with the bright light of approval in her eyes. Or maybe it was the reflection of the kliegs I saw.

Kane signaled his acquiescence with a nod, whereas I simply frowned at him. I noticed his reluctance—or should I say refusal?—to look me in the eye.

"Mr. Simon," said Cherry, "you've gone on record several times declaring Specials have no animosity toward normals, yet among the very first words you said in the studio contained a threat to people who had never harmed you, indeed, people you've never seen before. How do you justify that?"

"He can't," piped in Kane while my mouth was still hanging open.

"They were already afraid of me," I said, "thanks to the hysteria generated in them by our leaders." I nodded at Kane. "So I was just attempting some black humor, trying to put them at ease."

"Really?" said Cherry, raising her eyebrows like a Vulcan who'd just realized it was finally time to mate. "I'd like to hear your reaction to this, Reverend Kane. Bob—roll it!"

I overheard—and so did everyone else, in the studio and in the audience—myself saying earlier: *If I was here to kill you, then you would be dead already.*

I felt as though Jerry Montose—a.k.a. Pyro—had suddenly set my foot on fire.

"That's out of context! And somebody screwed with the sound, making my words and tone sound threatening!" I felt like an idiot, because I could have made it impossible for them to record any part of me. But I'd wanted to let down my guard a little, in the hope that if I trusted in them, however slightly, then they might trust me.

"My turn, John!" said Kane, his voice booming, his tone both enthusiastic and judgmental. "Once again you have inadvertently revealed your contempt for the common man. You ask us to take your word that you shall never use your powers to do harm to a mundane—pardon me, to a normal—and yet you have no problem joking about how easily you could lash out!"

"Is that it, Mr. Simon?" Cherry asked, intensely. "Are you saying you reserve the right to go postal on a whim?"

"I would never do that," I replied indignantly. "My dealings with the Post Office have always been cordial. Besides, anyone who knows me also knows I only use my powers when it was absolutely necessary, and then to save lives, not to do harm to others. And I have always been in complete mental control."

"Isn't that what they said about Stephanie Maas?" asked Steve, clearing his throat. "Wasn't she supposed to once be the very picture of mental health and, for that matter, family values?"

"Stephanie was misdiagnosed!" I said. "If you want to

complain to the right people, you're going to have go back several presidential administrations."

"You Specials have been adults for some time," Kane exclaimed. "And yet you still want the federal Government to subsidize your evil!"

"It still amazes me that after all these years, you persist in the delusion that we are evil. Do you think your own son is evil?"

Kane's reply was as pious as it was immediate. "I have guided him, all these years. I have stifled his temptation."

"Are you trying to tell me," said Steve, pouncing on the opening, "that you are solely responsible for the decency and benevolence we associate with the name Joshua Kane? That his goodness, if you will, is contrary to his true nature?"

"I have fanned a spark into a flame. Trust me, nobody knows my son better than I."

"You do *not* know him!" I exclaimed. "How could you possibly know what it means to be a Special?"

"Once, I confess, I was a sinner, all men are sinners, and thus have I known what it means to have evil in your heart."

"Phooey!"

Cherry covered her mouth so no one would see her smile.

"Furthermore," said Kane, leaning into my face, "don't talk to me about a father and his son. How would you know what we learn about one another through the bond between us? It's common knowledge you don't know who your real father really is!"

Talk about your cheap shots. The essence of what he had said was true, of course, and no surprise to the folks

12

in the audience. Since the Surge, aspects of Specials' personal lives that had formerly been off-limits to reporters were now fodder for every type of news broadcast, talk radio forum, and supermarket rag imaginable. It seems the public had never lost its fascination with the fundamental humanity shared between mundane and Special. "The question is *not* if a father is biological in origin—the question is, is he a good father? There's clearly something the matter with you, Reverend!"

Cherry and Steve looked at the director, a tiny, bowlegged man. He was ecstatic. He smiled at Billy, and Billy smiled at him. Then they both smiled at the hosts. They had a good show. Everybody was happy.

While I was watching them, Kane was haranguing me like the soapbox preacher he was at heart. I must say, the intensity of his verbal attack was stunning. I couldn't help smiling from ear to ear as he damned my soul to perdition, as he accused me of selling out my country, and as he intimated there wasn't a Special on the planet who didn't aspire to be the next Hitler or Stalin, just because it was our nature to be ambitious, greedy, materialistic, all because we were just plain bad. He also questioned the conventional view that I led a monastic existence, which during that period of my life was basically correct, but I have never believed my subsequent lapses constituted falls from grace. Especially a state of grace the good reverend never even pretended to attain.

"Not even your mother knows who your father really is," said Kane, with a distinctly un-Christian lack of charity.

That's when I lost it. That when I showed all the world what it was like when a Special performed the superpowered equivalent of going postal.

It happened in two stages. The first stage was the red hot flash of anger that swept up my face. The second stage lagged approximately two seconds:

The kliegs exploded, the cameras caught on fire, the electrical lines sparked. All at once. Instantly. It was as if I could alter reality with a simple blink.

Bill Myers and the crew reacted by making themselves scarce. The hosts and Reverend Kane ducked under the table like school kids protecting themselves from an atomic bomb blast.

I just sat there and tried to remain oblivious to all the flying glass while I reached under the table and grabbed Kane by the tie, then pulled him toward me until we were practically eye-to-eye. He resolutely kept his arms by his side. I knew he wanted to fight back, to hit me, but he couldn't. For not only was he was a man of peace, a man who gave lip service to the need to turn the other cheek, he was far from suicidal.

"See, people? Do you see?" said Kane, his voice trembling. "The beast within reveals himself."

"Oh, bite me!" I exclaimed, pushing him away.

He struck the floor with a distinct lack of dignity. "Everybody will see!" he said. "It's going to be on tape forever."

"No, it won't," I said. "I've already seen to that." I noticed the hosts peeking out from under the desk, and members of the crew—sans Billy—creeping back into the studio. "I've blocked the broadcast, I've erased the tapes. From now on, what happened here today will be just my word against yours and everybody else's—certainly no different than before."

"And I'll be telling the truth," spat out Kane. "You lost control."

"No, I just got angry for a second. And as for *you* telling the truth, I don't believe you'd know what truth was if it came up and bit you on the–"

A guard stepped up to me. He was a round man with slick black hair. I recognized him. His complexion had been ruddy when I'd walked in. Now it was pale, and beads of sweat poured down his cheeks. "Sir, I think it would be best if you left the premises now."

I looked him in the eye. "Of course, sir, I'd be happy to go on my way."

"You son of a bitch!" said Kane. "I'm going to sue you!"

My involuntary energy waves had somehow missed bursting a klieg directly above the set. It burst now, and Kane hunched over and covered his head with his arms as a thousand tiny pieces of hot glass rained over him. The pieces hit the floor in a single thunderous wave.

Kane remained hunched over and our brave hosts remained clinging to one another below the desk for several long seconds before they all realized the psychic violence was over.

The guard's eyes got wide and his fingers touched the gun in his holster. Evidently these security folks had gotten the delusion the Specials had turned the United States into the Wild West.

I waved a finger at him. "Not a good idea. Don't worry. I'm leaving now."

I'm sure that had it been possible for any camera to pick up my image while I was leaving the CNN headquarters—I flew up the stairs, by the way—I would have been photographed with the proverbial black cloud over my head. So much for turning around the public relation wars on television, at least for the time being.

SECOND
ANNIVERSARY

I spent the second anniversary of the Surge in the arms of an exotic dancer who worked at a gentlemen's club. Actually, that was how she was putting herself through graduate school; she was getting her doctorate in anthropology at Yale, and we had met at a literary event where I was invited to read my work to an audience of intellectuals who took me for a noble savage. She took me for an emotional roller coaster ride, one which I was forced to disembark eventually, but which produced a long-needed and much-yearned-for education. I also got the feeling she had had some experience in avoiding paparazzi, as she'd managed to keep both our names and pictures out of the tabloids, mainstream and otherwise. Since we had promised ourselves a total news blackout during that particular weekend, I had no way of learning about the hostage situation until it was long over.

The entire affair was Special Agent Paulson's idea, of course. During the closed-door Congressional hearings that came later, he testified that he had gotten the idea during a rare afternoon when he was supposed to be relaxing . . .

Paulson always thought it ironic that his brother Pat and his family had moved to Pederson. For it was in Pederson, Illinois that the Big Flash had struck the United States in 1968, setting the stage for the arrival of the Specials.

Pat's wife, Ann, had a well-paying job as a computer programmer, and Pat worked as a security guard. Pat was professionally unambitious, had been all his life. Paulson had to admit, he didn't understand his brother. Whatever amount of good he might accomplish in the world would be strictly limited.

On the other hand, perhaps none of it mattered; Ann made enough money for both of them, and their children would be well provided for in the event of an unfortunate occurrence.

Still, he envied Pat. He and Ann had two kids, a house in the suburbs, with a big backyard and a swimming pool. Pat was drinking a beer from a can that he rested on his burgeoning belly, and Ann was fixing dogs and burgers on the barbecue. The children were playing in the shallow end of the pool. The sun shone brightly, and the skies were clear and refreshingly free of flying persons. Paulson had no doubt the local Specials, who even though they could fly tended to maintain a facade of normalcy, knew he was visiting town, accompanied by a large security force, and were therefore keeping a discreet distance.

Paulson also had no doubt that the local Specials were making sure they all had air-tight alibis for this afternoon, just in case the uneasy peace between Special and normal was broken. Paulson couldn't blame them. He would be doing the same thing if he, instead, lived in a mirror universe where he was a Special. After all, the Surge itself had been caused by the death of several Specials—justified shootings, all—and that in itself provided them with the motivation to target him for revenge.

Truth to tell, many would not have hesitated to kill him, given the first opportunity. Only then, it would have been more difficult to escape the consequences of the law. Now, all one had to do was kill Paulson and then take off for Chicago, where he would no doubt be welcomed as a heroic equal among the ruling class.

For this reason, an enormous military and Secret Service detail accompanied Paulson wherever he went. Right now, the detail was parked outside his brother's home, and had commandeered the neighbors' back yards, just in case one of the fliers decided to zip overhead and drop a bomb in his lap.

It slowly dawned on Paulson that people were talking about him. He shook his head and realized his brother's entire immediate family had gathered round, smiling. "Have you heard a word we were saying?" Ann asked.

Paulson squinted and sipped his beer. "No, guess not."

"You're silly," said the youngest, who put his arm around his uncle's neck.

Paulson grinned. It put a strain on his muscles, but he was surprised at how easy it was. "I suppose I am. What did I miss?"

Ann pointed to the picnic table. Plates were stacked with burgers and dogs, and there were so many condiments and utensils available that there was hardly any room for anyone to eat. The oldest child was swiping a few flies away.

"You first, uncle!" said the oldest.

Paulson offered only token resistance. As he gathered potato salad and buns on his paper plate, it occurred to him he was no more or less safe in Pederson, home of his enemies, than he was anywhere else. And thanks to his security detail, he was a whole lot safer than any other ordinary citizen who might be targeted by one or more Specials.

Even a Special who wanted to live like an ordinary person and have all the things in life ordinary people do.

Things such as a mate, a home, a family.

That was when he got the idea. Specials had families too. Paulson had dealt with them, mostly in an adversarial relationship, all his life.

Then the next link in the syllogism came to him. The answer. The path he must take. A path he must take without Congressional oversight or even that of his superiors in the Bureau.

"Can I have another beer?" he asked.

"What's the matter, brother?" said Pat.

"Do I look like something's the matter?"

"Well, yeah," said his sister-in-law. "You appear almost happy."

Paulson grinned. It was a lot easier this time. "I have an idea. I can't tell you what it is right now, but I'm sure you'll read about it in the papers."

That was as much as he ever said about his plan before he actually began giving the orders that would set it in motion. Looking back on it, he had to admit that perhaps it wasn't one of his most successful notions. The first question he had to answer during his appearance before the Congressional Committee of Justice had to do with his choice of target:

Stephanie Maas, the woman who now called herself Critical Maas.

The woman who had conquered Chicago.

The most unusual thing about Stephanie's birth was that her mother had survived to deliver her.

Stephanie's mother, Molly, had been the wife of a successful businessman in Pederson, Illinois. She was the meek child of local landowners, and her husband loved her, took care of her, but was a philanderer who abused her verbally when he was drunk. Molly was pregnant with Stephanie that night when history changed in 1968.

The night of the Big Flash.

At first it just appeared to be a gigantic comet. A mile-long ball of ice and fire plummeting through the atmosphere. So bright it obliterated the night sky of the entire Western Hemisphere. Its speed was estimated at 200 miles per hour. Its very presence caused at least three thousand fatal heart attacks, in addition to countless automobile accidents, suicides, and sudden proclamations of eternal love. People believed, and quite reasonably considering the visual evidence, that the end of the world was nigh.

The comet should have exploded, leveling trees, crops, and buildings for miles around.

Pederson, in particular, should have been obliterated.

There should have been a crater, a very deep crater, with a diameter of at least fifty miles, where Pederson had been.

There should have been earthquakes. Tidal waves. Enough dust and debris in the sky to create a planet-wide cloud cover lasting for months, if not years—in other words, a rain of death, destruction, and doom of Biblical proportions. The wiping out of the sinful and the virtuous alike. A rapture wherein the chosen were taken into the arm of a God more fierce and savage than any who has ever been imagined. The condition of Europe after World War II would have been a utopia in comparison.

It was very possible, indeed likely that the arrival of the comet could have caused the utter extinction of mankind. Not to mention virtually every other species of plant and animal life on the planet, except maybe the cockroaches. And the creatures that thrived on the very bottom on the ocean, near the openings of volcanoes. A place for evolution to start over.

From scratch.

And yet Molly Maas was alive, alive and healthy so that she was able to give routine birth to a normal child whom she and her husband christened Stephanie.

One hundred and twelve other women were also pregnant at the time. They too, in time, gave birth to normal, healthy children.

Children, doctors and scientists realized in retrospect, who were a little too healthy. Children who rarely got sick and whose bodies recovered quickly from personal injury. Children who never should have existed in the first place, because the comet, if nothing else, should have wiped out their mothers.

As it was, the only impact was that of a blinding flash of light that lasted for about twenty seconds.

And then it was gone.

The night sky had returned.

People had died for nothing, because it seemed that after the big lightshow in the sky, the hullabaloo was over. The panic had been for naught.

Now the question remained: Just what *had* happened that night back in 1968? Had the present somehow bled over into the future or the past? Had this universe's continuum come into contact with another dimension? Was reality itself in danger of collapsing? In the final analysis, the only answers to these questions were metaphysical, as the universe and the space-time continuum both proved to be reticent about providing further information.

The event came to be popularly known as the Big Flash. The social ripples that could be traced back to the event were rather profound. Middle class America embraced the counter-culture with a renewed interest, and the generation that was born in the aftermath of World War II suddenly experimented quite openly with mind-altering drugs, sexual freedom, and alternative ways of thinking. Social and environmental activism increased. Experimental life styles became commonplace.

But for the folks in towns such as Pederson, in the heart of Middle America, the Big Flash might as well have not happened in the first place, for all the ripple effects to be found.

Stephanie Maas and 112 others were born and raised as if they were normal children, and for the first six years of their lives, nobody ever had any reason to think otherwise.

Then came the first grade photo shot, the rainstorm, and the collapsed roof. An event which should have been a local disaster, with an estimated sixty-five children and adults injured—and no telling how many might have died.

Only the unlikely—indeed, the unprecedented intervention of Matthew Bright averted the disaster.

The fact that he averted the disaster by catching and holding the detached section of roof was what made the event unprecedented. The fact that he held it as easily as a beach bum clutched his surfboard was what made it unbelievable.

A photographer's picture of the event triggered a worldwide sensation.

It was like switching on an electric current. Right after that, children—in Pederson and the surrounding area—began manifesting special powers: flying, lifting weights, walking through walls, or reading minds. Some had extremely specialized abilities; others were more generalized. Some had their powers switched on right away, and in others the switching was delayed, sometimes for as brief a time as a few hours, and in other cases, for several years.

Naturally the Federal Government, in this case spearheaded by Special Agent Paulson of the FBI, took an interest. A compulsory research program was introduced on the kids, and the statisticians quickly noticed a correlation between the time they were born and the Big Flash. That correlation being simply that the children had all been conceived, yet unborn at the time of the Big Flash. All their mothers had happened to be within a certain radius of Ground Zero.

Elsewhere, an Arizona child on a trip through the zoo began imitating the great apes and the chimps with remarkable fidelity whenever he was within a certain range, and another child, from North Dakota, became hirsute and began running about the fields on all fours. A third child, an American whose mother was ambassador to Nigeria, kept losing himself in a dimension where he no longer existed, only to eventually wander back into his own continuum again. It was quickly determined that the mothers of all these children had been within the Pederson radius at the time of the Big Flash.

23

Since there was obviously no fixed time-limit for the abilities to manifest themselves, Paulson got the politicians and bureaucrats to brand as Special any child who happened to be within the womb at the time his or her mother was within the Pederson radius. Paulson preferred the term "mutant" or at best "aberration," but bitter experience had taught him that tilting at cultural windmills was a fool's game.

Molly Maas was one of those mothers, and hence Stephanie, although she'd never given evidence of possessing extraordinary ability, was yanked into the same educational track as the other Special kids. That track wasn't exactly voluntary, even for someone as meek and mild as Stephanie, who through the entire term of her government supervision—indeed, for many years after her emancipation—gave no indication she had the power to perform any action beyond the ordinary.

Of course, if the doctors and scientists and reporters and academics had known that Stephanie's father molested her in ways unfathomable to any individual whose sexual predilections centered on individuals past the age of puberty, they might have taken a closer look at Stephanie. They might even have hypnotized her, and thereby discovered something that would have given them pause, a clue that within the meek, mild, mousy Stephanie Maas, there dwelled the most deviant, psychotic Special of them all.

Even before the Surge, Specials started turning up dead, with the result that each surviving Special's powers increased a notch with each death. The more dead Specials there were, the more difficult things became for Stephanie. It turned out that hers wasn't the only personality lurking in her fevered skull. The other personality belonged to a profoundly powerful high threshold Special who called herself "Critical Maas." CM's impulse control ranged from zero to non-existent, and since the Surge she had ruled Chicago with a whim of iron.

Meaning that her slightest, most capricious impulse immediately took on the effect of law.

Until, of course, she changed her mind.

Critical Maas flew above Wrigley Field and waved her torch high. Louise Schroeder, a Special who'd become a rather accomplished firestarter as a result of the Surge, kept the torch light blazing from afar. The light was a cool green. It swept over the ratty baseball field like gauze. The scoreboard cued the people to applaud and cheer, but today they were a little slow on the uptake. CM didn't mind. The show would have them going soon enough.

The torch itself was part of a statue's arm. Once the arm had been attached to the Statue of Liberty. While on a quick out-of-town sojourn, CM's right-hand gal, Deedee Noonan, had torn it off and teleported it to CM as an anniversary gift. A touching gesture, in CM's view.

She switched on her mike and heard a half-second delay in the echoes of her words as she said in a joyous spirit, "People of Chicago—thank you, thank you, thank you for coming out today. Welcome. Today is my birthday, and today is the day we'll get to ring in the new by ringing out some of the old, if you catch my meaning. I don't know what's going to happen today, but I can tell you this: there's going to be a lot of opportunity for advancement for those of you in government work. You'll have the chance to meet some folks who've displeased me at some point during the past year. I'll be straight with

25

you—some of these folks are going to die. But think of this as a good thing, because just as many will have a second chance with me. The chance to live another year. Of course, for a few folks this is a third or fourth chance, but the rules are the rules. And you know what Tina Turner used to say, eh? *Break a deal—face the wheel!* Am I right?"

The sign cued applause. The response was tepid, at best.

"A lot of folks seem to vbe vying for an opportunity to compete next year?" CM said, a sly note creeping into her voice.

The applause became noticeably more enthusiastic.

"Better! Now let me provide you with incentive." And CM hurled the torch toward the grass.

Toward the bleachers.

The audience barely had time to scatter before the torch hit, right smack in front of the bleachers. A few people were grazed by sparks and splinters, but none of the injuries were serious.

"Let me hear that taste for blood!" CM commanded, knowing she would be obeyed.

This time the people did not disappoint her.

A satisfied CM flew to her open-air box seat, shouted the words "Let the games begin!" and dropped down on her luxurious divan. "Beulla, peel me a grape," she said to a servant standing nearby.

"Okay," said the girl, a teen-aged blonde of limited intelligence. With trembling fingers she began doing exactly as she was asked.

"Oh, for God's sake." CM threw the nearest thing—an ashtray—at the girl.

It glanced off the girl's head. She fell down smack on her rear, more startled and afraid than hurt. She was on the verge of tears. "I'm sorry! Did I do that wrong?"

"Yes, dear. Now get the freel out of my sight."

The girl crawled off. CM turned her attention to something infinitely more important: the first contest, currently being announced sans electronic assistance by Bombast, who could control sound waves. He was a pedophile, possessed by a sexual desire beyond CM's ability to empathize with, but who was she to judge?

Coming out on center field was former stock analyst Roger Meredith, armed with a sword, a shield, and a can of Mace. And perhaps with his wits, but if CM knew Roger—and she did, because he had formerly worked for one of Stephanie and Ric's accountants—then instead of spending last night praying for a miracle or for victory, whichever worked best, he'd prepared by drinking himself into a drunken stupor. Well, on consideration, perhaps not even Roger was that stupid. Getting into a drunken stupor was what he'd done the night *before* he was sentenced on embezzlement charges, and he'd stood before the judge pasty-eyed and weak-kneed, about to barf any second, with cocaine in his cigarette case.

And standing at home plate: Joe Bond, State Senator, millionaire, Desert Storm veteran. His political career had been on a rocket trajectory before the takeover, but now he was a humble hydroponics farmer in one of the underground gardens the Specials had built for the feeding of the populace. He wasn't much of a specimen, physically, and was only here because he'd volunteered to take the place of his teen-aged son. But CM had hopes the opponents would be evenly matched because, in addition to his weaponry of trident, net, and state-of-the-art Swiss Army Knife, Joe was a truly ruthless cheater, easily capable of coming up with a killer strategy. Roger had better watch himself.

As they advanced warily upon the field, CM snapped her fingers, and five young men immediately burst through the curtain behind her and flocked about her like a swarm of carnivorous pigeons. Her cell phone rang, and one of them picked it up before she had an opportunity to threaten him with the most personal dismemberment possible if anyone permitted an interruption. She did make a note of his face, though, as she took the call.

It was Nick Peel. Since the Surge, his mind was capable of directly picking up radio frequencies; unfortunately he had no control over the ability and could no more switch it off than you or I can control our breathing. The lack of control had driven him insane. He lived in an abandoned gated community and only communicated with CM or her major minions when it was absolutely necessary.

CM listened to what he had to say. "Interesting. Thanks."

She hung up and returned her attention to the spectacle. Joe had stabbed Roger in the ankle, pinning him to the Astroturf. Roger was currently using his shield to fend off Joe's Swiss Army Knife. CM felt smugly satisfied that her assessment of the battle potential had been confirmed by events, but she found she couldn't keep her mind on the game. Indeed, her mind wandered so far off into never-never land that she paid no attention to Joe's vicious *coup de grace*.

"Damn," she said aloud. "I have to get someone to watch my back."

Ric Maas, estranged husband of Stephanie Maas, had a lot of reasons to be angry with the world. First, his wife had deserted him, and she had no problem dissing him in the most intimate detail with the slightest provocation, in whatever public forum she deemed appropriate at the moment.

Second, automobile sales at his dealership had plummeted with all the speed of the Big Flash, but none of the grandeur. Thanks to his association with Stephanie, he was known through the town—hell, throughout the *world*, as a man so stupid that he'd lived with a woman for ten years and never noticed that deep down inside, she was a total psycho, sicker and more twisted than Hitler and Stalin could ever dream of being.

Third, it was very difficult to get a second date after a woman discovered he'd been intimately involved with such evil. Surely some of it must have rubbed off on him.

Fourth, his children detested him, because they'd seen how he'd treated their mother before she'd embraced the dark side. The brats actually believed those damn *Star Wars* movies had given them clues to her motivation.

Fifth, such was his naivete that he actually believed his government always tried to do the right thing and uphold his Constitutional rights.

"Why are you doing this to me?" Ric asked of his captor.

Paulson looked up from the magazine he had been reading. They were the only two people in the kitchen, and only Paulson had freedom of movement. Ric was tied to one of his own kitchen chairs, and so was stuck at the kitchen table. His hands were bound on his lap, and his legs were tied to those of the chair.

This was the part of an operation Paulson always found the most frustrating: the waiting. He sighed, silently debating whether or not it would be worth his while to converse with this Maas fellow. He decided it would help pass the time. "Spoken like a genuine pawn," he said.

Ric looked as if his face had been doused with cold water. "I am not a pawn—I am a free man, with—!"

Paulson held up his hand. "Please. You are a prisoner in your own kitchen."

"Well, yeah. Where are my children?"

"Safe."

"Safe where?"

"Outside, under heavy guard. Don't worry. They are not the bait. You are." Paulson took out his pipe and stirred up the tobacco by tapping the bowl on the edge of the tabletop.

"Don't smoke in here," said Ric Maas coldly.

Paulson looked at the man in surprise and laughed.

The kitchen was airy, with blue walls and white curtains and a wide gas stove in the middle of the layout. A few toys were scattered on the floor, and the lunchboxes stood on the counter. It gave Paulson a good feeling.

"I can't afford to be sentimental, Maas," he said, lighting his pipe. "I've been entrusted with protecting the greater good of the nation and her citizenry. I have been entrusted with a certain degree of autonomy. After all—and I believe I may say this with but a slight touch of hubris—the path of history will depend on how I cope with the Special crisis."

"You don't actually believe that, do you?" said Ric with a sneer. "Everything you have ever done up to now has only made the situation worse. Sure, I may have been a little tough on Stephanie occasionally, but she was at heart a nice girl, and she would have stayed that way if you hadn't decided she was a traitor."

"She became that way because of the Surge. It would

have happened whether or not we'd included her in the round up."

"The Surge wouldn't have happened if you'd left well enough alone!" Ric was getting red in the face.

Paulson sadly shook his head. "You don't get it, do you? We are at war—an undeclared war against a clearly defined enemy. We have the right—*I have the right*—to use the weapons of an undeclared war."

"All this time I thought you were just a vigilante."

"You weary me," said Paulson with a sigh. "My mistake. I could have chosen either one of Stephanie Maas' parents, but I know the woman who is Critical Maas wouldn't lift a finger to save them. No, the only way to draw Ms. Maas out of Chicago is to use you. And the best way to use you is to flagrantly violate your civil rights. Who knows? There might be a firing squad in your near future."

Ric couldn't help laughing. "She hates me, you moron!"

"Stephanie loved you, and some part of Stephanie must remain inside her." Paulson tapped his temple as he spoke. "I leaked the story of our little get-together to the national media. She's bound to find out."

"She won't risk it!"

Paulson shrugged. "If not for you, then she will come out for the sake of her children."

Ric's spirit deflated at that point, and he began to cry. "Not the children . . . you fool . . ."

Paulson felt the blood drain from his face. "What do you mean—fool?"

"Don't you read your staff's own psyche evaluations? Critical Maas always does the opposite of what you expect. Just to spite you. And she doesn't care who she hurts."

That's when the shouting outside started. Paulson went to the window just in time to see two Specials carrying a diesel truck in the air.

They dropped it directly on top of an armored car parked at an intersection on the other end of the block—the car which he'd ordered the children be held in for the duration of the operation.

The noise generated by the impact was deafening. One side of the armored car was crushed, and the truck broke apart over it like a piece of bamboo. Metal shards buoyed by a gasoline tidal wave sprayed out like buckshot. Everyone was doused. Those who had been unable to find cover—to duck behind a parked car or tank—were invariably cut down, generally the same instant they were caught beneath the gasoline.

Those who'd managed to escape the radius of the shards and gas waited until they could be certain this foray, at least, was over. Then, upon the order of someone Paulson couldn't see, they hurried to the dead and wounded to administer first aid, and protect.

Meanwhile, Critical Maas hovered above her home-made ground zero. The Special Paulson recognized as Deedee Noonan tossed something to her.

"Oh, my God!" Paulson screamed into his handheld. "Get them out! Get out now!"

"You idiot, you stupid idiot," said Ric, his voice filled with both hatred and fear. He could not see what had happened, but he knew it was terribly, terribly wrong.

Meanwhile, Critical Maas switched on the flame thrower. The fire began at the top of the armored car wreckage, then spread out in an even circle as if it had been set on a match on a dessert served in a fancy restaurant.

Paulson backed away from the window.

"What is it?" Ric demanded. "What happened?"

Paulson found it difficult to catch his breath. Finally he was able to speak: "Sir, I am afraid I owe you an apology."

"What happened? Are my children safe?"

"Like I said, I owe you an apology."

"You son of a bitch!" Ric's eyes were filled with tears. "You got my children killed!"

Ric lunged toward Paulson, but as his legs were still tied to the chair, he only succeeded in falling on his side. He landed hard. His head struck a cabinet, he dislocated his shoulder. Through his tears Ric saw a lot of stars, exploding stars, filled with blood. He was unaware of his pain. His physical pain, that is. The pain in his heart was both devastating and eternal.

Paulson shook his head. Though the guy wasn't the most sympathetic of fathers, he surely loved his children. It was a damned shame.

Now, where was a good place to hide? The storm cellar?

Suddenly part of the wall opposite Paulson exploded and shot straight toward him like a stone expertly fired from giant slingshot.

Paulson kissed the floor. He felt the edge of a beam scrape the nape of his neck.

Paulson screamed. Ric had crawled over and was biting him on the ear.

He twisted away, rolled over, and was oblivious to the stream of red running down his neck only because Critical Maas, her face and arms scorched from the heat and nicked from the metal, was striding through the hole she

33

had made with her fist as if she was returning home after a long vacation.

"Good evening, Special Agent Paulson," she said pleasantly, smiling. "I want you to know how touched and deeply honored I am that you picked me to be the first subject of your current initiative."

Paulson went for the gun in the shoulder holster under his jacket.

But CM was faster. A blur, in fact.

She grabbed a butcher knife from a rack on the counter beside the stove and threw it at Paulson's hand with an accuracy he could later describe only as demonic.

The knife penetrated his hand and pinned it to Ric's left calf.

Paulson's instincts, stunned as they were, took over. He pulled the knife from both his hand and Ric's calf with one quick, efficient motion, and though the world was spinning, he attempted to return the favor with the same knife. He stumbled, and the throw was wobbly, its trajectory off, way off.

Critical Maas sidestepped it easily. She regarded the two injured men with a cold eye. "How sad. And yet how typical of the modern American male. I'm especially surprised at you, Ric. You deal with pain so poorly. You're definitely setting a bad example for the children." She paused, and slapped her forehead. "Oh, that's right, I forgot. We don't have the children to worry about anymore."

Outside, a slaughter ensued. Many of the soldiers and agents had managed to avoid the fire, but they were scared out of their wits, incapable of regrouping. The laughter of Deedee and the other Specials could heard easily above the pleas and screams. Maybe it was just Paulson's gruesome imagination, but it seemed the women were getting the worst of it.

Ric began calling his ex-wife a litany of names, most of them obscene, but all seemingly incapable of stinging her. They all elicited a smile. All except one:

Stephanie.

Refusing to acknowledge that her physical being had altered along with the shuffling of her personality, he called her Stephanie. Continuously, in between insults, he lectured her and tried to shame her, a technique he had apparently utilized to great effect when she *had* been Stephanie. None of that worked. It was clear the only thing that could possibly cause her emotional damage was the use of her former name.

And when Ric finally got the response he required, Paulson realized the man was intent on committing suicide.

Because he barely put up a fight when Critical Maas half-ran, half-flew to him, picked him up, and slapped him briskly, just once.

With just enough strength to tear his head half off his shoulders.

He was still gasping in vain to take a breath when CM shattered his breastbone with a single brutal fingertip and tore out his heart.

She looked down at Paulson and held it for him to see. It took one last, reflexive beat. Then she crushed it like a tomato.

"Any more hostages you would like me to kill?" she asked. "I can't believe you were so naive as to think I would surrender myself to of all people *you* in order to protect *that* insipid dweeb. You must be more deluded than even I can imagine, and believe me, I can imagine a lot." She casually tossed her ex-husband's pulpy heart into the garbage disposal. "You see how I treat the people I once thought I loved. You can imagine how I must treat the people my sworn enemies love."

Paulson gasped in horror.

Critical Maas smiled. "I'd call your brother, if I was you." She tossed him a cell phone. "Here. I still have a few free minutes coming to me."

THIRD ANNIVERSARY

I spent the third anniversary of the Surge at a secret location doing a remote broadcast for a Pacifica radio station. I was being interviewed and taking calls and answering e-letters. I quickly discovered a certain segment of the audience was easily willing to believe that the Federal Government was at best stretching the truth, and at worst lying about the planned Special uprising that would have, in effect, turned the entire nation into a larger version of what Chicago was now.

Another segment had no problem accepting the Government's side of the story, namely that the Specials—all except the "good" ones—were plotting revolution, and that, furthermore, we had been the aggressors during the Surge, when surrounded by the troops at the ranch getaway of one of Chandra's wealthy lovers. The truth was that while many soldiers died that day, seven helpless Specials had died first. The unused energy that fueled their power, energy that normally would have been tapped into gradually, like a battery, through the natural course of their lives, was upon the event of their deaths distributed

37

among the remaining Specials. This influx of energy transformed most of the low-powers into high-powers, made most of the high-powers even stronger, and unimaginably augmented the abilities of those whose talents placed them beyond category.

For all Specials, the influx of power was quite a rush, and while Matthew Bright, Patriot, and myself had had a lifetime to adjust to our exceptional might, the others were psychologically unprepared to deal with the sudden ability to bridge the difference between whim and reality with the ease of one thought. Perhaps it was to be expected, if not excused, that they would use their powers indiscriminately, without regard for the law or morality of the mundane world.

Critical Maas was the head cheerleader, of course, the main instigator, and those who had gone so far off the deep end they were unlikely to ever regain their respect for conventional mores quickly joined her in Chicago.

As for the others, once they settled down and regained some perspective, they went quietly underground, changing their identities and in some cases their appearances with the help of a network of libertarian sympathizers that had grown up in the wake of the early civil rights violations perpetrated on the Specials. They still wanted what they had always wanted: A normal life, with a spouse, two point five kids, a house in the suburbs, and a terrific job with swell stock options.

For despite everything, they still loved the good old U.S. of A. They could have fled, gone underground in Europe or Nigeria or wherever. But that dream house existed only in a narrow frame of reference, and they lacked the desire to envision themselves living anywhere else.

Mostly, that is. I'd tried to keep track of everyone, but

naturally that was impossible, and so it was very likely that certain Specials whose location was unknown to me had re-established themselves outside the borders. While on the radio, I had to field several questions from right-wing paranoids about the potential for Specials to prop up dictatorships hostile to the United States, like that of Iraq. The lack of evidence never seemed to dissuade them, and after a while I gave up on trying to prove the Special community innocent to those who had already decided it was guilty. Hell of a way to spend a day. I liked last year's news blackout better, but unfortunately my partner had fallen for a wealthy stockbroker. My adjustment to my current bout of celibacy, I'd discovered to my dismay, was quick and painless.

I wondered how Chandra was doing.

Celibacy is the last word one thinks of in connection with Elizabeth Chandra, who is, simply, the most beautiful woman in the world. She had the power to cloud men's minds so pervasively with the hypnotic aura of her beauty that they loved her unconditionally—albeit shallowly. She had possessed this ability since puberty.

We had been sitting in class when it happened—suddenly none of the boys could take their eyes off her. She was still skinny, with a mere hint of the handsome body she would later develop, gawky, and giggly, yet the Flash had endowed her with uncommon charisma. Whether in her presence, or viewing her in a photograph or in a home movie, hell, even in a drawing, the guys were devoted to her and would do anything she asked, so long as it did not violate the dictates of their conscience. When it came to Elizabeth Chandra, a teen-aged boy was like a robot incapable of violating the Three Laws; he would obey her unquestionably, except in cases where it would do harm to himself or others.

Full-grown men, as it turned out, had exactly the identical problem. Even Dr. Welles had trouble taking his eyes off her. And in those eyes I read a peculiar combination of lust and guilt—she was after all barely twelve.

Rumor had it Chandra's power was especially tough on the men in her family, especially her old man. They should have seen her as a daughter or a niece; instead she made their mouths water.

To make matters worse, Chandra's power was entirely involuntary. She could not turn it on and off. Men were destined to be her playthings. The only exception was myself, not that I was immune to those incredible pheromones, but that I was able to control them, put them into perspective, so that they could not influence my emotional response to her presence.

In time I convinced myself that it was as impossible for me to love her as it was impossible for me to love any one else.

As Chandra aged and her body changed, the sway she held over the opposite sex only intensified. Needless to say, it affected her attitude toward boys and men profoundly. For her the average male was never a person; he was only a means of getting something that she wanted. I'm not sure exactly when she became sexually active— probably around her fifteenth birthday—but from the beginning she was especially ruthless with the emotions of mundanes, driving them to acts of desperation and even suicide. She was only moderately easier on the Specials she went out with—I don't think any of the guys ever contemplated suicide, although there were the occasional periods of fury, tears and temper tantrums.

The Homeland Special Security Act mandated that she attend all four years of high school and then earn a college diploma; otherwise I'm certain she would have had herself emancipated at the age of sixteen and embarked upon her career in show business earlier than she had. That was when she shortened her name, dropping the "Elizabeth." I'm convinced she was one of the worst actresses who ever lived, but her abilities permitted the men in the audience to overlook that, and they inspired her leading men to give intense, committed performances that at best revealed searing emotions, and at worse were over-the-top, accidentally campy extravaganzas.

Women didn't give a damn. They didn't give a damn while she was in high school (although because she was a Special, she did manage to be friends with a few girls until she distracted their boy friends in the most intimate way possible). Nor did they give a damn when she was on television or in the movies. Women didn't want to be with her, they didn't want to give her the time of day.

So Chandra stayed with men. Men who adored her. Who wanted to please her. Who would obey her without question. She believed men were interchangeable because they always acted the same around her. Time only confirmed her understanding of the opposite sex, which remained limited because her own sex, by and large, rejected her friendship. Only the Specials she'd known as a child and teen interested her as human beings; their rejections and rebuffs of friendship hurt because they were the only rejections she had ever experienced.

Her homes were gifts from her wealthy admirers, her possessions something to be held for today, and then discarded tomorrow. Her sex life, though of great interest to the media, meant little to her. To her way of thinking, aroused men were automated sex toys, nothing more. Her lovers wore identical, faceless silver masks, in part so they wouldn't have any illusions about the romantic significance of their trysts. She had no friends, no confidantes, not even among her agents and personal managers. She avoided her fellow Specials, mainly because most hadn't forgiven her for the advantage she had taken of them in the past. For that reason she could not understand them. They'd all been adolescents, after all. Wasn't adolescence the time when you made mistakes, learned your limits, and moved on from there?

Chandra had only one secret in life, really, and it had been revealed to me by the ghost of Clarence Mack, the dreamwalker Jason Miller (a.k.a. Patriot) had murdered in order to prevent disclosure of his plan to betray the Specials and siphon their energy. Clarence told me that during the act of making love, Chandra would pretend she was with the one Special who'd seemed relatively immune to her mastery of pheromones, the one Special she liked exactly as he was, face and all, the one Special she could she give herself to in the most profound meaning of the phrase.

Me.

Clarence said it like I should be taking a bow. What I could have had, had I displayed the slightest bit of interest, he had been dreaming of all his life. Even in death, it seemed, he could not lose his passion for Chandra.

To think I'd never known. Never noticed her eyes boring into me while I looked away, oblivious.

Naturally, when she couldn't get the one man she truly wanted, she treated men only as conveniences, sex objects, employees, and co-stars, nothing more nor less. How else could the most desirable woman who ever lived have been expected to respond?

Rarely do I find promiscuity poignant, but in Chandra's case I had to make an exception. Of course, by the time I got around to seeing if she wanted to change the situation, we were interrupted. We and the other Specials who'd made it to safety were sneak-attacked by the United States Army, acting under the command of Special Agent Paulson.

What happened after that was fairly simple, though you'd never know it to listen to the Government spokesmen. Men were nervous, tempers were quick, leadership was slow on the uptake. Shots were fired. Defenseless Specials were killed, plus a few defenseless civilians. Suddenly there was a lot of released energy to be spread around. Most of the low-powers graduated to high-power status, and those with particularized abilities found them expanded and augmented.

The Surge had begun. It was quite a rush for most Specials, and there were many incidents, many crimes and transgressions committed, before the brand new high-powers regained their perspective and began to regret the damage they'd done, both to others and their own cause. The Federal Government made it clear that a temporary insanity-by-reason-of-unprecedented-rush defense wasn't going to work, but it was just as clear that the Federal Government wasn't going to admit all those incidents never would have happened in the first place if it a) hadn't been so gullible and b) had followed the Constitution.

In any case, most of the survivors went on the lam. Most were too powerful to be kept in prison, and it took them a while to grasp the full implications about how the balance of power had changed. Chandra and I were separated. Being one Special was trouble enough—the Feds would try to contain those on the wrong side of the law even if they couldn't arrest them—but two Specials together was too much of a dare. We stayed underground.

I bobbed to the surface occasionally, making appearances at university rallies and at various media outlets, attempting to make the case to the American people that while the Specials might have gotten a little out of hand, most of us were still the same wannabe mundanes we'd always been. Fat lot of good it did me, or anybody else, but I had to try.

Chandra, meantime, remained in hiding. It was easier than you might think. For not only was the male half of the species ready, willing, and able to fulfill any request she might have for food, shelter, clothing, and extracurricular activities, but since the Surge, her abilities expanded to include her own sex. For the last three years women found her just as irresistible as men.

And by irresistible, I mean that straight heterosexual women who had never had the remotest inclination to take a walk on the wide side found themselves getting hot and bothered by being in Chandra's presence. They were just as willing to help Chandra as men. And they were especially enthusiastic about fulfilling her personal needs.

I'd heard rumors that during those trysts, masks were not required, so maybe she never thought of me when she was with a woman. The truth is, it was probably better that I didn't know.

Such was Chandra's sway over the human individual that I don't know if any agent of the Federal Government would have ever arrested her, even if she had been cornered. Though she probably could have talked her way out of any situation, she moved discreetly from house to house, neighborhood to neighborhood, city to city, always depending upon the kindness of strangers. Another rumor had it that she even convinced Reverend Kane to let her use his remote cabin getaway in the Rockies once.

God only knows how many hearts she broke just in the first three years she spent on the lam. She never killed, as she was constitutionally incapable of such brutality, but she could be considered a terrorist of love.

Word of her exploits reached me occasionally. Heaven help Paulson, I often thought, if he was ever stupid enough to be alone in a room with her. The things some people did for love. . . .

His old school crush Chandra was the last person on Matthew Bright's mind as he flew over New York City on the night of the third anniversary of the Surge. He was too busy watching the crowd, too much on the lookout for signs of trouble, to reminiscence about great lost loves. Chandra had made her choices, he had made his, and now they were on opposite sides of the law. Matt was certain his choice had been correct.

Tonight Matt flew directly over the crowded streets. Normally he hugged buildings as he flew through the city, so as not to unduly distract the average neck-craning citizen, and not to draw the attention of potential felons. But tonight he wanted everyone to see him. Last year's Surge anniversary had inspired, for complex sociological reasons whose logic eluded Matt, a spontaneous outburst of revelry in the citizenry, who immediately deemed it a carnival. If so, it was like the carnival on a Guy Fawkes Day flashback, with the normal sexual and conscious-altering mores of all social strata being turned topsy-turvy for the duration.

As far as Matt was concerned, though, that was a nice way of saying that the very people he had sworn to protect had decided to celebrate the existence of outlaws on the run by indulging in a most public sex and drug orgy. This year's event was more organized in that the city fathers had decided to sanction and attempt to regulate it— stationing teams of paramedics on every corner—but someone had to be available who could maneuver through crowds and stop any destructive behavior before it led to serious damage of property. Last year's property damage had probably been the impetus for the city fathers to facilitate the very behavior they disapproved of the rest of the year.

Matt certainty couldn't say he approved of what he saw happening below—the booze, the wild dancing, the performers, the kissing, the groping, the first base, the second base, the home runs. Some of the home runs were performances for public consumption involving noted members of the adult entertainment industry, while others, the majority, were reasonably private endeavors in alleys or at windows, involving respectable members of society. Matt supposed it was the people's right to misbehave, if that was what they chose to do, but as a self-confessed straight arrow, he could not help but disagree.

Something caught his attention: a woman walking alone.

She wore a white fur hat and a long sable overcoat. She kept her head down, deliberately avoiding eye contact with revelers and abstainers alike. Her walk was purposeful, yet she hesitated at every intersection. Matt did not need to note the looks people gave her as she walked by, nor the way some folks moved toward her before they thought better of it; her posture and general demeanor were unmistakable.

It was Chandra. On the move again.

Matt swore to himself. He was duty-bound to take her in.

Matt increased his altitude, went high above the buildings so that it wouldn't be obvious that he was following her. Since the Flash had strengthened his power of sight way beyond that of the average mundane, there was no chance—at least as far as he was concerned—that he would lose her.

He waited until she had turned a corner down a street lined with brownstones. There were few pedestrians, and most brownstones were dark, implying the residences were either unoccupied at the moment or those inside were too busy being preoccupied. He descended and landed facing her when she was halfway down the street.

"Hello, Chandra," he said.

She took a step backwards.

"You can't escape."

The fear in her eyes was replaced by a steel glare—the relentless yet neutral look of a hawk that has sighted her game. The instant she turned it on, Matt's heart began pounding and he became nauseous. The surefire symptoms of puppy love, yet so powerful and pervasive, it was all he could do to maintain his focus on his true goals.

"You're right. I can't escape," she said. "But neither can you." She spoke without malice, without arrogance, and certainly without an inkling of the love he felt for her.

"I survived the lonely nights and the depression the first six or seven times I had to live through it," Matt said. "You're a fugitive from justice, Chandra. I have to arrest you."

"No, you don't. And how could you be that crass anyway? Do you really believe for a moment you love your duty more than you love me?"

He began to reach her, but ceased when she took a step backward. Not because he was afraid to touch her—quite the opposite; how he yearned to crush her body against his and kiss her with all his heart—but because he was afraid she would stumble while stepping off the sidewalk. That was the kind of consideration Chandra could inspire. He resolved to make sure her stay in custody was as comfortable as possible, and that Paulson's people had minimal access to her.

"My love of duty is constant," he said, "whereas my love for you shall pass. Eventually."

"What kind of love is that?" she said with a sneer.

"The artificially induced kind," he replied. "Time was when it wouldn't be difficult to imagine myself loving you for real, Chandra. After you got over your initial glee at how you could rake teen-aged boys over the coals, when you were still a considerate person, with a sense of the greater good. I watched you become a world-famous celebrity before you graduated from high school, and I knew that even without the Flash you would have found fame and fortune."

"What a thoughtful thing to say." Her smile was enigmatic, provocative. It was a familiar smile, like the Mona Lisa's. He'd seen her use it on camera. A documentary was being filmed about her preparations for a cable TV show, and remembered quite vividly her referring to it as "Smile Number 17".

"But would you have found love?" he asked. "Yes, I think you probably would have. Thanks to the Flash, you are perhaps the only person on the planet who isn't a master criminal who has yet to find love."

"There's love in my life," she said sharply. Obviously his barb had been successful.

"I'm sure there's plenty. Love you take, that is. But how much love can you give? And is not love, in the final analysis, something you give, rather than take, without expecting recompense? The Flash has eliminated the possibility of your having that experience, Chandra. The Flash has ensured that you will forever be a case of arrested emotional development."

"I know what love is!" she protested.

"You mean there's someone you could give unconditional love to?" Matt couldn't keep himself from taunting her. He had a vague notion that if he could somehow make her miserable, if he could defeat her emotionally, her sway over him and everybody else might be diminished, at least until she was safely locked up. It wasn't much, but it was the only plan he had.

Chandra opened her mouth to speak—then hesitated.

"There is someone!" Matt exclaimed. He didn't know if he should be glad for her or be jealous. "Who—?"

Chandra sat down at a bench at a bus stop, covered her face, and began to cry. Her shoulders shook uncontrollably.

"No, I understand," said Matt, approaching her softly. "There would be someone, but he or she is unavailable. Oh, Chandra, I'm so sorry. I had no idea—"

The pity he felt for her was profound and true. The Flash had visited many ironic cruelties on the Specials, and on one level this was yet one more. Only this instance was especially unkind. The Flash had decreed Chandra would be forever denied that which she so unfailingly inspired.

He knelt beside her, and touched her shoulder. With all his being he yearned to make love to her, right here on this bench, with all the passion and tenderness he could muster. Heck, with the goings-on tonight, nobody would even notice—but no, that was just her power wrapping itself around him.

"Chandra," he said gently, "I have to take you in."

"You bastard!" she said. With surprising strength she pushed him to the ground.

Before he could get up she was halfway down the block.

Of course, he couldn't blame her for running. Though he couldn't say he would have done the same, because he never would have made such an effort to avoid such richly deserved punishment. On the other hand, he never would have betrayed his country in the first place, but he loved her so, he found it easy to forgive her.

He moved, his combination police-and-superhero uniform creating a brief blue streak over the street.

The second he grabbed her—by both arms—she opened her mouth and yelled at the top of her voice, "Rape! Rape! Help me!"

Matt was so startled by the tactic that he called her something impolite. At the same time he lifted his feet from the ground, intending to take her into the air with him. However, he inadvertently loosened his grip.

Chandra was able to pull away and she ran into the onrushing crowd, comprised mainly of those who had heard her plea.

"Stop him! He's trying to rape me!" said Chandra. "Look!" And she opened her sable coat and, without even trying to be subtle about it, tore her own blouse on the right side, exposing her black bra over a breast that Matthew could not help but think of as perfect.

"That bastard!" one man said, as he fell to his knees and began kissing her hand. Women felt the same way too. The crowd's anger was palpable, seething.

"My God," said Matthew to Chandra, "have you been taking vitamins?"

A man wielding an umbrella in a threatening fashion advanced. A woman advanced swinging her pocketbook the way a rock star swings his microphone; she was oblivious to the personal items flying out of it, striking the folks behind her. One man pulled a knife, another had a gun, a third had an acoustic guitar.

"Hey, look," said Matt, pointing at the badge pinned to his chest, "I am a duly-appointed officer of the law. You people don't want to do whatever it is you're contemplating doing."

They came closer.

Matt began backing away. "You know, I am authorized to use force to defend myself."

The crowd evidently did not care, because the people did not stop advancing.

Realizing that his quarry had slipped into the crowd and that he was in danger of losing her altogether, Matt took off, flying straight up into the air.

That was when the bullets began flying. One whizzed past his ear, another struck him, to no avail, on the sole of his boot. That really ticked him off. He was getting tired of buying new boots. For a fleeting instant he wished his powers included those of Timothy White Owl, who could identity anyone instantly and who never forgot a face. Then he'd be able to have most of Chandra's dupes brought up on misdemeanor charges, just to teach them a lesson about the relationship between the heart and the head.

Oh well, he thought, *I'll just have to be satisfied with tracking down Chandra.*

Which was more difficult this time, because she had traded coats with a homeless person and vanished.

Even so, an hour after she'd first eluded him, Matt's super sense of smell caught a slight whiff of Chandra's distinctive apricot perfume.

She had to be nearby.

The only problem was, the street was deserted.

Matt grimaced. The woman had a talent for finding deserted streets.

He landed in the middle of the road and tried to listen. Beyond, on the streets he could not see, the revelry and rebellion continued. He perceived the sounds of the laughter, the music, and the debauchery like a distant echo. The intonation of ghosts. The people he served had become a dream.

He stood there and tried to shut out their noise. It was an annoyance to him, a distraction.

He wanted to hear a voice. *Her* voice.

Funny, he hadn't thought of her in years, other than in the most fleeting fashion. She was the one person he found easiest to put out of his mind. Such was the incentive she had, without meaning to, provided him.

Tonight she was the only person he wanted to think of.

He concentrated, listened, tried to find the sound of her voice emanating from the walls of the dark homes on either side of him. Tried to catch another whiff of that blasted perfume.

52

Not that it did him any good. After a while he knew he was wasting his time, Chandra had eluded him completely—for the time being. Yet he did not leave the middle of the street, he simply walked back and forth, slowly, vaguely hoping she might slip and reveal herself.

How long he engaged in the hunt he did not know. Only when the revelers began straggling onto the street, in search of either privacy or new territory to conquer, did he leave.

He flew up, up, into the sky, losing himself in the night, and remained high above the city until the dawn, when the squares and angles of the street lamps and highways dimmed into nothingness, and civilization began to emerge once more.

FOURTH ANNIVERSARY

Jason Miller awoke with blood on his hands. He spent twenty minutes at the sink trying to wash it off before he realized that the blood was just another mental delusion, the manifestation of his guilt.

The guilt came and went. He had no control over it. Some days he was glad to feel as powerful as he had when he was twenty—truth was, he was even faster, stronger, and perhaps smarter, thanks to the Surge—but on other days he was weighed down with a spiritual burden that would have weakened the knees of Atlas. He did not regret having branded his childhood friends traitors to their country—often their subsequent behavior seemed to have backed up the charge—but he knew his motivations had been selfish.

More than selfish. Self-centered in the extreme.

Furthermore, he could not understand why they had dictated his actions so heartlessly. Granted, he was just as human as any one, Special or mundane, and just as prone to temptation. But before the incident with Joey Drake, the temptation had been confined to blurry dashes through the girls' locker room, or stepping out on his wife once in a while. Normal man stuff. Nothing that had conflicted with his basic moral code. However, when confronted with the certain knowledge that the power bequeathed by the Big Flash was running down, he had not hesitated to harm another human being.

Nor was Joey the last. Peter Dawson died next. The man who could not be hurt, cut, or poisoned was suffocated in a plastic bag. Then there was Charles, who had to die before anyone found out. Then of course John Simon found out anyway, by walking with Charles in the fields of the dead. Obviously the only thing to do, the only way for Jason to maintain his position and still get what he wanted out of life, was to change the rules, to frame the Specials so they would be in custody or out on the run, and to place Specials whose loyalty to their own country was unquestionable, Specials such as himself, in unassailable positions.

The plan had worked, basically. The place of Jason Miller, a.k.a. Patriot, in history was assured. He would go down as a super-hero, good corporate employee, husband, family man, and savior of democracy. What better legacy could any man have, or want? If only it wasn't for this goddamned guilt . . .

From the bedroom, his wife asked him was wrong.

"Nothing, honey," he said, with a grim uneasiness. Lying to her came so easily, so naturally to him. "I just have to go somewhere."

"Great," she said, sarcastically. "Just try to get back in time for Little League, okay? Joss wants you to see him play. It would mean a lot to him."

"Sure, honey."

Five minutes later he was dressed and out the window,

headed for the clouds. He wore his standard red-white-and-blue costume, with its billowing cape and the helmet with the single white star surrounding one eye, representing his fundamental angelic decency—at least, that's what the costume people kept telling him.

He flew toward Pederson, several hundred miles away. He took his time, so the flight took him nearly an hour. The entire way he seethed, thinking of his wife and the demands she kept putting on him—didn't she realize by now how important his work was? Didn't she understand how much the average citizen needed the strong arm of Patriot as a shield from rogue Specials?

After a while he calmed down, and realized he was in truth angry at himself, angry for what he had done and what he had to do.

As soon as the lights of Pederson came into view, he slowed down to reduce wind sound and took out his cell phone. He punched a number that should have been private.

"Dr. Welles?" Jason said into the phone.

"Yes?" The voice was hesitant, suspicious.

"I need to see you."

"Jason? What do you need to see me about?"

"I have to talk to you. Don't worry. I'm alone and have no hidden agenda."

"You mean, this is not a trap?" said the doctor with a sour laugh.

"I hoped to be more diplomatic about it, but yes, it is *not* a trap. You told us years ago you would always be available, regardless of circumstances, regardless of anything that might happen between us. *Regardless of anything.* Your words. I must confide in you."

"*Must?*"

"Yes."

"You could have done that a couple of years ago, when it would have meant something. We could have avoided a lot of tragedy."

"I'm asking *now*. Where, exactly, are you?"

Dr. Welles told him. "I must warn you, though. I—*We're* expecting company."

"I don't care. Patriot out." *Oops!* He felt silly, he had absent-mindedly signed off as if he was on duty for the Nexus Corporation.

Flying over Pederson filled him both with nostalgia and with regret for all the things in his life that hadn't gone as planned. The downtown area was run down now, and judging by the unkempt lawns and the houses with shabby roofs and peeling paint, the surrounding neighborhoods had descended from middle class to lower class. Another change was the expansion of the suburbs, the adjacent shopping malls, and of course the amusement park devoted to Special themes. But the fields and the forests and the wild areas were still the same—only there was less of them—and nestled between the river and the hills was the place that had been Camp Sunshine. The place where the young Specials had been interned and the place where they had eventually gone to high school, after their parents had secured the rights to weekend custody.

It was the place where he and Peter Dawson had tested the extent of Peter's invulnerability.

The place where he and Matthew swore a blood-oath over a campfire that they would never harm a mundane, regardless of the provocation.

The place where he scored four touchdowns against Princeton High, without his feet leaving the ground once.

The place where he and Chandra had made out for the

first time. At least, he imagined he was the first for her, but with Chandra one could never be sure.

The place where his future had once seemed made of Teflon.

One thing about blood: it sticks.

He looked at his hands. He could not see it, but it was there all the same.

He spotted Dr. Welles standing in the backyard of a modest home at the end of a cul-de-sac, smack in the middle of a new housing development. Jason knew it was new because none of the trees were older than five. As he came in for a landing, he perceived immediately how Dr. Welles had aged during the last five years. His face was lean and haggard, and his posture had deteriorated significantly. His eyes were sad. Well, it was perhaps to be expected. The man had spent several months, off and on, in custody, before the authorities got tired of losing facilities to irate Specials.

Jason landed and strode across the yard to greet Dr. Welles. Jason held out his hand, but Welles pointedly lit his cigar. Jason frowned: many times during camp or school, he'd seen Dr. Welles light a cigar to show contempt for an official without actually saying something directly. Generally their protests went unheeded; only pulling serious rank could get him to acquiesce. Jason hid his hand in his billowing cloak.

"Good morning, Doctor. Thank you for seeing me."

"It is good to see you, Jason," Welles said coldly, suspiciously.

"I'm alone. Everybody knows where you are, Doctor. Nobody needs me if they want to arrest you again."

Welles nodded. "That much is true."

"Who is it, honey?" asked a woman from inside.

"Just a visitor. He'll be flying off soon enough." He turned back to Jason. "You will, won't you?"

"Sure. Is that who I think it is?"

"You really don't keep up with current events, do you? Yes, that is Mrs. Simon."

"John's mother?"

"She's not a patient, merely the mother of a man who once was."

"Well, I need you as a patient, for a little while. Will you hold our conversation in professional confidentiality, like you promised when we graduated?"

"You know, or should know, the lengths to which I've already gone to preserve it. Sit down." He indicated the lawn chairs. "Would you like a cup of coffee?"

"Uh, a glass of water." He sat. He hadn't expected hospitality.

Welles returned, made himself comfortable leaning on the brick barbecue in the shade, and said, "What is it you expect from me, Jason? Don't ask me for forgiveness. I'm not capable, yet."

"I want to know your opinion about certain matters."

Welles shrugged. "Easy enough."

"I want to know if you believe it is possible a good man can do something bad and bring about good—a greater good than if he ever could without transgressing."

"Jason, do I detect guilt?"

Jason's eyes narrowed beneath his mask. "I don't think so," he said coldly.

Welles realized his cigar had gone out. He relit it. "You might ask if it is possible an evil man might do something good—"

"Yes, of course he could!" Jason exclaimed.

59

"And yet still bring about a greater evil." continued Welles.

"I don't get it."

"Imagine if in 1943 Adolph Hitler had an epiphany and realized he'd wasted his entire life by trying to conquer the world and wasting the Commies and the Jews and that from now on he only wanted to use his considerable power and influence to do good in the world. He'd make it up to the Jews, the Poles, the Russians, the gypsies and everybody else, and he'd put the German people on a path that would bring them closer to realizing the ideals of Christ and Buddha and any other great religious thinker he believed worthy of emulation."

Jason sighed. "Okay. I don't know a whole lot about World War II, but I don't think that would have been possible."

"Please. Haven't you ever watched an episode of *Xena, Warrior Princess?*"

"Sure, those women are—"

Welles silenced him with a gesture. "They are, but that's not the point. The point is the story of Xena is the story of a mass murderous and torturer, an outlaw and a plunderer searching for redemption by wandering the world and fighting the good fight. She has caused perhaps thousands to die, and yet you root for her."

"Well, sure, that's because Lucy Lawless is incredible to look at."

"Imagine she looked like Hitler instead. Would you buy the story of her redemption?"

"No. What are you trying to get at?"

"I'm saying that the sort of dispensation you're looking for never happens in real life. The only way you're going to alleviate your guilt is to die."

"I can't die. I've got children to raise."

"Then you've already made your decision. Why did you come to me in the first place?"

Jason blinked and looked away. "I—I don't know. I just was wondering . . ."

"If there was a way out."

Jason nodded. "There has to be!"

Dr. Welles looked away from him. A shiver went up the doctor's spine. What if his next words caused Jason to lose his temper and kill *him?* The authorities wouldn't care—the only reason he was a free man was because of the possible retaliation should he be taken prisoner. But the words escaped him, eluded all caution:

"Jason Miller, Flagg, Patriot, whoever you call yourself, I am many things. A psychologist, a teacher, a thinker, a man who obeys orders, a man who disobeys when he thinks he can get away it, an authority figure, a role model, a cigar smoker, a lover, an occasional philanderer, and I was even bi once—"

Jason looked like he had been poleaxed. "What?"

"But that doesn't matter. The point is, there is one thing I am not, and that is not a priest. You are not seeking absolution. You will not find here."

I decided it was time to speak: "I don't know about that."

Jason crouched like he was about to take off.

"I can go just as fast you, Jason," I said, finishing my walk through the wall. I had business in town and noticed Jason flying in. Naturally suspicious, I followed him, little realizing that I'd be following him to familiar ground.

"There will be no fighting here today," said Dr. Welles sternly.

I looked at him. "What are you doing here?"

"Good morning, John," my mother said. She was making her entrance in a robe and nightgown. She stood beside Dr. Welles and put her arm around his waist. He put his arm over her shoulders. The whole image was surreal. "We've been seeing each other, John."

"You're two consenting adults," I said, unable to mask my disapproval. "But you—you're supposed to be my doctor, my therapist."

"Oh, I can be objective about you, John," said Dr. Welles. "On the other hand, the one person I can't be objective about right now is your mother." They exchanged a hasty kiss.

"Why don't you two go inside," I said.

Jason and I began circling each other. I hadn't even thought about what I was doing, I had so anticipated a time when I could devote my undivided attention to an encounter with Jason that my maneuvers were sheer instinct.

It was clear he felt the same way. His jaw was set hard; he was steeling himself from his guilt, finding that ruthless corner in his soul he found it so easy to scurry to, like a rat going for a hole.

"I said no fighting!" Dr. Welles reminded us.

Jason squinted at me. The sun was in his eyes, but he was peering directly at my heart. I sensed that's what he would go for first.

My right hand balled into a fist. At that moment I had only one question in life: should I wait, or go first?

Mother answered the question by stepping between us. Christ, I remember thinking; she could be so reckless, almost insane, when she felt like it.

"Boys," she said, "I want you to cease right this instant! Jason, go home!"

"Yes, ma'am," he said.

"Before you go, Jason . . ." she said.

He had floated a few inches from the ground, but now he hesitated. "Ma'am?"

"I think you went down a path without knowing where it would lead. That's true for most of us, but you of all people should have known. When you find the right path again, you'll know what to do."

Jason sneered at her. "Damn you!" And he took off, streaking toward the horizon.

Mother watched him go with her mouth open. "That ungrateful puppy! After all the cookies I served him!"

"You served him cookies!" I asked, surprised.

"Yes, when you both were in college."

"You served him cookies?" asked Dr. Welles, his complexion suddenly very pale.

"Yes," Mother said, answering him more seriously than she had me.

Dr. Welles looked at me and shook his head. "She makes great cookies."

"Oh, you two *are* a couple of children," said Mother, and she stalked off.

FIFTH ANNIVERSARY

D amn," said the duchess as she put down her cigar. "Lost another round." She stretched her long legs, unsnapped her garter, leaned over, and took off her pantyhose. Now she was down to her black bra and black underwear, not that she seemed to mind.

Jerry Montrose a.k.a. Pyro, one of the most powerful firestarter Specials, was down to his shorts as well. He'd hoped to reach this state of undress in a more passionate manner, but it turned out the duchess was a better poker player than he'd expected. The duchess was a middle-aged, svelte redhead, who had a tendency to run the tip of her tongue over the bottom of her nose ring every time she thought she was going to get something she liked. Right now that nose ring glistened brilliantly. It was certainly his lucky day when he'd met her in the casino downstairs, while she was on leave from her husband, a member of the Moroccon royal family who donated his time to the UN.

Of course, Jerry had had a lot of luck the last five years. He'd been a rogue almost from the day he graduated high school. He spent years on the run, under pressure, in fear of being discovered. Usually he had a right to be afraid, because he got caught all the time. Either because his temper was too quick or he'd called attention to himself by helping some innocent in need of rescue. Ultimately it didn't matter why. He would get caught by Paulson and his gang of Keystone Agents and he would go to jail. For a couple of days. Until he got tired of the three squares and the warm if Spartan bed and had to get some fresh air. Then he'd burn his way out, go to the libertarian underground and beg for funds to buy a new identity. He'd hated that. The underground gave him what he needed, but only after swearing this would be the last time.

It bothered him occasionally that the only reason the Surge happened in the first place was because he'd thrown in his lot with Jason, Joshua and Reverend Kane at the first opportunity. Together they'd convinced Congress the Specials were poised for a hostile takeover of the US Government. In return, Jerry got some payback against those he believed had deserted him in his greatest hour of need.

But when seven more Specials died that terrible day, Jerry began to grasp the implications of the bargain he'd made. At night, he dreamed of the time to come when he would most need mercy at the hands of the mundanes, and how they would refuse to grant it. It was almost enough to make a man feel guilty.

And perhaps he would have felt guilty, gladly and with great gusto, were it not for the fact that the Surge had bestowed upon Jerry Montrose an almost molecular control of fire. A firestarter with that kind of control had a talent mundane society could use, and since the Surge Jerry had been working as a bodyguard and all-round troubleshooter for the city of Las Vegas. His generous salary was paid by the corporations running the casinos and hotels, but he was answerable only to the Mayor and the high-ranking members of his staff.

All things considered, it was a great gig. His hours were pretty much his own. He got to help out the police on occasion, catch bad guys, and occasionally smack around an old school chum who was getting out of hand.

And the sight of the half-naked duchess, puffing on her cigar while shuffling the deck here in his very upscale apartment, more than made up for any sense of nostalgia he might be feeling about the so-called good old days.

"So," she said, "is that a dying ember in your pants? Aren't you glad to see me?"

"I think you'll find some fires never go out," he replied.

The phone rang.

He scowled. He cursed. He almost melted the phone with a thought.

The duchess dealt.

"I have to get that," he said.

The duchess inspected her hand with utter neutrality, but she kept glancing at Jerry suspiciously.

Jerry nodded several times, said "uh-huh" a lot, and put down the phone. "Sorry, babe, but I gotta split. Duty calls."

She threw down the cards, began to snap something at him, thought better of it, relaxed and took a more kittenish approach. "That's not fair! I will make a formal protest to your ambassador!"

"You do that. Look, these gigs usually don't take long. I just have to see the mayor for a few minutes, maybe mess with someone's head a few hours, and I'll be back. It won't take long. I guarantee it."

"Then we can leave the ambassador out of this?"

"That would be my preference."

She ran her finger along the top of his shorts. "All right, but if you stumble across anybody interesting, I won't be averse to sharing. So long as you share me."

"Okay," he said, stepping back, "I'll keep my eyes open." He pointed at his shorts. "These are flame retardant."

"We'll see about that," said the duchess, the cigar between her teeth.

Jerry's apartment was located in the middle of downtown; it was a straight shot over the high-rise hotels to the Mayor's mansion. Below him, the neon lights he loved so well beckoned like coral in a hellish night sea. Beyond the neon lay the street and store lights of the more modestly illuminated suburbia. For the people who lived in the tiny cubes and boxes, Vegas suburbia was nirvana on Earth, a place where they could practice their family values at home, right next to the most family-friendly Sodom and Gomorrah of all time.

And beyond that lay Jerry's practice range, which most people called the Mojave Desert.

One of Jerry's favorite stunts was to fly through a wall or window, burning or melting the barrier while leaving the area surrounding the hole intact. And he would have loved flying into Mayor Squire's game room or bedroom, just to have the pleasure of making a fancy entrance. But because Jerry wasn't the only surviving firestarter among the Specials—and the mundanes had, for some reason, the sneaking suspicion that Jerry might turn against them if his interests ever demanded it—a certain protocol had to be observed whenever he approached.

Jerry flamed off as he came in for a landing at the guard's station at the front gates.

"Don't you think you oughtta get a tighter pair of shorts?" asked the beefy guard standing outside.

"Don't tell me I take your mind off your work," Jerry replied. He looked at the other guard—a freckled-faced youngster—sitting at the window in the booth. "I believe I'm expected."

The youngster nodded. He was probably a rent-a-cop, like most of the guards, but two of the five guys standing around being armed on the other side of the gate were moonlighting from the Vegas police force. The others were there for inexpensive numbers' sake; the pro cops were the genuine bodyguards, in case of an actual situation, usually an assassination attempt. During his unprecedented six terms in office, Mayor Squire had made many enemies in both the mob and corporate America, not to mention among the Specials. So far all his enemies' efforts at extracting revenge had proved to be annoyances, but his luck was bound to run out someday.

Jerry figured as long as the Mayor's luck held out, so (probably) would his, and so he felt a personal kinship with him, rare in his relationships with mundanes.

A mundane, indeed. Most Specials would have found the long and winding driveway to the mansion still too warm from the hot afternoon to be comfortable walking barefoot. That aspect was very comforting, as far as Jerry was concerned. But the occasional gravel and loose rock on the surface was an altogether different matter. Jerry's body was barely toughened by his outdoor activity, and the bottoms of his feet were not an exception. By the time he reached the front porch (where the butler was practicing his fast draw), his feet were throbbing from gravel-inflicted bruises.

"Go on in, sir!" said the butler, whose name was Rajah. The guy was Caucasian and from Minnesota, but his name was Rajah. Jerry suspected his parents had named him after a cartoon character.

Jerry found Mayor Squire in the kitchen.

The kitchen was the size of Jerry's entire apartment, with a high ceiling and a bank of lights that would have been better suited for a stage show. This was one room too big for Squire to fill with his unctuous charisma. A short, round man whose most appropriate ability, if he'd been a Special, would have been that of bouncing from room to room, Squire was a hedonist who liked to pretend to possess self-control.

Jerry noted from the ashtray filled with fresh butts that tonight his friend had dropped the pretense. Indeed, even as Jerry entered, Squire was lighting up, striking a long kitchen match with trembling fingers. The match broke.

"Here, let me do that for you," said Jerry. He flamed on, lit the cigarette, then flamed off.

Squire took a deep appreciative drag and promptly coughed.

"I think maybe you better cut back," said Jerry.

"Very funny," said Squire. "If anything, tonight's a bad night to quit smoking."

"What's the matter?"

Squire nodded at something. A piece of paper next to the telephone. The message on it was pasted from words cut from a newspaper.

Jerry read the message. Judging from the fonts, the paper was a local singles register. The message read:

Howdy, Mr. Mayor.
Interested in a trade?
Your daughter for Pyro.
Jerry. Baby. Meet me at the Funhouse.
Love and Coitus

Deedee

Jerry gave the message back to the Mayor. "Your daughter, eh? She's a fox."

"She's too young for you, and I want her back safe and sound." Mayor Squire had intended his words to sound like an order, an unquestionable order, but his eyes were wide, his breathing was labored, and sweat glistened on his forehead. The man was worried.

An open wine bottle stood on a counter. Jerry reached for a wineglass and helped himself. "Deedee Noonan. If ever a girl had been destined to be a truck stop waitress, it was her."

"Who is this Noonan?"

"She used to be the kind of girl you'd expect to see wearing a coal miner's daughter's dress to school. She only flew because it was easier than walking." He took a swig of wine. "Before graduation, we went parking a couple of times." He sighed and sat down. "I get weak-kneed just thinking about it."

"I can see that," said the Mayor, giving the man a towel.

"Later she stopped talking to me. I never thought about it this way before, but she treated me the same way a guy treats a frail."

"She probably wanted to beat you to the punch. What does this have to do with my daughter?"

"With Rhea? Probably nothing. She's just a device for Deedee to get to my attention."

"An interesting approach. Was this Deedee a closeted sadist, like Critical Maas?"

"No, that's the strange part," said Jerry, pouring himself another drink. "Don't worry; I'll burn this off the moment I flame on. "

"Just don't catch my house on fire."

"It was only after the Surge that she lost control of her id. The influx of power caused a kind of rush that sent her over the edge."

"She obviously still has the hots for you, bozo. Now give me back my towel and then go return my daughter, safe and sound. After that, I don't care what you do. " He threw Jerry a set of keys. "Here, use my golf cart to go to the front gate. That'll save you some energy."

The Funhouse was an amusement park built around a combined theme of Indian and Occidental desert lore, complete with rides, neon, and cotton candy. That lore included all forms of ritual, especially the aberration of cannibalism, plus ghost towns, wild west lore, and alien abductions. Most of the rides and games were linked to the themes in some fashion. The Trickster Roller Coaster and the Area 51 Ride were among the Funhouse's biggest attractions.

The evacuation was complete by the time Jerry arrived. All the electricity was still on inside the park, but at the gate the police had deployed several searchlights, in order to augment, somehow, their fleet of cars, paddy wagons, ambulances, and helicopters.

"We've been expecting you," said Captain Osbourne, who was taking the lead in this operation.

"Is anybody inside?" Jerry asked. He noticed Osbourne had been reluctant to shake his hand.

"Of course not!" Osbourne replied, obviously quite amused by the absurdity of the suggestion.

"Great. Do we have any idea where she is?"

"No."

"Where the Mayor's daughter is?"

"No."

"Do you have a plan for me to follow?"

"No. Personally, I think you oughtta just stroll inside. If she wants to find you the way people think she does, then she'll find you."

"What if she kills me instead?"

"Then we're going to have to hope the Mayor's daughter is still alive."

Jerry nodded, flamed on, and flew into the park. He tried to think. This place was a couple of acres large, and contained children's, family, and adult sections in equal measure, all with distinctively individual styles. If he were Deedee, where would he be?

Maybe it depended on which Deedee was luring him. The Deedee of today was nearly as ruthless as Critical Maas. What she lacked in CM's uncanny ability to pick just the right sadistic action at any given moment, she more than made up for in robust execution. All the profiles emphasized Deedee's propensity for impulsive action. The only reason why Rhea was probably still alive was because killing her would complicate achieving the overall objective.

On the other hand, the Deedee of yesterday had occasionally intimated he was a boy she believed could one day truly care for her, in the most profound way it was possible for two people to truly care for one another. At the time Jerry hadn't the faintest idea what she'd been talking about, which, come to think of it, might have been the reason why she'd rejected him so forthrightly. But it was possible, just vaguely possible, that Deedee was searching for someone who could truly love and care for her in between the times when she was busy stomping the crap out of defenseless mundanes.

Which would mean she was waiting for him in the vicinity of the Tunnel of Love.

The Tunnel of Love wasn't an old-fashioned slow boat ride into a long, dark, stinky tunnel where couples could get away with public displays of affection without actually being seen. This tunnel, in the tradition of the raunchiest part of the adult section, was a long, dark, stinky maze where it was recommended the couples wear roller blades. It had been inspired by the video of an old Dire Straits song, which had featured a svelte young babe making love to the camera. Huge stretches of this convoluted maze were places where couples could go as far they wanted without being seen, though they could certainly be heard, or tripped over, or joined in communal activities. Just the sort of place that might be appreciated by a more sophisticated version of the Deedee of old.

Jerry stood, flame off, at the Tunnel entrance and pondered the matter. The huge silver and pink door was in between the legs of a gigantic neon outline of a Vegas showgirl. Huge portions of the walls had been kicked in by someone with superhuman strength. Deedee, of course. She was marking her territory.

It occurred to him that Deedee was like that preacher Robert Mitchum played in *The Night of the Hunter*, the preacher who had "love" written on the knuckles of one hand, and "hate" on the other. She had the choice of loving him to death, or just straight out killing him. The problem was, she didn't know which fist she intended to use.

Jerry found himself hesitating. He didn't mind taking on drug dealers, thugs, mob muscle, lawyers, CEOs, celebrities, religious fanatics, and individuals who'd gone postal. In all those situations, the chances that an opponent could kill a fellow whose body was made of fire were rather slim. Jerry never had to worry about coming home at the end of his shift.

Tonight, however, was proving to be an exception. He knew for a fact that Deedee's invulnerability protected her against his flame. She'd have no problem tearing him apart, assuming she found something she could grab hold of. Jerry considered that a good reason to be cautious. He flamed on just enough to rise a few inches off the ground.

He flew between the neon legs.

The corridors were either dimly lit or totally dark, just as they were normally. The operators had left the music on. The music consisted of a loop of peppy instrumental music, of the kind he'd always associated with adult movies. Jerry flew down the corridors cautiously, at a steady clip, ever on guard for a surprise attack or a booby trap.

Just being on guard wasn't good enough, however.

Jerry was flying out the other side of the maze, into a virtual reality lover's lane—the cars and the back seats were real, but the mountain rise and the starry sky were computer images.

That was when the foam hit him.

So much foam that it extinguished his fire and buffeted him beneath a crushing force at the same time. He shouldn't have been surprised. The park people had installed the innovative fire prevention device because not all firestarters were friends of Las Vegas.

The foam swept him along as if he was caught in a wave. He hit a wall, head first.

He struggled to get to his feet and stay there. He had a visceral fear of being smothered and dying from lack of oxygen. Probably all firestarters had the same phobia, but that was a small consolation indeed as he found a loveseat and hung on for dear life.

When the onslaught of foam ceased, and he was merely up to his neck in the stuff, he glanced up and saw Deedee Noonan hovering overhead. She held a duffel bag over her shoulder.

A duffel bag with feet protruding from the top.

The feet were kicking. Jerry breathed a sigh of relief. Whoever was in there was still alive.

The feet appeared to belong to a young woman. In fact, Jerry recognized the elegant cut of the ankles. Rhea!

Jerry's heart soared even as he realized Deedee had him, for the moment at least, entirely at her mercy. "Hello, Deedee," he said in tones as neutral as possible. "To what do I owe the pleasure of this encounter?"

Deedee landed. She pointedly did not put down the duffel bag, and instead allowed it to dangle into a small mountain of foam.

A muffled plea from inside the bag indicated Rhea was having difficulty breathing.

Deedee said nothing. She looked at Jerry with her head half-cocked, like that of an eagle eyeing its prey.

"Why are you doing this, Deedee?" Jerry asked. "She never did anything to you."

"She didn't have to do anything," said Deedee. "She's a mundane. She doesn't matter."

The muffled voice became more agitated. *Get me out of here!* she seemed to be saying.

"Does this have something to do with our past?" Jerry asked. He had the feeling the more he got Deedee to talk, the better the chances were he could extricate both himself and the girl from this situation alive.

"No, I just wanted to see you naked," answered Deedee, with a maniacal laugh. She produced a knife from a sheath in her belt and hurled it directly at Jerry's chest.

Usually it did not require much will on Jerry's part to flame on. Generally he found it as much second nature as running or swimming. But the foam covering him was a definite impediment.

Only for a few nanoseconds, however. He needed to generate enough heat to turn his entire body into flame so the knife would pass directly and harmlessly through him. The foam would evaporate in the process.

He succeeded, and shot a bolt of flame at Deedee's hand, the one holding the duffel bag.

She gasped and dropped the bag.

Rhea landed on her head, but fortunately the drop wasn't too far.

"Don't even think about it," said Jerry, pointing a flaming finger at Deedee before she could glide down and pick up the bag.

"Okay," she replied, with a shrug.

"What was this all about? Why did you risk leaving Chicago just to kidnap the Mayor's daughter?"

"I was bored," she said. And without another word, she flew off.

Jerry watched her disappear down the tunnel. At that particular moment he felt he could have been knocked out with a feather. He had known that many of the Chicago rogues were insane, but he had had no idea matters had gotten that . . . irrational.

Rhea in the duffel bag was kicking wildly. Her protests were becoming more and more obscene.

Jerry loosened the bag and helped her pull it off. She was disheveled to be sure, but she had the loveliest porcelain skin and bright green eyes. He had known from the time she was just jailbait that he wanted her. Now more than ever.

"You saved me," she said breathlessly. "How can I ever thank you?" she added, with a wink.

Jerry returned to his apartment, Rhea in tow, to find the duchess was gone. She'd left behind a note, indicating she had to return to Morocco because her husband's mistress had just had a baby.

"I guess it's just the two of us," said Jerry with a wan smile.

"Sorry, once you promised a threesome, I had my heart set on it," Rhea replied. "All of a sudden I'm not in the mood. Can I use your phone? I need to call my dad."

SIXTH ANNIVERSARY

The President of the United States spent the sixth anniversary of the Surge out of the country, attending a G-8 conference in Glasgow. This was an unprecedented event. Not merely the fact that the conference was being held in Glasgow, the Scottish port which had been struck by several terrorist bombs recently, or even the fact that the President chose to spend the anniversary out of the country, but that he'd chosen to attend a very public forum.

For previous anniversaries, you see, the President had hunkered down in secret locations, just in case a rogue Special decided the time had arrived for some payback on the Oval Office, in retribution for the historical sins and inconveniences that its predecessors had inflicted upon our kind. But by number six, either the hooey surrounding the event was becoming routine, or this Prez, J.C. Harris—the first black, the first female, the first Reform Party member to hold the office—thought perhaps the time had also arrived to signal the rogues that they were expected to adopt a lower profile in the eyes of both the media and law enforcement.

Late that night I watched one of the press conferences on a cable news channel. Harris wasn't the greatest looking dame who ever existed—actually, she resembled a youthful Margaret Thatcher, but with soul—however, she was still good looking enough for the eyes of two of her fellow world leaders to keep straying to her rear end. For most of the conference it looked like standing between those two was going to be President Harris' riskiest move of the day.

Then the newscast cut to a shot of the reporters and the staff, and I almost jumped out of my chair with enough velocity to crash through the ceiling. Luckily my television was equipped with one of those devices that lets you play back what you've just seen while recording the present, so you can watch it when you're ready. I checked the instruction booklet real fast, so I'd be reasonably assured I knew what I was doing, and then in the tradition all great minds, pushed buttons until the picture began to back up.

At the proper moment, I froze it. Then I selected part of the picture and pushed in. There was no mistaking it. I had been right.

Laurel Darkhaven was attending the news conference.

Doubtlessly she had false reporter's credentials, but the questions remained, who was she working for, and what was she doing there?

I remember Laurel, vaguely, from kindergarten. I'd apparently had trouble mastering the fine art of tying my shoe-laces, and she'd helped me out on more than one occasion. Even then though, I'd had a tendency to think of the fairer sex as mysterious plant creature invaders from another planet, so I can't say we had much of a relationship. I suppose Laurel was normal enough. She laughed and hung out with the other little girls, she didn't take much effrontery from the boys. Maybe she listened and was obedient in class, I don't recall. I suppose I'm taking a roundabout way of saying that although she showed me a measure of kindness and consideration, there was nothing distinctive about her personality at that young age.

Then came the storm, the photography session, the crashing ceiling, the revelation of our powers. Even the slightest, most nondescript nuances of our nascent personalities took on great significance to the doctors, scientists, politicians, and family desperately trying to figure out what to do with us. The doctors were concerned, the scientists curious, the politicians ambivalent and the families still loving, but their otherwise divergent attitudes toward us all had one thing in common: they were afraid of us.

Children are like dogs in that they have a tendency to reflect whatever emotion is directed at them. Treat them with indifference, they are likely to treat you the same way. Hate them, and they will hate back. Hurt them, and they will bide their time until they can hurt you back. Love them, well, chances are they'll love you in return too, most of the time.

Treat them with suspicion . . . you get the picture. Laurel was more deeply affected by this phenomenon of human nature than most. Within the period of a few months, she evolved from a reasonably garrulous kid into a munchkin with a perpetual scowl stapled to her forehead. Kids have a tendency to withdraw into their own skins for brief (or in my case, longer) periods, during which they either set free their imaginations or try to make sense of the world. You can tell when they're gone by the faraway look in their eyes. Laurel soon ceased to get that look. She never took her eyes off those also in the room, and during playtime she never took her eyes off the entire breadth of the field.

We approached one another occasionally, always warily, usually to no great effect. Any curiosity we might have had at sensing a kindred soul was quashed beneath the weight of our indifference rather rapidly.

We weren't the only withdrawn ones, of course. The adults didn't seem to mind the fact that the Force had sired such a high percentage of moody, withdrawn children. As I grew older, I realized an equal percentage of mundanes would have signaled the need for intervention, whereas in the Specials' case, the adults totally refrained from tainting the natural course of events unless it was absolutely necessary. I had the feeling they were afraid to do otherwise.

Only Dr. Welles, as it turned out, had the intestinal fortitude to stand up to us, break down our emotional barriers, to do whatever was necessary to improve our well-being, no matter how afraid he was. With Laurel, this required double the dose of fortitude.

How it worked out, I have no idea. Dr. Welles tended not to betray confidences unless the fate of the world was at stake. And from what I gathered, Laurel kept the relationship strictly to herself.

All this meant Laurel was predestined to develop a certain detachment from humanity. Even her fellow Specials weren't particularly real to her.

Now the relationship between one's character and abilities bestowed by the Flash has never been satisfactorily established. What sort of power Laurel might have possessed had she been able to overcome her instinctive suspicion of others will forever be a matter of conjecture. As it was, she possessed exactly the sort of ability you'd expect a person of her personality type to have: subtle, discreet, and willful. Not the sort of power that would stand out in a crowd.

Laurel could move small objects for very short distances. By small and short, I mean she could pass the salt gram by gram without lifting a finger, but she couldn't change a tire the same way. Not exactly the world's most promising power. Most kids would have settled for a modest future as a magician or Ping-Pong hustler, but by the time she graduated from high school, Laurel figured out that a person with her ability, plus her natural tendency to blend in with the crowd, was an asset to her country in the fight against those who would harm our national interest.

The CIA and the FBI came to similar conclusions, and began bidding for her services. The CIA won. The agency stationed her at a variety of embassies around the world, to see how she might best fit in.

They needn't have bothered. Nobody knew how she'd fit in better than Laurel herself. And she had exactly the proper demonstration in mind to prove it; she merely had to bide her time until she found an individual deserving of the procedure.

She found that person in King Juluka, an African warlord whose hands had been stained with blood for twenty awful years. His personality turned out to be equally objectionable. When he intimated to Laurel that her personal safety while a guest in his country depended a great deal on how cooperative she was when they had their first date on Saturday night, she simply smiled and with but a thought closed his carotid artery, shutting off the blood flow to his brain. He died soon thereafter.

It took investigators about a week to put the pieces together and conclude Laurel had been personally responsible for the man's execution. Confronted with the evidence, Laurel confessed, adding that she failed to see what the big deal was. King Juluka was a scumbag and the human race was a lot better off without him.

The CIA begged to differ. King Juluka was the *United States'* scumbag and was a known quantity in a continent full of surprises. Exactly the sort of quantity the United States needed to work with in order to advance its corporate interests in the name of democracy.

Laurel's punishment was light. She was ordered to cease being a temp and become a full-time employee of the U.S. Government. She had to follow orders and only kill when ordered to kill. She also had to kill the right person.

All this she eventually found rather inconvenient and certainly too restrictive. One day she offed her CIA handler and disappeared in Eastern Europe. The ethnic conflict currently raging through the land came to an abrupt conclusion when leaders on both sides began dying mysteriously during routine public appearances. The leaders and went into hiding, and the conflict died down, briefly.

The first flare-up was equally brief. The leaders were completely hidden underground, and thought they were safe to resume their bellicose behavior. They were wrong. Family members started to die. Wives, siblings, children, they died almost as soon as they thought they might not be recognized in public. Then the second cousins began to die. Family members of campaign supporters.

The war was over, temporarily.

Not long after that, an occasional mobster or white collar criminal died just as suddenly, the victim of a heart attack, stroke, or spinal injury. But that pattern was controlled. More mannered. Rational.

A thorough CIA review of recent Swiss bank accounts uncovered evidence of suspicious accounts making new transfers into a hitherto unknown secret account. The transfers were timed before and after such incidents. The amounts of the deposits were modest, enough to live on comfortably, even while underground, but never enough to tempt one to make an ostentatious purchase, one that might draw attention to one's self.

A CIA agent made a request to the World Supreme Court to investigate further. The agent died. The World Court got the message. The CIA got the message.

The investigation was over.

Laurel's discretion remained constant, even after the Surge.

And, judging from the unsolved high-profile murders I read about in the papers from time to time, she remained equally successful.

Even so, I felt sorry for her. Surely happiness was an elusive thing for the world's leading hit woman.

And now all of a sudden she had popped up on my TV screen, the President standing squarely in her narrowing sights. I was thousands of miles away and could do nothing about it.

I screamed in frustration, shaking a few pictures off the walls, and knocking a few books off some shelves. I threw a can of beer at the screen. Fortunately I had consumed most of the beer, so the glancing blow didn't do much damage to the set, and I could still watch the rest of the proceedings between the world leaders and the legit reporters. There was no way I could travel overseas in time to make a difference. Jason and Matt were fast enough, but Matt had sworn off foreign entanglements, and there was no way I'd trust Jason with a simple request, ever. Besides, we weren't exactly a big super-hero club, with secret signal devices that told us to reconvene so that we might defend civilization against its enemies.

I watched, helplessly, as President Harris delivered some innocuous remark, promptly rolled her eyes and fell over backwards as if she'd been socked in the jaw.

"You bitch!" I screamed at the TV set. "How much did they pay you to sell out your country?"

I calmed down after a second though. I'd forgotten I had never voted for her party, even when I could vote. That said, I watched with great concern, feeling as if the earth herself had ceased to rotate in the wake of the supreme media drama being generated by this one heinous act, as the world leaders swarmed around the stricken President, and as the world leaders were then shunted aside by medics and security.

It looked bad. Surely some of the security people suspected a certain rogue Special might be responsible. I knew of course she was, and I spent the next few minutes feeling my soul sink deeper and deeper into a mire of futility.

One of the cameras panned across the faces in the crowd. Laurel was still there. She had changed her hair since the last time I'd seen her, hell, she'd changed her face, but it was her, no mistake. Why she hadn't taken advantage of the confusion and hightailed it, I had no idea.

Until the medics and security began cheering.

And helped the President stand.

She was all right. The incident, for whatever reason, was over.

Laurel Darkhaven had never intended to kill the President. She had wanted to make the point that she could kill the President anytime, if she wanted to.

Why she had chosen that time, that place to make that point, I had no idea. She was so far underground that theories about her state of mind and/or thinking processes were total conjecture. For all I or anybody else knew, she was merely acting on a bet.

As good a reason as any, but it only underscored the problem faced by world leaders, particularly American ones:

The Specials remained unpredictable. Ultimately, we were beyond mundane control.

SEVENTH ANNIVERSARY

I spent the seventh anniversary of the surge making the rounds to various media organizations, attempting to assure the general public that in the final analysis Specials were no different than any other minority. Some of us were good, some were bad, some were indifferent, most were morally conflicted and/or imperfect, and the majority of us could hardly be blamed if a minority had misused their great powers to inflict as much gratuitous violence upon the human race and the planet as possible. I know what you're thinking. I didn't believe it either. I'd made a resolution to make progress on the PR front for a change, though, and I'd listened to and heeded the advice of a few political consultants who had poll numbers indicating what the best spin on the overall situation should be. Or so they said. I discovered, much to my dismay, that there really wasn't much positive spin you could put on the fact that a major American city had been subjected to a ruthless, capricious tyranny from which there was no escape for seven years. The American public tended to be skeptical about these things.

The Right Reverend Samson B. Kane happened to be wandering the streets of Seattle around ten that night, Pacific Daylight Saving Time. He also happened to be alone. Usually he spent the anniversary of the Surge denouncing the Special phenomenon on every media outlet he could jack himself into, but his doctors had advised him this year to skip it. The Reverend had ulcers, bad ones, so painful they made acid reflux disease seem like mild gas, and they tended to get worse during periods of extensive media appearances. So he decided to listen to them for a change; only now as he walked the streets alone, save for the presence of the Lord, he wondered if he'd made the correct decision. It went against his natural inclinations, to shun the good fight. But then his weariness of spirit was uncharacteristic too.

He had come to Seattle to assist in the audits of the charities his ministry managed. A couple of deacons he thought he could trust had been juggling the books, at the expense of the poor and afflicted; these were good men who had succumbed to temptation. They were truly remorseful and Reverend Kane felt for them. He was undecided what to do. Should he turn the matter over to the authorities, jail time and scandal would surely ensue. The deacons had families who would surely suffer disproportionately. Would it be enough if they simply returned the money and unofficially donated a considerable amount of time to community service? Or should he set a more rigorous example?

Answers were not easily forthcoming. No wonder his ulcers were acting up.

Suddenly, the Reverend stopped dead in his tracks. He looked around. He was in an area of dark brick buildings. Windows were smashed, boarded up. Half the streetlights were out, and there weren't too many of those to start with. The sound of passing traffic was distant, and he hated to admit it, but the presence of the Lord seemed somewhat diluted.

"Nice watch," said a deep voice behind him.

Yes, it cost about a thousand dollars, Reverend Kane almost said. The chill running up his spine cautioned him, however, and he turned to see that three youths with menacing eyes and complexions that appealed to the racist tendencies in what he referred to as his lizard brain had emerged from an alley.

"What are you doing on our turf, man?" the largest one asked.

"Just passing through."

"Not so fast, little man. I complimented you on your watch."

"It's nice," said another.

"I think it should be my watch," said the third, pointing his pistol directly at Reverend Kane's forehead.

"Donate it to our cause," said the large one.

"Yes," said Reverend Kane, groping for his wrist. "Of course."

Suddenly, the world turned black. Pitch black. A dark smoke sprang forth, as if another rift in the fabric of reality, similar to the one responsible for the netherworldly comet that had created the Flash, had occurred, for no purpose other than to complicate the Reverend's unpleasant situation.

The Reverend cupped his hands together and dropped to his knees.

He heard cursing. He heard three hard *raps!* that he instinctively knew were blows against skin and bone. The blows came so fast that they were over before the first body had even hit the ground.

"How you do like my new blackout bomb?" asked a voice, disembodied in the darkness.

"Randy Fisk?" stammered the Reverend.

A soft breeze began dissipating the smoke. And the tall, caped form of Ravenshadow, artist, sinner, and self-styled superhero towered above Kane like the Colossus of Rhodes.

"The one and only," Randy said. His metallic mask, which appeared to be inhumanly bolted to his face, could not disguise the smile and laughter in his voice.

"You saved me," said Kane in a stunned whisper.

"Well, only as a side-effect of putting these bozos out for the evening," said Randy. "I'm correct in assuming that despite my good deed, you won't be cutting us Specials any slack in the near future, right?"

"I do God's will."

"Well, I've got news for you. It was God's will I save you from the beating of your life. See ya around. Give my best to Josh."

Kane watched in confusion, and in wonder, as Ravenshadow rose into the air and disappeared against the vast backdrop of glorious, indifferent stars.

EIGHTH
ANNIVERSARY

By this time, the media's interest in anniversaries of the Surge had declined, not because things in Chicago were any less dire, but because the status quo of the standoff between Special and mundane had remained the same. Indeed, from all appearances, it was beginning to settle into the perpetual state of tension and conflict one normally associates with the Middle East or civil wars in Africa. Even the political pundits had begin to notice their observations had undergone very little metamorphosis from year to year (evolutionary enlightenment was out of the question), and consequently were becoming bored with the subject.

My personal guest shots were down, too.

I had to admit, it had been a tough year between the seventh and the eighth, so far as planet Earth was concerned. There were at least three civil wars in Africa, including one between the Zulus and everybody else in South Africa, and the Saudis had to put down an armed feminist revolution. The Communist party was swept into power in the Russian elections, and a fungus began wip-

91

ing out what was left of the Brazilian rain forest, propelling the Green Party into power there. Christian fundamentalists began targeting the Green Party with their propagandistic wrath, because they feared the Greens, being the only international party, were a harbinger of the world government they so deeply feared.

In the United States, Rhode Island threatened to secede from the Union, and a contingent of Navy SEALS had to storm the beaches and occupy the state capital building until the local branches of government came to their senses. Hula-hoops came back into style; there was even a sport known as extreme hula-hooping, that caused a lot of bodily injury. The Rap Star Wars became more violent than usual, and the crime rate increased in general. Pundits tended to blame the outlaw Specials, claiming our little clan inspired social anxiety, but the number of crimes committed by Specials remained roughly the same for that year.

The day of the eighth anniversary did confirm one thing about human nature in a democratic society, though: Regardless of the amount of social unrest and uncertainty, there was always the time, energy, and inclination to protest police brutality. And that was what was going on in Cleveland that afternoon when things got out of hand.

A Cleveland police officer had been caught on videotape roughing up a black teen-aged male who was suspected of shoplifting, of all things, a van Cliburn CD. The kid later died of his injuries. Not only was the poor black community inflamed, but so was the rich white community, as the kid's mother was the daughter of a local real estate czar with political connections up and down the social ladder of the city. So it was a very rich racially and culturally diverse demonstration before the local police station that degenerated into a riot, and permitted the police to test their riot control training on an entirely different class of folk than they were used to. Not that the insults were any more sophisticated.

In the midst of the riot, the singing began. It was not an amplified voice. The song did not boom from the speakers in the square, nor was it sung through a megaphone. And yet it permeated the entire locale, as if it somehow rose through the sidewalks and the streets and the grass or had come down from the sky to wash away the dirt and grime of the petty concerns of man like a phantom storm. The song had no words, it had no melody or rhythm, and was even devoid of that zoneless ethereal quality one associates with spacey synthesizer music.

Everyone heard it. And everyone who heard it stopped what they were doing. They stopped regardless of whether they were insulting someone, or being insulted, or arresting someone, or resisting arrest, or throwing a rock or full beer can at someone, or spraying pepper spray or firing rubber bullets at someone. A few even stopped so fast they forgot they should have been ducking and were consequently decked, but once they regained their senses, they didn't seem to mind.

Because what they really wanted to do was to listen to that song. To that song which had nothing whatsoever to do with peace, love, and brotherhood. It had nothing to do with political protest or social commentary. It had nothing to do with abstract composition. It was simply a transcendent work of art that everyone, regardless of their personal taste, found incredibly beautiful.

It became common knowledge that the Special known as Paula R. had stopped a full-blown riot that day. No one had seen her—though many theorized she must have been disguised as a bag lady or had otherwise transformed her appearance—but they all knew she was there. Those who had heard her concerts in the days before the Surge knew at once it could have been no one else but her, and everyone else suspected it was her. She had given both the protesters and law enforcement personnel the opportunity to step back from the abyss, and such was the beauty and power of her talent they had no choice but to take it. On the eighth anniversary of the Surge, a Special had performed a good deed, and perhaps had saved many lives.

Most of the newspapers buried the story somewhere around page ten.

NINTH ANNIVERSARY

The miracle happened in the tiny mountain hamlet of Norfolk, West Virginia, population 541. A severe thunderstorm was causing the creeks and the rivers to rise. Some of the run-off was coming down new and different routes thanks to the fact that the mining companies had been topping off mountains and many of the streams had been clogged with rock and soil. One result was the flash-flood that shot through Norfolk. Judging from what happened in its wake, its size had to rival that of a tsunami. The people waiting out the storm in the church basement never had a chance. Ten people drowned.

It should have been a tragedy.

But once the waters receded, a man pulled the bodies upstairs and a woman tended to them. After the woman finishing tending, the bodies returned to life, as if the drownings had never taken place. Actually, a couple of bodies were in better condition than they'd been before the incident. At least two cases of cancer went into complete remission and one heart condition disappeared as a result of the mysterious revival.

I don't know how the media found out, because at first those who had been revived were absolutely mum about who had brought about the miracle of their recovery. Gradually, under the pressure of relentless professional curiosity, enough details about the woman's appearance and/or manner had emerged for an enterprising muck-raker to decide that the miracle worker was none other than quiet, self-effacing Kathleen Hunt, the local grade school teacher.

Upon seeing her picture on CNN, I realized instantly that I knew her as Cathy Holmes.

Once upon a time Cathy had been a Special without powers, an individual the scientists who studied us believed had been unaffected by the comet that had landed—if landed is the term—on Pederson and conferred superpowers upon the unborn children. We all thought Cathy was untouched, that not even the Surge could provide her with abilities beyond those of an average mundane.

Obviously she had been keeping a secret from us, from *all* of us, and only this emergency, coupled with her natural compassion and propensity toward sacrifice, had forced her to out herself.

The bottom line was, Cathy had saved ten lives, but in so doing, she had placed herself in danger. She was going to need help.

I took to the skies.

Usually I took my car. I didn't like to be seen, especially around town, but I had to take the chance. I had to fly.

I arrived in Norfolk too late. I found her husband and her children at the local police station, filling out reports, talking to the FBI. Neither the police nor the FBI wanted me to talk to the man, but they didn't want to try to stop me either.

"They've taken her," was all he said. "They've taken her."

I didn't have to ask who. By now, Cathy was undoubtedly in Chicago, the prisoner of a crazy woman.

TENTH
ANNIVERSARY

I spent the tenth anniversary drinking, sick at heart, completely bummed, dispirited beyond belief, convinced future generations would judge my life as if it was a R. Crumb cartoon gone horribly wrong.

"Mr. Natural! Mr. Natural!" I'd say, stepping into the panel with an over-anxious, worried expression. "What does it all mean?"

"Don't mean shit!" the old man with a beard would say, somewhat amused. He was skateboarding out of the panel, toward an infinite white expanse I could barely imagine.

The next panel didn't have to exist, I would have been glad to skip it altogether. But I was living it anyway, sitting alone in my study in Pederson nursing a parade of scotches. I was intensely moody, naturally, and spent over an hour of the evening listening to Ralph Vaughn Williams' *Sea Symphony*, which uses a choir and the words of Walt Whitman to evoke man's complex relationship with the glorious, eternal, enigmatic sea—not only the sea, but the equally indifferent sea of life as well. Though he

98

may have been an intellectual, Vaughn Williams was the scion of an island race who'd taken to the oceans with the strength, skill, and numbers of army ants. Swarming the world with their proper British attitude. His music evoked the sounds of the sea as heard through British ears, through chanteys and hymns, as well as orchestral flourishes.

The Sea Symphony affected me profoundly. Listening to it, I could not help but equate the lives of the Specials with the piece's view of nature, which could inspire death with the same ease it inspired awe. Before the Flash, mundane historians believed the currents of life and history had already been laid out, their currents mainly mapped. The Flash itself, and after it, the Surge had disturbed the waters, and mankind was forced to sail on seas of rampant unpredictability, where doom could strike capriciously and awe could be denied.

And for what reason? To what avail?

All the struggle, the pain, the loss—what had it gotten us, in the end? Seemed to me life was like war, and what was war good for? Like the song said, nothing. Absolutely nothing.

And if I for a moment doubted the severity of my admittedly inebriated conclusion, there was always the latest issue of *Mediaweek* lying on the floor beside the john to remind me. With the picture of the newly revealed Critical Maas carrying Doc Welles out of the rubble of the jail where he and the Specials had been held prisoner—carrying him while using her new power of flying.

A power she and the other Specials visible in the shot behind her had acquired thanks to the massacre of seven helpless Specials who had been looking to me for leadership, for direction.

And for protection.

I had failed them. And in so doing, I had failed myself. I had failed Dr. Welles, who had put his trust in me. I had failed Chandra, Ravenshadow, and Willie—all those who at one time or another had broken through my self-erected walls and extended the hand of friendship.

A hand, I hasten to add, I always regarded suspiciously. Even I had had to admit, occasionally, there was something about the unruly potential of my enforced childhood friends that severely disturbed me. For that reason, I'd kept to myself as much as possible.

Perhaps I had Dr. Welles to blame, in part, for my isolation. He befriended me as had no other. He raised me in ways more profound than my folks could ever conceive. Through my childhood and adolescence, he'd emphasized the day would come when my fellow Specials would need me, and would depend on me.

To do the right thing.

To kill them, if I had to.

Or to save them, if I had to.

So far I'd done neither.

Which isn't to say I hadn't had the opportunities. Ten years had given me lots of opportunities. But I'd never been able to take advantage of one, to build up momentum of cause and karma. I'd failed Welles, both my enemies and my friends, and myself, all at the same time.

Must be some sort of world record.

The *Mediaweek* summed up the results of my failings rather succinctly:

—Critical Maas had made Chicago a haven for the worst of us, and that no mundane who was in, or who went in, ever got out. Chicago had become a black hole; even the reconnaissance planes were shot down, or tended to be destroyed by a Special using only his bare hands.

—Jerry Montrose was still working as a protector of the city of Las Vegas, though by this point the Mayor and the corporations were becoming a little wary of his volatile temper.

—The scientific community and the general public were still debating over whether or not the massacre ten years ago had precipitated the redistribution of energy among the Specials, an event popularly known as the Surge.

—The most powerful Specials, even those with basically a good heart and good will toward their fellow man, don't use money or pay taxes because no one could arrest and hold them anyway. They have stepped outside the boundaries of society, and in most cases, the love of a mundane is their only anchor in reality. Reminds me of Ivan the Terrible's love for Anastasya, and what happened to poor old Mother Russia after she died.

—Criminal Specials are dropped in barren wastelands outside the country—preferably Africa, where the governments aren't too strong—in the hopes that it will take six or seven weeks for them to return to the United States and do more damage.

—They could be killed by another Special, theoretically, but the most logical candidates are reluctant to spill blood. Matthew Bright has always been a beacon of virtue, while the one known to be unnecessarily brutal occasionally, Jason Miller, a.k.a. Flagg, has apparently, and without making too big a deal out of it, taken to prefer negotiation to the use of physical force. Though not exclusively, of course.

—Randy (Ravenshadow) Fisk operates *pro bono* to help small cities that cannot afford the NexusCorp fees to deal effectively with Special incursions.

—Cliques of Specials have formed in several major cities, carving out slices of urban territory, claiming it as their own communal property.

—Young people of today regard Specials as role models—even the rogue Specials—in much the same way previous generations regarded JFK and Jello Biafra. Young people of today dress like Specials. They seek the flair of punks in zoot suits, the dissident spirits of '60s radicals. They have their own ideas of what the sexual revolution should be about, and those ideas have radically altered the playing field of sexual politics. They also have their own ideas of what an equitable economic system should be, and it does not resemble capitalism.

—This includes the ones who emulate that paradigm of corporate virtue, Patriot. They are just as rebellious, just as radical as their fellow cultural travelers. This is the first time in history when extreme right-wing mundanes are upset that a bunch of kids are dressing themselves up in the American flag.

—Reverend William Kane, founder and head of the Cathedral of Light in Urbana, Illinois, blames the popularity of the Specials among the young on the media. The media he uses so well. Much better than I.

—The politicians, the country's representatives, are too preoccupied with their strategy and squabbling to try to come up with a solution to the so-called "Special problem" that won't piss off the Specials and won't endanger mundanes.

—The common man doesn't care—he just wants to stay out of the Specials' way.

—The common woman, on the other hand, has brought about an exceptional number of paternity suits against Specials.

—Many Specials have sold vast amounts of sperm and ovaries to the pregnancy farms. Then they usually give the money to friends or relatives.

And there was more, of course. The gossip column had paragraphs on the latest rumors concerning the bedroom exploits of former celebrities Chandra and Paula R. I didn't care what Paula R. did, though it bothered me that she did it in order to survive in the style to which she had become accustomed, but what Chandra did filled me with such regret and loss that my soul swam in a sea of tepid wash water. I had become convinced a long time ago, you see, that if it hadn't been for the Flash, Chandra and I would have been destined for one another. Now we were like passing shooting stars, well on our way to flaming out.

The irony was, it still might have been that way for us, if I had controlled my life instead of letting it control me.

Someone let himself in through the front door. One thing about having a lot of Specials around Pederson— burglary was a rare crime, so rare most households were unlocked most of the time.

Personally, I was hoping it was a burglar. I could have used an opportunity to turn someone's molecules inside out. Instead, it was Randy.

"John? You here?" he called out from the kitchen.

"Yeah, back here," I said hurriedly, hoping to distract him from the refrigerator. Specials of our wattage tended to have large appetites, and I hadn't laid in supplies for company.

It worked. He stood in my darkened office with his hands balled in fists by his side, half-looking like he was itching for a fight. I figured he probably was, but not with me.

"Love what you've done with the place," he said. "Early American *blech*, if I'm not mistaken."

I took it back. Maybe he did want to fight with me. "It's a lifestyle choice," I said.

Randy indicated his overcoat and his black shirt. "See how I dress? This is a lifestyle choice. You're just living in a world of crap."

"Sit down," I said. "Care to make yourself at home?"

"I will when I get back to the kitchen. You realize how many calories I have to consume every day to keep up my fighting prowess?"

"It certainly must complicate the underground life," I observed.

By then he was already in the kitchen and at the refrigerator. "Christ, man—no wonder you're so frailing skinny!"

Fifteen minutes later he had wolfed down three sandwiches, cleaning me out of cold cuts, chips, and beer in the process. "I like your diet, too. Early American cholesterol, is it not?" he said, sitting cross-legged, making himself right at home, on the chair nearest mine. "Took me a while to find you. Nobody's heard from you in over a year. You know, nobody blames you for what happened."

"Cathy's *there*, because of me. Nobody else."

"Incorrect. Cathy's *there* because of Deedee and the rest of CM's swine."

"I should have saved her!"

"I should have been there to help her!" said Randy, with his mouth full. "How do you think that makes me feel?"

"I know how it makes you feel: not good. Still, you don't feel as bad about it as I do. And maybe that's what's making *you* nuts."

That startled him. "I do have a thirst for justice, that's true. And I realize it's a thirst probably destined to remain unquenched."

"We live in a desert of inequity, don't we? And we are doomed to die there."

"Doesn't mean we should give up, John. It's taken me months to find you. I should have given up. Logic dictated I give up. But I had to see you. Never would have thought to look for you in good old Pederson."

"How did you find me?"

"Wasn't hard once I thought about it—even though you don't have a phone or e-mail, and you live in a rented home under the assumed name of a childhood friend who's been sworn to secrecy. And he keeps this secret, despite the possibility of revealing your location to tabloids for profit, because he's afraid the authorities might harass him or subject him to tax audits as revenge for helping you." He blew a layer of dust off the top of the chair. "*How* can you live like this?"

"I mean, how did you narrow the search to Pederson?"

"First off, a villain always returns to the scene of the crime."

"Very funny."

"But seriously, folks, your powers have always been in the area of pure energy. Figured they've been harder to control since the Surge, so I ran all the stats for power blackouts, brownouts, and cable outages until I came across a John-shaped anomaly."

"Still playing the world's greatest detective, eh?"

"Hey, it worked, didn't it?" He paused. And pointed. "Is that a dead rat?"

"It stopped stinking a long time ago. Seems like you've gone through a lot of trouble to locate me."

"We *are* old friends."

"And you've never looked me up unless you want something."

"Sorry, it comes with being the world's greatest detective."

"Now that you've found me, Mr. Wayne, what do you want?"

"I've got a job for you," he said, walking to the window. He nudged the rat with his toe. I didn't have the heart to tell him a recently deceased house cat had come with the premises, and the furry object on the floor was a stuffed toy.

"Not interested," I said.

"You said that the last time."

"So I'm in a rut. Sue me."

"If I could walk into a courtroom without being busted, I'd think about it. Don't you think it's time?"

Before, Randy was simply annoying; now he was being downright irritating. My spine communicated to me a dim impression of a succession of brownouts running down the entirety of the Mississippi River. I felt a distinct chill in my lungs, and a hollow of fear deep in my gut. "You're talking about going outside, aren't you?"

"I'm not talking about a house outside of the house, if that's what you mean."

"When you put it that way, I don't know what you mean. I am not going anywhere, Randy Ravenshadow, and I am not doing anything pro-active this week, this year, or any other decade. I am out of the affecting reality business. I've done enough damage already."

"John," he said with that smarmy empathic pose he liked to use on suspects, to get them to crack, "just because things haven't worked out so far doesn't mean you should stop trying."

I laughed. "Yes, it does. You don't know what it means, what it does to the heart, to get out of bed every morning knowing you're a failure, knowing that the next thing you accomplish is apt to make things worse, and you have the historical evidence to prove it." I waved the *Mediaweek* at him. He winced, snarled, and regarded me contemptuously, all with one face. "It doesn't matter what you think about this piece of dreck—it's an indication of how the world sees us—and it means I have failed, every day of my life, I have failed."

"Whoa, whoa, let me get a word in edgewise. I want you to think about something. Think about this—think about, oh, George Washington."

"What?"

"He wore the enemy down until luck, circumstance and his own persistence created the formula for victory. That's what we have to do with the mundanes, John: wear them down until we maneuver ourselves back to the right side of the law. We have to wear them down until they can trust us again."

"It's true what *Mediaweek* says about you," I pointed out. "You did fry your brains on something."

"Just weed," he said defensively.

"Doesn't matter. I've made my decision and it is final. I don't have any business being out in the real world. I screwed up, Randy. I failed, I failed you, I failed Chandra, and—"

"Oh, what bull—"

"Don't interrupt. I failed everybody, Randy. That's what it means to be a failure. You fail other people, and you fail yourself. And I have to live with this, all the time."

"I see you're savoring the experience. Even if what you say is true—which it isn't, but let's assume, for the moment, that you're more inept than The Tick—don't you think everybody deserves a chance at redemption?"

"No. Not anymore." Lately, when I'd gotten tired of brooding indoors, I'd taken to brooding outdoors, just for a change of scenery. I walked outside into the back yard, into the chill night air, so I could savor the sensation of being a failure while looking at the stars. Stars that swept across the sky like dust, frozen in motion. Their distance beckoned me. For one brief instant, I imagined the possibility of leaving this godforsaken planet.

"What were we supposed to do?" Randy called out from behind me, bringing me crashing back to earth. "Take on the whole government single-handed?"

"I should have figured out what was going on faster. I could've stopped Jason before he put us all on the wrong side of the law."

"I get it! You're in search of hindsight!"

"I have plenty of that," I replied, grimly.

"Should've, could've, would've—we can second-guess ourselves to death, John. You can—" He stopped in mid-sentence. He blinked at something. For a moment I thought he was on a pot-induced brainlock, but then he walked toward a rusty old swing set in the corner of the yard. "Nice set of swings. I used to have one, when I was a kid."

"Yeah."

He looked around, dreamily. "I bet this place was real nice before you moved in. Now look at it."

"The house is a tad run-down, isn't it?"

"I've seen mummified hookers who weren't as run-down as this joint."

"I wonder if these swings can still hold me."

"They should. They're stronger than they look—"

"So you've tried them?" he asked, with mock surprise.

"—And you can walk up walls. So I think the chances are slim you'll land on your arse. Much as I'd like to see it."

He patted his "arse" in my general direction, then sat down on a swing. A little gingerly, I thought.

"Yeah, these swings are stronger than they look—and so are you."

"That was a cheap shot."

"Hey, excuse me, these are desperate times, and therefore I have the right to use any rhetorical device I need to, in order to get what I want."

"How can you trust a man who's mastered the art of diplomatic manipulation?"

"You don't have to trust me, personally," said Randy, kicking off the ground. "You just have to trust me to do the right thing."

"That's the most preposterous statement I've ever heard—!"

An unlocked gate squeaked open. "He's right, John." It was—

Chandra! My knees turned to water, my spine to jelly, and my feet into sponges.

I cleared my throat. "Hello," I said.

I'll say this for her: she still knew how to strike a dramatic pose. She stood at the entrance with one hand on top of the gate and the other on her hip. I couldn't see her eyes for her dark glasses—which I'd heard she'd taken to wear as often as possible, in order to dampen her ability to cloud humanity's minds—but it didn't take psychic powers to feel their intense focus on me.

"Thought I'd get in on the action," she said, by way of a greeting.

"It's been a long time," I said, lamely.

"Too long," she replied. The accusatory tone in her voice was difficult to miss.

"I've been ashamed."

"I know," she said, with a unique blend of compassion and sarcasm. She glided close to me, slid her glasses above her forehead, and looked me in the eye with smoldering honesty.

"In on what?" I asked, belatedly, feeling like a character from a James M. Cain novel. You know, the hero who dies or is otherwise ruined for love of a woman.

"About time you asked," said Randy. He was walking up the wall. "I said I had a job. I think we can pull it off. But we'll need your help."

"What kind of job?" I asked, fearing a bad punch line.

It was worse than I'd feared: "Chicago."

"Chicago is a city, not a job," I said.

"John!" Chandra exclaimed.

"You been to Chicago lately, John?" Randy asked.

"No."

"Neither has anybody else. Not anybody who wants to get out alive anyway. People used to go in, because they were curious, wanted to escape the land of mundania, for whatever reason, or were looking for a honorable way to commit suicide that was quicker than smoking. In the final analysis, the reasons don't matter, because damn few people ever leave Chicago, and that was only in the early years of the post-Surge period. Now no one in their right mind voluntarily goes to Chicago. The only people who do are kidnapped, like poor Cathy. They say in the last year the borders have been guarded by voracious creatures of a patchwork nature. Want to give me three guesses who's responsible?"

"No!" I stared at him, horrified. "I haven't heard that before!"

"Been skipping the news too?" asked Chandra, sweetly.

Randy's smile was razor-edged. "While some people were brooding and feeling sorry for themselves, I've gotten some of the Feds to trust me. They're prepared to offer us amnesty if we can clear out Chicago."

"Who's us?"

"Whoever goes in with me. That's you two, and maybe a couple of the others I'm talking to."

"And you really think you can trust the Feds?"

"I got it in writing, signed, sealed, notarized. It's legally binding, and a first step toward legitimacy for us."

There are some Indians who said the same thing."

"Yeah, but they lost. We're gonna win. We'll have to change of course. Some of us will have to go back to using money, instead of renting our professional services, bartering, or just taking what we want. But as long as we stay outside the system, we can never fight for our inalienable rights. We can never fight the ones who put us in this position. Once we're back on the inside, we can fight them in the courts and in the arena of public opinion. We can drag the truth about what happened to cause the Surge kicking and screaming into the courtroom."

"Surely we can get coverage on Court TV, at the very least," Chandra said. Always the mistress of the media.

"What kind of opposition are we looking at?"

"You mean, Chicago?" she said, with a laugh. "Our competition in Chicago is unknown. Stephanie's still out of control, and Randy thinks she's made the city a safe haven for the worst of us—even the law-breakers the media call the disappeared."

"So the competition is still pretty stiff."

"Plus," Chandra continued, "we have no idea of the extent of the city border defenses. There are rumors which Randy has referred to."'

"That's why we need power," said Randy. He kicked off the wall, did a somersault in the air, and landed feet first with feline proficiency. "That's why we need *you!*"

Chandra stepped close to me and put her hand on my shoulder. Her soft touch generated enough heat to make my blood vessels sizzle. She looked me in the eye. "John, I'm not good at asking—I've never had the practice. But I'm asking you to come out of your shell and face front like I know you're capable of doing. You've always been the strongest of us, John. You've never strayed from your path. Don't stray now, not when we finally have a chance to reach the end of this road."

I shook my head.

"Don't you get it?" said Randy. "It's a chance to get back in the game on our own terms. We might not get another one. So what do you say?"

I shook my head again. "I can't."

"Oh, John!" Chandra exclaimed. She turned away, fuming. "Don't you want to tell me, John?" she asked, between her teeth.

Her super-charisma had the same effect on me it always did: nothing. Her mundane essence and her mundane essence alone provided the raw inspiration for my emotional attachment to her. "I still can't," I said.

"Why not?" "I have an obligation I haven't told anybody about."

"I'm not surprised," said Randy sarcastically.

"I ... managed to sneak the Doc back into town. I've got him hidden in a place near here. If I go, there's no one to take care of him."

Chandra turned pale. "Oh, my God! What's the matter with him?"

"Accelerated decrepitude," I said. "And don't forget, ever since Paulson tried to frame him for the death of my mother, he's either been laying low or outright on the lam. Last few years, it's mostly been on the lam. His heart, lungs, and kidneys are about to fail, and while I've 'convinced' a few doctors to make house calls, there's no hospital that will take him in. The Feds have ways of retaliating against those who assist the officially disfavored, even when they're performing their sworn duty. So I have the Doc hidden in a place near here. Needless to say, he's not doing well. He's even declined to the point where he's watching daytime TV."

"It's okay," said Randy. "You forget, I have resources. I can have a nurse there by morning, and a kidney dialysis machine there by the afternoon. He'll be all right, I promise."

It occurred to me I was running out of excuses. "So when do you want to go?"

"Now."

"Not so fast." I had to say good-bye to Doc first. I used to think of myself as an unsentimental sort, but the thought of all this senseless violence—that which had happened and that which was to come—was starting to have an odd effect on my emotions. Imagine: This from a man who wasn't used to having any.

Warily I knocked on the door and opened it. "You awake?" I whispered.

"Yes, I'm awake, goddamnit," came the hoarse response. I'd always believed experience was supposed to make a man wiser, and that wisdom brought with it serenity and the kind knowledge of truth. But if anything, Dr. Welles' hard-earned wisdom, coupled with his current physical discomfort, had turned him into a cantankerous son of a bitch, loveable but infuriating. "I want to watch some television."

"You can't," I said, sitting on the corner of the bed. "You need your beauty rest."

He laughed, then coughed. "Don't make me laugh," he said angrily. Barely able to move, he leaned over to deposit some spittle in a pot on the rug.

"I have to go, Doc. Randy says he'll have someone here in a few hours."

"Good. I'm getting tired of having you wipe my bottom." He was exaggerating, I hasten to add. He wasn't that far gone. Yet.

"Believe me, I don't get that much of thrill out of wiping your bottom either. Listen, we have a chance, not a good one, considering what we're up against, but a chance to set right some of the circumstances we've found ourselves in. Randy and the others—"

"Who are the others?"

"Chandra. I don't know who else yet."

"Chandra? That vixen? Damn it, I told you not to make me laugh."

"I thought you liked her."

"Why do I have the feeling that you and Randy—and Miss Chandra—are charging off half-cocked somewhere?"

"Chicago, to be exact."

"Even better. What would you like carved on your tombstone?"

"One of my poems. That way I'd be ensured some privacy. Listen. I know you expected much of me, and I wanted to live up to all your expectations. I feel like I let you down. I *know* I let you down. Maybe now, I can change that."

"Nuts! You haven't let me down!"

"You've been like a father to me, for so long. Certainly you've been more of a father than my real one was. A thousand times you've tried to get me to leave you, and I've been tempted every time. Now I really do have to go. I hate leaving you like this—"

His fingers slithered toward mine like spider legs and he touched my hand with a ghostly strength. This was the most tender gesture he'd made since my mother died.

"John," he rasped. "I'll be okay. You go, boy, you go. Okay."

I don't know what happened. One moment I was looking at him suspiciously, as our relationship had trained me to do, and the next moment, my arms were around his neck, hugging him so hard I almost broke his neck. "I love you."

"I know. I love you too. Now will you let go of me? Before you break my neck?"

"Sorry. Goodbye, Doc."

"Goodbye, John. Give them hell."

I was a mite surprised to see Chandra and Randy standing in the backyard of Doc's safe house as I came out the rear door. Chandra was quietly puffing a cancer stick, while Randy was eating what appeared to be, judging from the trash at his feet, the sixth of a series of protein bars.

"Are you ready?" Randy asked, impatiently.

"I'm ready," I replied. "Chandra, you can't fly. How did you get here?"

"How do you think? Randy carried me. But I'll gladly go the rest of the way with you," she added, somewhat breathlessly.

Randy said, in mock sincerity, "I never touched her inappropriately, man. I swear."

Chandra raised an eyebrow in his general direction. "But you wanted to, right?"

"Of course," said Randy, "but how flattering can it be, knowing I don't have any choice?"

"Uh, it isn't, actually."

"Don't get me wrong, Chandra," Randy said sternly. "I like you and we need you, but I've always resented your power."

Chandra gasped. "But I can't help using my power! And I can't help what it is, either!"

"You can help how much you enjoy using it," said Randy.

"Aren't you being a bit judgmental?" I snapped at Randy.

"Oh for God's sake," Randy said, "can't you see this woman is the Typhoid Mary of heartbreakers?"

And he took to the air.

Chandra put her arms around my neck before I had a chance to think about what he'd said.

"Take me," she said. I shrugged, grabbed her by the waist, and achieved liftoff with a light kick.

She snuggled close into on my shoulder, and wrapped her ankles around mine, so she wouldn't be hanging in the air. I had no idea where Randy was leading us, and at the moment I really didn't care. This was the first time Chandra and I had ever touched from head to toe, and I felt like I was flying while under the influence.

Even so, Randy's words had had the desired effect. I would give my life for this woman, and she would give her life for me, of that there was no doubt.

But there was no way I could give her my heart.

Blood splattered against the wall. Critical Maas hit the FBI agent again.

"When will they be here?" she demanded. It was all she could do not to crush his skull between her fingers like it was an empty eggshell. Already the man's face was bloody as hell and battered almost beyond recognition. What was it going to take to get him to talk?

"I don't know," he managed said between bloody lips.

CM did not know his name. She didn't care. While doing reconnaissance, he'd strayed too close to the no-man's-land between the city limits and the outside world, hence had been an easy capture by the rogues. Now he sat before her, his arms tied behind a chair, and he was at her mercy. That was all she needed to know. She hit him again.

"Soon," he spat out, along with a few of his teeth.

"Now we're getting somewhere," said CM, squatting in front of him so she could get a good look at the man's puffy eyes. "How soon?"

"Next few days . . . maybe . . ."

"And who's leading the charge? Paulson again?" She regarded Paulson as one of the luckiest people on the planet. Three times during the last five years he'd been within easy reach of her anxious fingers, and three times he'd escaped with his buttocks reasonably intact.

"Don't know . . . Specials . . . maybe . . ."

"Well I'll be damned! You've just earned a reward." She

hit the man gently, just hard enough to knock him out, so he wouldn't feel his pain for a while. Unfortunately, judging by the way his head moved, she might have struck him a little too hard.

"Oops," she said with a smile, as she glided past Deedee and the other rogue Specials present in the ruins, and curled up on the back of a ruined statue of a lion.

Everyone stared at her in silence, waiting. The only sounds were the soft hiss of a gentle breeze and the steady drip, drip, drip of blood from the FBI agent's nose and mouth.

"Sounds good to me," CM said. "Anybody else up for a war?"

PART TWO

11

THE GATHERING

She dreamed she was in her kitchen, fixing breakfast for her family, when the flash flood hit and decimated the kitchen along with her entire house. Which, come to think of it, wasn't her house exactly, not the one she had been living in when the flash flood hit the town, but instead was the one's she'd been living in when she was six, before the family had been required to return to Pederson. She choked as the water smothered her in the dream and—

She opened her eyes.

And immediately felt nauseated. Miserable. So full of self-hatred that she wished it was possible for her to commit suicide.

Because she was still in jail. The dream had been sufficiently vivid to make her forget, if for a few moments, that she was still in jail.

Cathy Holmes knew she couldn't commit suicide because she'd already tried, and her unique abilities prevented her from dying as a result of the application of her will—though whether the initial Flash was responsible, or the Surge years later, was unclear.

It wasn't invulnerability, exactly. It was the fact that after she'd consumed an entire bottle of Liquid Plumber—at the cost of great personal agony—her body had "miraculously" healed itself and she had returned to normal without actually dying.

Soon thereafter, the rogue who brought her next meal noticed the empty container under her bed, and CM took very unkindly to Cathy's suicide attempt. Cathy was punished, severely, and thus she learned that her body healed much less quickly when the damage wasn't fatal.

In the meantime, the mundane who'd brought Cathy the substance in the first place endured the punishment of having her arms and legs torn off one at time. After that, no one was likely to help Cathy again, and so she had resigned herself to her fate.

She was doomed to live, until she had the opportunity to burn herself alive in a big fire, or dive into a vat of acid.

"Hello, Cathy Jean," drawled the rogue guard, a muscle-bound high power named Hugh Dinger. "How ya doin'?" He was rolling in a handcart, on which lay a mis-shapen body covered in a white blanket. He called her "Cathy Jean" because CM had christened her thusly for some capricious reason, perhaps intending to paint her as an unsophisticated country girl in the eyes of the worldly rogues.

Cathy said nothing. She was tired of these people seeing her cry.

"Still not talking?' Dinger observed. "Suits me, just as long as you do what you're supposed to do."

Cathy concentrated on preventing her gorge from rising.

"Touch it," said Dinger impatiently. "I have but a single life to live. Touch it. You heard me."

I used to think I was the only one of the Pederson 113 to be born without powers, she thought.

"*Touch it,*" Dinger said again. "Or else . . . well, you know what else, don't you, Cathy Jean?"

I used to wonder what it would be like to truly be Special, to be with the others on a plane more profound than those we already shared. She reached through the bars and slid her hand between the blanket and the cold, furry skin of the corpse beneath it.

Her arm glowed. She tried not to look at it.

Her hand became hot. She tried not to notice the energy draining from her fingers.

Not that she missed it.

The person or creature beneath the blanket, which now was a living person or creature, shivered and growled.

"Good girl," Dinger said, rolling the cart away. "I'll be back in a few hours with another one. Plenty of time to get your strength back."

I had no idea, Cathy thought, as she stared through the bars in her window at the setting sun. *And now all I want to is to go home again, to be normal again, to be clean again.*

She watched an eagle fly toward the horizon and disappear into the sun. It seemed to her the eagle was taking her future with it. From now on, there would only be the present in her life. The grimy, perverted, evil present. How long would it be before there was no turning back, and she became one of *them?*

* * *

123

Twenty minutes to showtime. Joshua Kane knew he should be downstairs in the studio. Reverend Kane liked to have all the participants in the televised services to gather in the green room twenty minutes early, so he'd be sure there wouldn't be any surprises.

Standing on a balcony surrounding the tallest spire of the crystal cathedral his father had had built to further the ends of his ministry, Joshua Kane—a.k.a. the Special known as Sanctuary—decided that, given his druthers, he would rather be doing what he was now—looking at the sun setting magnificently—than sit in the stodgy old green room listening to one of the deacons pontificate endlessly on human failings that had existed since the dawn of man. He was a Special who despite one very glaring episode of sinful behavior had always tried to live his life in accordance with the highest moral standards. The sky was ablaze with such crimson he easily imagined it reflecting the horrific light he had once believed existed below the Earth. In Hell.

He now knew that Hell existed on the surface of the Earth, and he had made his own significant contributions to its unique character, while Heaven was like the sky—the closer you came to it, the more elusive it became, until you got so close it disappeared altogether and became just a vacuum.

By now it should be apparent Joshua wasn't a deep thinker, but he was a sincere one, and his heart was heavy with a burden largely of his own making.

"Joshua!"

"Yes, Father?" said Joshua, not turning around. The flock of birds passing above filled him with awe and envy.

"What was that call earlier?"

Joshua ground his teeth. Not a day went by when his

father didn't ask that question, or one like it. "Just a prayer request from one of the Lazarus Club contributors."

"Never say 'just'," Reverend Kane snapped. "Contributors are what built this place. Did you take the request?"

"Yes, Father, I heard his prayer." Joshua noted that his father didn't even ask the nature of the request. One of the contributors could have requested a prayer that he would get away with murder or child molestation, and his father wouldn't mind so long as the check cleared.

"Good. Well, better come downstairs. We're almost ready for the evening broadcast–I mean, the evening service."

"Yes, Father."

"Didn't know the Lazarus Club had your direct line."

"God works in mysterious ways," said Joshua, still not looking at the man as he went back downstairs. He knew that was one answer his father would have difficulty finding fault with.

"Mysterious indeed," added Joshua aloud, to himself, after he'd heard his father close the door.

He stepped off the balcony, kicking off the rail, and sped up, up, up toward the crimson clouds.

The Congregationalists below uttered a collective gasp. For ten years people had believed that despite the Surge, Sanctuary's abilities consisted of the power to float and to glow beatifically. The truth was, Joshua/Sanctuary had kept the fact that he had become a high power as a result of the Surge a secret from everyone, including his own father.

Especially his own father.

And for this one brief moment, when he was flying above the masses and revealing himself for who and what he truly was, Joshua Kane knew what it meant to be free.

* * *

Dusk. Ten miles outside the buffer zone between Chicago and the rest of the world.

Below, waiting for us in the wood: nine Specials. Three the reader has encountered before. The first, and foremost in the clearing, Eli Kindler, with whom I'd exchanged fist-icuffs ten years before. The Surge had been good to him—he was built like a titanium shithouse, and was twice as strong as he looked. Of course, his head was twice as thick as it looked too, but even so, I was glad to see him.

Plus his wife Susan Kindler, the former mistress of mane, standing just behind him, also looking like she'd been taking Steroids-In-a-Drum. Third was Ian Erwin, for-mer mid-power flier, former milksop, who now flew so fast that when he went in circles he created small torna-does that did a lot of damage. He and Jason had had something of a long-running duel through the years, and several people had died so Ian could elude capture. Sev-eral innocent people, I might add, though that didn't make much difference in the eyes of the law. I'd liked to have been able to blame Ian somehow for the loss of all those people. Unfortunately, I don't know that I would have acted any differently under the same circumstances.

After all, the only reason Paulson and his goons hadn't captured me was because they knew they couldn't do it without killing me, and I would kill them in the process.

"Here we are, folks," said Randy, as he landed. "Right on time."

"Hi, guys," I said, making my landing. Chandra was still in my arms. Already the other guys were looking at me as if they wanted to hand my nuts to me on a silver platter. "Ian? How's it shaking?"

"Very well," he said with a smile. His unerring accuracy

while high in the air was infamous among the law enforcement community. And had been highly praised in rap songs playing on the radio and on the silver screen.

Big Bob Hardy pushed his way past Ian to be the first to shake hands with Chandra. The Surge had made him a shapeshifter; like all shapeshifters he was unable to gain or lose mass during the change. Bob liked to change into a giant mangy rat-creature. In fact, he'd changed so much he was having trouble losing the soft gray down all over his face, and the whiskers from his nose.

Chandra moved past him with diplomatic aplomb, and attempted to shake hands with the ladies. They instinctively backed away from her, practically in unison. Chandra recovered quickly, pulling back and just nodding a silent greeting. The ladies were Lucy Stradella, Rita Young, and Marcy Finn. These three had been among the plainer ladies before the Surge, but that extra influx of energy had idealized their physical appearance as well as their abilities. They all had a bit of blood on their hands, but I wasn't sure how much. Probably enough to get us through the first part of a fight, I hoped.

Luigi Moline and Mick Green rounded out the male contingent. They were slender yuppie types, who wore sweaters and stylish jeans. They stayed close together and I caught a glimpse of them holding hands once. They were being extraordinarily brave, I thought, considering CM's attitude toward male homosexuals. Capture would certainly mean torture of the most humiliating sort.

"I do love technology—e-mail, auto-dialers, programmed voice mail . . . makes my nipples hard, just thinking about it," Randy said, mordantly.

"I don't believe you," said Luigi.

"Well, you'll just have to take my word for it!" said

Randy, grinning. "Still, I'm glad you all made it."

The others tended to have quiet, determined responses. This was a very sober reunion, and of course, we had good reason for regarding it so. It might be the last reunion for some of us.

"You don't have to do this, Chandra."

Her voice trembled as she said, "I know. But I want to. I want to feel that I'm carrying my weight."

"It's dangerous!" I said.

"Hey!" Susan snapped. "Why should she get special privileges?"

"Sorry," I said. "I was just trying to be objective about our strengths and weakness."

"And yours isn't exactly between your legs, from what I hear," said Rita.

"Ladies!" said Chandra soothingly. She touched Rita on the cheek.

Rita flinched, but then touched Chandra's hand in turn and left her fingers there. She looked Chandra in the eye. "Sorry, I'm just a little anxious, that's all."

Susan rolled her eyes, but stepped away from Chandra and remained silent.

All the men were too busy looking at Chandra to notice.

All the men except me, that is. Only I had the freedom to like or dislike Chandra, depending on what my feeling of the moment was. At the moment I didn't like her, though I understood what she was doing: making the peace between us before we lost focus on our real mission.

"I know it's dangerous," said Chandra, so all could hear. "But I'm okay with it. I'm not as physically strong as you and Randy, John, but I'm no anorexic weakling either. Besides, I may be the only one who can help get us past Stephanie's security. Well, quietly, anyway. That may count for a lot when the time comes."

"Okay, here's the game plan," said Randy, calling the meeting to order. "I chose you people because all of you are on the run, same as John, Chandra and myself. All of you can benefit from the deal offering us immunity if we can take out Stephanie Maas and retake Chicago. All of you have abilities we can use if this turns ugly."

"Which it probably will," said Eli.

"Probably," added his wife.

"But we'll do this in stages," continued Randy. "We need to know what we're walking into in order to use our forces wisely and avoid casualties. So the four of will go in first, scout out the area. When we've got a clear plan of action, we'll send word to the rest of you."

"Wait a minute, Randy," I said. "You said the four of us."

"That's right, John," he said with a sly smile. I should have known something was up from that expression alone.

But instead I just charged ahead with my ramblings: "But I thought it was just us going in first: you, me, and Chandra. So who's the fourth—"

"That would be me," someone said, stepping out from behind the trees. A familiar voice, one I hadn't heard in years.

They told me later that my expression was rather amusing, not unlike that of a certain coyote who's just seen his road runner prey disappear on the horizon of a vista he's just painted on a boulder. The last person I'd expected to see, even as a surprise ally, was Joshua Kane. He wore an outfit I hadn't seen before, a yellow and white satin tunic and black satin pants. The tunic had a large yellow cross sewn over the front.

"I thought about it," said Joshua, talking fast, "and prayed about it and got word to Randy that if there was some way I could help—"

I was faster than his talk, though, so fast my hands were around his throat with but a thought and a blue haze of energy was building up in the fist of my right hand. "You son of a bitch!" I exclaimed.

"John! No!" somebody—Randy? Ian?—said.

"You sold us out! Gave us up to the government!"

"John—let him go!" That, I was certain, was Randy.

"I—" Joshua managed to say.

"You think I'm gonna trust you *now?*" I shook him like a toy, and restrained myself from sucking the life-force out of him.

Randy stepped between us. His hand on my shoulder was gentle, but firm. "I said let him go!"

"Don't you see? He's here to—"

"He's here because I asked him to be here!" Randy said. "Go on, Josh. Tell him."

At that moment you could have knocked me over with an errant mosquito. I calmed down with an effort, permitted my surging energy to dissipate, and released Joshua's throat. "Yeah, Josh, tell us," I said. "Tell us why we shouldn't kill you right now for selling us out."

I had to admit, his expression of sadness and regret appeared genuine. Not that I bought it for a moment, but it looked good. One of his hands shook; he steadied it with the other. He had difficulty looking us in the collective eye as he said:

"I know that I did do that. I sold you out. My father and I did some . . . terrible things. I did them because I was more afraid of him than I was of the truth. I've suffered the burden for ten years. I can't . . . bear that burden anymore. I need to atone. I need to try and fix this, somehow. I've prayed on it, and this is the only way for me to set things right. I can't ask for you to forgive me now. All I can do is try to earn your forgiveness at the end of this."

"He's not going," I said. "Don't you know how much blood is on his hands? How much blood there is on *ours*—" I waved at Eli and the others "—because of him."

"Yes, he is going," insisted Randy.

"Not a chance in—" I began, only to be absolutely stymied when Chandra slinked up to Joshua.

"I can't forgive you either, Josh," she said, "but I guess I can give you the chance to try."

I trembled with anger. For the first time in my life I felt like punching Chandra. This was probably the first time in her life anybody had wanted to punch her, as well, but she was clearly oblivious to my feelings as she searched Josh's eyes for an indication he was under her spell.

I don't know if she noticed one, but I certainly didn't. Joshua simply nodded. Tears slipped down his cheeks. He glanced to the sky a couple of times. Searching for divine guidance. I guess that's what it took for the average person who wasn't me to be oblivious to Chandra's pheromones: that or complete and utter self-absorption.

"You paid her to do that," I said to Randy.

"Nope." A beat. "Hey, she's your friend."

"I wish. It's not fair."

"What is?"

"That he has a chance to redeem himself. There's an old curse that says you have sinned so grievously against man and God that you should die, be resurrected, and then

131

die again, a thousand times, and still it wouldn't be enough to set things right again."

"I'd like to take care of the first part of that curse," said Eli, raising his hand.

A few people took one significant step toward Joshua, and for a second I thought I'd be witnessing my first lynching, but Randy immediately came between them. I don't think Joshua even noticed the threat or the rescue. Like I said, he was being self-absorbed.

"Look, in all this time, I've never let you down," Randy said. "Most of you are alive right now because of the plans I've made for emergencies, and several of us are dead because of mistakes Joshua has made in the past. But that's all they were: mistakes. And like you, I've wanted to extract a little payback, street justice style, for those mistakes."

"Why didn't you?" Susan asked. "You're like John. Nothing can stop you."

"Why haven't you set his hair on fire?" Randy shot back. "Or given him a telekinetic Mohawk?"

"I dunno," she said with a shrug. "Don't see what good it would have done, I guess."

"Because what happened to us would have been the same whether or not Joshua was involved. He wasn't one of the movers and shakers on this deal, honey. It was Jerry and Jason, working with the so-called Reverend Kane, who shafted us Specials big time. Even so, I know how you feel. I feel the same way. But now we have a chance to correct the historical balance between us and the mundanes, and we don't have a lot of time. We have to go *now*.

"We don't know what will happen once we cross the perimeter," Randy continued. "We'll need a witness, somebody the Feds have already certified as sufficiently credible to get us all indicted in the first place. Somebody they'll have no choice but to trust. Somebody who can force them to admit how easily they swallowed those lies, and how Paulson and his ilk have tried to use our existence as their own political staircase through the years. Anybody else fit the bill?"

Bob and Mick looked at one another and shrugged. Rita and Marcy glanced around, while the others looked essentially unhappy. They'd smelled blood, and had wanted to taste it.

"I dunno," Bob said.

"Then it's decided," said Randy. "Josh is going."

"I don't like it," I said, knowing I'd already lost.

"You don't have to," Randy replied, with a broad grin.

"I won't be responsible for him. He gets into trouble, you save him."

"Somebody'll have to."

"What's that mean?"

"He missed getting physically enhanced. He's as vulnerable now as he was before the Surge. His strength is what it always was—that of a below-average mundane. His power of illumination is the same, as is its control and range. He can fly now, rather than just float, but that's about it. Otherwise, it's as if he received absolutely zero energy from the general transference."

"An exception?" I asked. "How's that possible?"

The others mumbled among themselves, as suspicious as I.

"I don't know," said Randy. "Can't say I've given it a whole lot of thought, mainly because I never believed I'd have to. All I know is, sometimes the way we feel about ourselves affects our power. I don't think Josh believes he's worthy of being protected. I don't know whether it's guilt or the need to atone, but he's always going to be vulnerable, no matter how many of us die."

"Wonderful sentiments," Lucy said, brushing a thick lock of blonde hair from her eye.

"I'm not doing this to get killed," said Marcy. She was black and plump, with a round face that wore, tonight in any case, a perpetual long frown. "Randy," said Susan sternly, "you're not giving us any more of this-is-a-good-day-to-die crap, are you?"

"Oh, you may die," said Randy lightly, "but not tonight. Not tonight."

Marcy crossed her arms. "Well, there have many times when that was the best I could expect."

"I think *he's* got the best chance of dying tonight," said Ian, pointing toward Josh.

Through it all, Josh stood silent, looking away, pre-occupied with his own funk, presumably. We were just wishing he wasn't here, while he was actually acting like we weren't.

Then Rita, who had a stern, freckled face, puckered her nose and said, "I think it all has to do with his old man."

That spoiled it. Josh glared at her.

"You mean his puppeteer, don't you?" said Luigi, putting a stick of chewing gum into his mouth.

"I know who my father is," said Joshua grimly.

"All right," I said, gathering Chandra in my arms and taking to the sky. "Let's get this over with."

"Hey, wait for me!" shouted Randy, bolting past us.

Josh said nothing; he just began to display his usual holy, blissful lightshow and followed us, not really lagging behind, but not exactly being eager either.

Couldn't say I blamed him. Getting in Chicago would

be—was the easy part. Getting out, on the other hand, was going to be the problem.

And I had this sneaking suspicion that getting out was going to be a big priority very soon, once the gang and I began our recon. Though an ocean of fluffy white clouds was billowing in from the north, otherwise the sky was bright, and the moon full. We came in over the harbor and had a clear view of the ghost ships that had been scuttled and stacked up like a beaver dam near the mouth of the Chicago River. The Art Institute was totally deci- mated, its walls and roofs lying about like the pieces of a child's log cabin set, carelessly kicked over.

"Jesus," said Randy. "I'd seen the satellite pictures, but seeing this mess up close is mind-boggling. I had no idea . . ."

"Where do we land?" I asked.

"Arms getting tired?" asked Randy.

"No, I just don't want anybody to see Joshua."

"Well, you really know how to compliment a girl," said Chandra with mock chagrin.

I only noticed the chagrin in retrospect. I stammered out an explanation that Joshua was conspicuous in his Sanctuary mode. Randy found my explanation less than believable, but as Chandra had dug herself a little deeper into my shoulder while we had flown over the harbor, I decided her opinion was the only one worth considering.

Joshua wisely had kept his mouth during the entire trip. He kept it shut now, as Randy guided us over Lake Shore Drive and we landed between several slabs of road that appeared to have been shifted by giant ants burrow- ing to the surface.

"Here is as good a spot as any," said Randy. "In fact,

it might be the last, best safe spot. This is as far as most of the people trying to escape over this route ever got. Yet the Specials who've hooked up with Stephanie are never seen patrolling this area. I want to know what's out here stopping people from escaping."

"Think we'll figure it out standing around here and jawboning?" I asked.

"No, we're going to have to do some sightseeing," Randy replied. "Remember: we size things up, figure out where Stephanie and her followers are hiding out, get an idea on how the civilians are doing, and then call in the rest. No heroics. Not yet, anyway."

"That's kind of funny, coming from you, Randy," said Chandra. "I mean, as the first one of us to put on a costume and decide he was a super hero, don't you think it's—"

"Do you hear something?" Joshua exclaimed.

I shook my head. I hadn't heard anything. "Hey? Did you notice the lady was talking?" I asked.

"I thought I heard something."

What a nervous Nellie, I thought. His eyes were wide and he looked like he was about to have an asthma attack. He was trying to look in every direction at once.

Near as I could tell, all he could perceive was the eerie silence emanating like radiation from the deserted ruins of this once-proud urban thoroughfare. I had the distinct feeling he was wasting our collective time.

"What did you think you heard?' I asked, only to see a rather definitive answer charging directly at us. I think I got as far as uttering the word "Holy—" before I realized this was one occasion when words were truly inadequate.

Creatures were emerging, squeezing through crevices in ruins, through broken windows, popping up from manholes, from behind walls.

Creatures with wide mouths and sharp, pointy teeth.

Jigsaw creatures that looped toward us like great apes on a rampage. They had the faces of giant rats and the bodies of Frankenstein monster hunks. They wore trousers. They had beady red eyes.

They were very large.

They had us surrounded in a matter of moments.

Had we been a bunch of mundanes, trying to sneak in or out of the city, we would have been doomed.

As it was, we just had a fighting chance. Judging from the way they sprang forward, they could have easily leapt to intercept one of the fliers before it was too late. This was one case when the better part of valor meant to stand and fight.

Already blues waves of energy were cascading through me. Since the Surge I'd become a human fission machine, with enough energy to give the phrase "scorched earth" a whole new intensity, should I have so desired.

One of the creatures sprang at me. I let him have it.

He hit a wall like a bug smashing into a car window. The sound was so sickening that the others of his kind, dumb as they were, were momentarily distracted. At the end of that moment, of course, they immediately recommenced their attack.

I let another one have it. I had to be careful, slow and systematic, otherwise my blue bolts would become rapid, indiscriminate, and involuntary. I'd kill not only my friends, but everyone in Chicago.

Randy acquitted himself well, straight off the bat, as I knew he would. But Chandra surprised me—the first creature to lunge toward her got a punch in the nose that sent it reeling back.

Joshua, meanwhile, just stood there as a creature with

six arms sprang to meet him, all open arms and open mouth. He appeared worried, I'd give him that, but talk about being as dumb as a tree. Either he was putting himself entirely in God's hands or he was looking for an honorable way of committing suicide—maybe a bit of both.

I was trying to suppress an involuntary surge that was way too powerful, while Randy was busy elsewhere bashing two heads together. It was Chandra who stepped in, connecting to the creature's jaw with both fists, knocking it so askew that I thought its body was going to be torn from its head.

"Josh! Get behind me!" she yelled.

But he simply stood still, mute and downtrodden.

"Randy!" she yelled.

"Just a sec!" he said. "I'm busy." A gaggle of the beasts were trying to pile on him. He had one by the throat, another by the foot, and a third had his legs wrapped around his neck. Randy released the other two, grabbed number three by the legs, and swung him to the ground as if he was casting off a sack of potatoes. "The name's Ravenshadow. Glad to meet you."

He grabbed yet another attacker by the throat and squeezed so hard the creature's head was in danger of exploding like a pimple. Randy studied the contorted face. "Speaking as an artist, I must commend you for possessing an interesting design. Sort of Picasso meets a patchwork quilt. Wonder if the artist signed his or her name anywhere on or in you. Let's find out."

And he tore the creature in half with the ease of a strongman ripping apart a paperback novel.

"I think it's pretty, don't you?" said Critical Maas to Cathy Holmes in the latter's cell.

Cathy could barely bring herself to look at the creature CM had rolled into the cell. It was an abomination, a jigsaw concoction sewn together from dead animal parts, some parts with muscle and bone still intact, while others had obviously been stuffed at some point during the past three hundred years.

"I call it a rat-bat-cat-dog thingie, with bits of rabbit and parts of a hyena we got out of the zoo. I'm saving the lions and tigers and bears for the entertainment of the masses." She paused. "Now, touch it."

Cathy could not bring herself to move.

CM thought this was amusing. "Yeah, I'd heard you were pulling a work stoppage. Bet you'd like to smash my face in right now, wouldn't you? Too bad the only power you got was bring dead stuff back to life."

Cathy silently agreed. She'd never so much as suspected her gift until after the Surge, and then so much about her life that she had thought only slightly unusual made perfect sense: her green thumb, coupled with the frequent insect infestations in her apartments and gardens; the fact that all her friends' pets had lived to a ripe old age, and then tended to die only when she wasn't around to say good-bye; and her unerring ability to pick the freshest vegetables without paying much attention to it, regardless of the overall quality of selection. Now she missed her husband, her children, all the friends she'd made under the pretense of being a mundane. No mere touch was ever going to bring back *that* life.

"But your life's just been one big irony after another, hasn't it? I mean, for most of your life you didn't even know you had this power. Can you imagine the money you could have made using this energy to bring rich dead folks back to life?"

"Stephanie, please . . ." Cathy knew that was a mistake the moment the words left her mouth, and she cowered a nanosecond before CM responded:

"I AM NOT STEPHANIE! I'm . . . not . . . that . . . that frightened little mouse who couldn't keep her own father's hands off her! I'm the one she hid behind when she couldn't take the pain anymore!" Then her anger evaporated in an instant and she began to giggle, insanely. "Mouse. That's funny. Stephanie Mass. Stephanie Mouse and Maas and round and round—it's just downright funny, you know?" Then her mood bounced back. *"BUT I'M NOT HER!* I'm *Critical* Maas. Don't forget it! Don't confuse the two of us again. It's insulting! *DO YOU UNDERSTAND?"*

"Yes," said Cathy, deliberately sounding as frightened as possible. "Yes. I understand."

"Good. Now touch it!" said CM. She shook her hand at the thing on the cart. "Touch it or the next one I design with be a cat-bat-donkey-nun-Cathy's left-leg. All I have to do is leave you one arm and one hand. I'll take the rest and your power will keep you alive throughout the entire process. You know I mean it."

"All right," said Cathy, hating herself intensely. She concentrated, and her right hand began to glow. She tried to rationalize what she was doing, but how could one rationalize creating an abomination? She was no soldier, she had never steeled herself to the possibility that she might one day have to endure the unendurable. The thought of having to bear more pain frightened herself almost as much as the thought of staying alive.

The thing stirred and coughed up some putrid liquid that Cathy strongly suspected was embalming fluid.

"Could you do me a favor, now," she asked, "and get this thing out of my sight?"

"Sure," said CM. "I wouldn't want to offend your delicate sensibilities."

But before CM could wheel the cart away, Dinger walked to the cell and said, "Hey, Crit. They're here. Picked up the word. We got four of 'em just inside town."

Critical Maas smiled. The most evil smile Cathy had ever seen.

"Par-tay time . . ." CM said.

"I don't like it," I said, watching what was left of the gaggle of creatures bound away into the ruins. "Any one of those creatures could have warned the others that we were here."

"Not a chance," said Randy, pretending to brush the bloodstains from his gloves. "It's vaguely possible they have some sort of telepathic sensory transference gift, but I didn't see any sign of real intelligence in them. They're intended for intimidation, to hunt down the average mundane trying to leave, not—"

"Someone's coming!" Chandra hissed.

"How do you know?" Josh asked, a mite awe-struck.

Without much forethought, we ducked into the nearest rubble and crouched down. Randy was the exception: he hugged the nearest wall.

In the sky were two squads of flying rogues. The squads had been flying separately, but they weren't making a formation now. They both just happened to be heading deeper into the city.

"This could be our break," said Randy, waving us over. "One of those groups has to be heading back to their base. We follow them, find the base, and call in the rest. I'll take the one on the right. John?"

"I'm on it," I said. "Better stay low to the ground in case they've got spotters."

"What about us?" asked Chandra.

"Wait here," I said, levitating and moving off. "We'll need backup in case something goes wrong."

I couldn't resist a smile as Chandra put her hands on her hips and huffed at me in disgust. "Well, that's just freeling great!" What am I supposed to do? Read a fashion magazine?" She calmed down, with an effort, then said: "I hope they'll be all right. We should find someplace close to wait."

"Yes . . ." Joshua replied. Somewhat absently, she realized in retrospect, but not so absently that she considered for a moment he might be doing something rash.

"You know, come to think of it, I do prefer fashion magazines to those covering current events," she said. "What sort of magazines do the women in your church read, Josh? Other than your father's publications? Josh?"

There was no answer.

"Josh?"

Still no answer. She looked around.

And there was no Josh. He had slipped away.

Randy stuck to crawling, walking, and running along the sides of buildings, leaping from wall to wall when he had to, as he followed his designated squad of rogues who were flying through the city. It occurred to him, with much satisfaction, they weren't hard to follow. He'd had more difficult times trailing murderers, drug dealers, and white collar criminals.

They're overconfident, he thought. *Happens when you think there's no one else in town who can do what you can do.*

He believed he recognized them, even though he rarely caught a decent glimpse of their faces and he obviously hadn't had contact with them since the Surge. The flamehead was Bob Hillman. The thin guy who had to flap his arms occasionally to stay airborne was David Clarke. The zaftig babe was Jackie Crosby; before the Surge she had been a happy homemaker with three young children. After the Surge she'd murdered her husband, then as many members of Operation Rescue as she could find, thus leading some to conclude she was rebelling against the very conventional standards of morality she had adhered to previously. The last Randy had heard, the kids were all in foster care; eligible parents were afraid to adopt them.

At least they're still alive, Randy thought. *More than you could say for some family members.* The initial headrush of the Surge had induced Selma Burke to change her husband into glass. With a wave of his fingers Randy extended the shadow of a building across an empty lot and scurried across it.

The three rogues he was tailing had turned the corner around an industrial factory. When Randy made the same turn, they were nowhere in sight. He deduced they'd gone inside.

It made sense. A factory was a good prospect for a base of operations. Easily fortified. Rock solid.

Well, there's always a soft spot, he thought, bending apart the steel bars across a window on the first floor.

The hall inside was long and dark. The perfect environment for Randy, who bragged that he could evade a bat's sonar, if need be, and indeed had evaded radar on more than one occasion.

Randy heard voices: people laughing bitterly, sadistically. *So far, so good,* he thought. He'd hide in a corner and listen just long enough to get the information he and the others needed, head back the way he came in and—

BANG!

It was only a sound, but it was as if the hand of God had reached from the ether to crush him like a spider.

Randy spun around, taking in every angle of the room in search of an escape route. None was immediately apparent.

Then came the hissing.

"Oh, crap," he said to no one in particular. "Gas."

Randy struck the nearest wall as hard he could. He only made a slight dent. The wall was made of reinforced steel—thick as a bank vault's door.

He struck it again and again—and he coughed, more than once. His coughs progressively made him feel as he'd swallowed sandpaper; his eyes watered and his sinuses expanded. He was in deep doodoo, and he knew it. He was damned near invulnerable, but he had to breathe like everybody else. CM and the rogues had set up this trap a long time in advance, knowing he'd probably show up eventually to wreck havoc on their new urban order, and he'd followed them straight to it with the single-minded intensity of a dog headed for a meal, oblivious to all other concerns.

His blows became weaker. He attempted to concentrate on just one spot, but he couldn't stand straight. Even so, he was constitutionally unable to surrender. There was no way he'd die just because he couldn't resist the effects of the knockout gas . . .

Randy had no idea how long he'd punched the wall—probably not more than a couple of minutes—but he knew that his time was about to run out. He concentrated, gathered all his remaining strength, balled his hands together, wound himself up like a baseball pitcher, and struck.

The sound of the wall being ripped off its welded bolts was the most satisfying he'd ever heard.

The wall landed on another floor, he landed on the wall, and his feeling of satisfaction proved most elusive. The gas was dissipating, but he was weak from its effects and suspected he would be for several more minutes.

More than enough time for Critical Maas and her entourage of rogues to have their way with him.

"Welcome to Chicago, Randy," said CM. "Now you have a good sleep, hear? This'll all be a lot more interesting when you wake up."

"Sleep? Not a bloody cha—"

Suddenly, Randy's mind was embraced by the one form of darkness he could not manipulate, that of his own sleeping brain. He did not know it, but he had fallen asleep at CM's feet.

He snored. Loudly.

"Ravenshadow's always been gadget man," said CM, "so he's probably got some way of signaling the rest. Find it."

The women in the room giggled and commenced searching Randy and his Ravenshadow costume thoroughly.

"The others are in place," said Hugh Dinger. "Do they go?"

"They go. John's always been the most dangerous one of us all. Word is he can take any one of us in single combat—maybe even two or three at once. Yeah, he's a real tough guy. So we can't take any chances. Kill him."

Somehow, I had been under the delusion I was being discreet. I was trailing Deedee and two other fliers to what was left of Wrigley Field, staying way behind, indeed, only barely seeing them when I was following them through a tunnel leading to the stands—

And when I emerged, looked around, and discovered they'd eluded me, I was struck from the rear by what felt like a Mack truck.

I slid across the tattered Astroturf like a hockey puck until I dug a gully a few inches deep with my shoulder.

I was pretty groggy, but had a fighting chance of shaking it off—until I was hit again by the same truck.

I fell straight backwards, my back as tense as a board of wood, and slapped the ground like I'd taken a bad dive into a swimming pool. A swimming pool without water. I saw stars. I blinked. I saw galaxies. I saw the gigundo fists of Bart Franz ready to take another swipe at me. And they were big too. Bart's ability had to do with the manufacture of calcium and steroids, and it had gone out of control since the Surge. Probably affected his mind too, though judging from the way he was grinning at me, he wasn't too upset about it.

He wasn't alone. Bob Hillman was there, with not just his head aflame but his arms too. Randy had been trailing him, so I had the sneaking suspicion that a disaster was imminent, if it hadn't happened already. Deedee was there, naturally. And the phosphorescent flaming Tina MacIntyre, the sturdy Ryan Middleton, plus several others, flying and grounded, whose faces I couldn't make out because I was having difficulty focusing.

I suppose I should have been afraid. Or overcome with worry for Randy, or more importantly, worry for Chandra. Instead I was none of the above. Basically I was just extremely pissed off. My only option was to try to take off, to get the hell out.

A fist to my jaw, a kick to my chin, and a roundhouse

blow to my nuts indicated it was perhaps too late for flight to be a valid option.

I concentrated, as best I could, and perceived that the blue energy emanating from my hands weren't as strong and as dense as they usually were, but my good right arm was strong enough, nonetheless, to connect a haymaker to Deedee and send her on a trajectory to center field.

An energy burst sent Bob flying.

I broke Ryan's nose, gave Tina a black eye, and think it was Gretchen whose teeth I knocked out. All in all, I gave as good as I got, for as long as I could.

But in the final analysis there were too many. Too damn many.

It wasn't long before even I realized my blows fell with all the force of an angry butterfly.

Even before that I realized I was in trouble because their devastating blows to my body caused me no pain whatsoever. I was going into shock.

Even before that I realized that Bart crushing my shoulder in one of his giant hands ultimately wasn't going to cripple me, because I wasn't going to be around to not enjoy it.

Remember the scene in *Robocop* when hero Peter Weller has been mortally wounded and the last thing he sees—after he's shot in the head by Kirkwood Smith, playing the villain—is complete and utter blackness? There's no white light, no feeling of euphoria, just an ending.

That's what happened to me.

The last thing I thought of was Chandra. And how sorry I was that I'd allowed her to be trapped in Chicago with this series of maniacs running loose.

The only good thing about oblivion: no regrets.

12

TELL THEM WILLIE BOY IS HERE

My name is William Corealis. But the last name wasn't always Corealis. Used to be Smith. Willie Smith. Sometimes known as "the one that got away."

And nobody calls me "Willie" anymore.

I'd been living in Chicago throughout the occupation. It wasn't easy, of course, living here all this time without giving myself away. I had to witness many terrible, terrible things. I knew better than to intervene. I knew that to intervene meant giving myself away, and giving myself away would mean I would have to get involved; I would have to make a choice. Long and bitter experience had taught me making a choice was tantamount to suicide.

And considering what I had witnessed during the decade Chicago had been under the jackboot rule of that modern-day Caligula bitch, I'd perhaps made what was ultimately the most intelligent, most honorable decision. Because if I'd acted at any point before today, it surely would have been in vain, and I'd be dead, not alive to act now, when it might make a difference.

How odd. Making a difference was the one thing I'd

never counted on doing in my life. All I'd ever wanted to do before was survive. But a strange tugging of personal obligation was awakening an unaccustomed ambition in my soul. Once upon a time I'd dreamed I'd add up to something. Once upon a time I'd believe the Special kids who'd made fun of me and who had put me down would look at who I was today and admit they'd been wrong. Once upon a time I'd had something approaching a human heart.

Today I couldn't help but wonder why I'd changed, and if it wasn't too late to make a difference. After all, why had I stayed? I could have gotten out at any time. And if I'd died, so what? I wouldn't have died alone.

There had to be a reason, a rationalization, if not a justification.

And the dead man lying in front of me was it.

"You sure he'd dead?" one of the rogues asked. The stupid redneck.

"He's dead," said another. 'We killed the hell out of him."

A couple of intellects, these bozos. They hadn't changed so much.

"We'd better get back," said the flamehead, marginally brighter than the rest. "Now that the main threat's eliminated, we can mop up the rest."

They all took off, leaving the dead body for the patchwork varmints to find—burial was never necessary, or even practical, in Chicago, not with those abominations running around. I avoided them too—

Just like I avoided getting near fresh corpses; the opportunities to draw attention to myself were too plentiful.

But I had to get close to this one. I had to go into the open, under stars as white as death, and make sure.

149

Before I did anything, I had to be sure.

I looked into the battered face. The skull had been crushed—horizontally, from the top down to the lower jaw, like a crumpled cardboard box.

He wasn't just dead, he was very dead.

I knew him. Rather, had known him.

He had been John Simon. Johnny Simon, back then. We'd called him Poet, because even as a kid he was always writing. Seen him on television, down through the years. Read some of his later stuff in magazines here and there. Some of it was good. Some of it—well, poetry is a subjective art form. I just can't say a facility for words was one of his super-powers.

But I'd always gone out of my way to find his stuff. Except for the past decade, of course. I wondered if he'd ever gotten any better.

Didn't matter. I felt sorry because he'd always been good to me. I never forgot that. Never.

I remembered the first time I'd thought maybe he was all right, that I could trust him. A little. Let down my guard when I was around him. A little.

We were about ten. He was one of those proto-heavy metal kids with long black hair, long limbs, a narrow torso and a perpetual black cloud over his head.

Me, I was round. My head was round, my belly was round, and I had tits. I stuttered. I never stuck up for myself. I was always afraid something even more humiliating would happen to me if I did. I was everything a bunch of normal kids couldn't help taking out their aggressive impulses on.

We were sitting on a hill watching the rest of the little heathens roughhouse or play games in the recreation area. If John noticed me walking up the hill to sit next to him, he didn't show it. He didn't seem to mind, either.

"So you d-don't hang out w-with them much either, huh, John?"

"No." He didn't look at me.

"D-don't you like l-like them?"

"Does it matter?" he asked.

"N-no."

"Do you?' he asked. "Like them?"

"I guess not. They m-make fun of me 'cause I'm fat, and 'cause of the way I t-talk."

"What's wrong with the way you talk?" he asked.

I turned to face him. He had been waiting for me to do that, so he could look me in the eye.

"N-nothin'."

"Damn straight."

"Humph," I said. I felt strange inside, as if a tourniquet inside my chest had been loosened. I can't say we became friends at that moment, because we never became friends, and maybe what he'd said wasn't as a big a revelation as God talking to Moses, but sure as Hell it was what I needed to hear at the time.

Couple of days later Doc Welles was putting a group of us through our paces, seeing how our powers or our control over our powers had developed—or not—since the last time he'd check us out. It was my turn, and I was having a hard time, as usual.

"Okay . . . that's three feet, two inches. Are you sure you can't fly any higher than that, Willie?"

Actually, I was floating, moving back and forth with the changes in direction of a slight breeze. It was the best I could do. Indeed, it had been the best I could do for a long time. About six years, in fact.

Two of the fliers, Matt and Jason—they would grow up

151

to be a police officer and a corporation lackey, respectively—were showing off their not-inconsiderable flying techniques by buzzing over everyone who couldn't give them literal hot feet.

Jason was always one of the worst, far as I was concerned, and from above he shouted loud enough for me and an entire army to hear: "It's cause he's too fat! Right, Matt?"

"Leave him alone, Jason," said Matt. "It's not his fault he's . . . well . . ."

They buzzed around one another as Jason said, "I think the word you're looking for is FAT! Fat, fat, fat, fat—"

No one thought Jason was being particularly funny, but no one was doing anything about it. Heck, the Doc was so intent on making his notes on my abilities that he was oblivious, as he usually was at such times, to the interaction between his charges. And both Jason and Matt were so powerful that when either was one was feeling his oats—usually it was Jason, but Matt was no angel either, at that stage of the game—the others tended to leave them alone until they got tired and turned their attention elsewhere.

But this time someone *did* intervene.

Someone whom we couldn't see for the foliage reached out and grabbed Jason by the foot and yanked him as hard as he could.

Jason bent like a whip being cracked, smashed through several branches, and landed unceremoniously on the ground. A normal kid—heck, a lesser Special—would probably have been killed by the fall, but Jason didn't even bother to shake it off before he jumped to his feet and looked around with frightening malice in his eyes. "Who the heck did that?' he demanded of the universe in general. "What the heck are you doing?"

He wasn't used to being treated that way. He particularly wasn't used to seeing John walk up to him with clenched fists and say with no uncertain intentions, "Lay off Willie, Jason."

"Why? What's he to you?"

"A: it shouldn't matter, you shouldn't be treating him that way in the first place. B: he's my friend. Now leave him alone. I won't tell you again."

Jason thought about it. I had the distinct feeling he was as surprised as everybody that John stood up to him with such confidence. John had always avoided Jason; that wasn't strange—he'd avoided everyone else. But up until now only Matt hadn't treated Jason with a certain amount of deference, mainly because only Matt was his equal and there was nothing he could do about it except show Matt respect in return. And now John—this busybody—was regarding Jason with the same respect, or lack thereof, and it was clear Jason didn't like it.

"Yeah?" said Jason. "And what are *you* gonna do about it? Make a little sparkle and try to scare me?"

John scowled. He didn't back down an iota. And the fact that he didn't made me and probably everybody else gasp.

"Let's find out."

Even Jason gulped. I could hear it, like a big raindrop hitting a puddle on the other side of a field. He didn't back down an iota either, but he did hunker down, as if he wanted to see what John had before he made his first move.

But by then Dr. Welles had noticed. He stepped between them. "Okay, that's enough. Jason, I want you to give me fifty laps. Around the whole perimeter."

"Doc—" said Jason ineffectually. Flying might have been easier on the knees than running, but it was an expenditure of energy just the same, and Jason was going to be totally exhausted by the time he was done.

"Now," said the doc, "and stop picking on William."

"Fine. Whatever," Jason spat out, and he took off.

That wasn't the last time John stuck up for me. He stuck up for me a lot, even if we didn't hang out all that much. But he couldn't save me from the worst thing anybody could do to a kid that age.

I was the kind of kid who was lost in his own world, even when he was surrounded by others. So one afternoon I was practicing during the recreation period. Actually, practicing is too strong a word. I was just idly floating, trying to see if I could break the three-and-a-half foot barrier without Doc watching, when Cathy said:

"You shouldn't feel bad, Willie. I don't even *have* any powers yet. Neither does Chandra or . . . well, three feet isn't so bad, Willie."

She meant well. In retrospect I can see that. At the time I had another interpretation. I could look down into her eyes—and those of the other kids—even as she, and they, looked up into mine. And I saw the one thing a kid that doesn't ever want to see in another kid's eyes.

Pity.

"Such a wuss," I overheard Randy say. "Look at him, he's pathetic."

Randy was one of the kids who openly wanted to grow up to be one the good guys. Which is not to say he had any intention of becoming the loyal soldier of society that Jason and Matt aspired to become, but coming from him, the truth especially hurt. And I guess something inside me just snapped.

I realized they didn't matter anymore. None of them. Not my folks, my teachers, or my fellow Specials. They meant nothing to me and I would never mean anything to them.

And with that realization came release, and freedom.

I rose.

I rose higher in the air. Higher and higher.

Higher. Up, up, and away, as they used to say.

For just a second, I thought about going back down again. I was afraid I'd get into trouble. Then I saw John Simon, jumping up and down and waving, encouraging me, and I felt more than heard what he must have been saying:

"Keep going. Live free."

So I did.

I lived free.

In that time, I've been places, I've seen things, and I've done the one thing none of the Specials ever had a chance to do.

I lived as a normal man.

Sure it was pretending. I knew who I really was, but that didn't matter, most of the time. I worked my way up, learned how to survive. I made a life for myself and eventually I made a home in Chicago. When all hell broke loose ten years ago, and CM came to Chicago, bringing her scumbags with her, I could've left. But I stayed on. I hunkered down and made sure I wasn't noticed.

Even so, I tried to do right by the normals. Helped them when I could. Helped some of them escape. It wasn't their fault the Specials had come to town.

155

As for our kind, well, can't say I missed 'em. Frankly, I never gave a damn about any of them.

Except for John Simon. Poet. The dead man who lay at my feet.

He had done okay by me. And now I had to do okay by him, regardless of the consequences. Maybe I hadn't done as much good during the occupation as I could have, but one thing was certain: I wouldn't be able to do any more if I got caught. Chances were, doing okay by John was going to get me caught.

Fortunately, I knew just who could help me.

I picked up John and flew toward the tallest building left standing in the Grant Park area. I left him on the rooftop. It was the safest place I could think of to leave him.

Then I headed toward the Cook County Jail.

I seethed with anger. A luxury I usually did not permit myself. Usually I detached myself from the emotional ebb and flow of existence as much as possible. Objective decisions were the only safe decisions, and they could not be made in anger.

Tonight, however, I did not care.

I found Cathy just as she was being fed. As I watched, a normal minion wearing a coat and tie slipped a paper plate holding a stale hot dog in a bun and a few pieces of celery under the barred cell door.

"Let's see you bring *that* back to life," said the minion. "Hah!"

Not only was CM sadistic, but she was stupid as well—how could her most prized secret weapon be expected to perform properly if she was underfed? I hoped Cathy had enough Flash-power in her to do what I needed her to do.

The minion went off laughing. Cackling evilly, like a

movie villain. Some people just don't know how to act without using the media as a role model.

Cathy looked down at the plate. I imagined she was wondering what good a hunger strike might do her, or if she could get some common medicine if she got food poisoning off that so-called meal.

I called her name.

She looked up and saw me looking through the bars of her window. Judging from the gradual change in the look on her face, it took her a few moments to remember that her window was on the tenth floor.

"Time to go," I said.

"Willie . . . ?"

It was time to make a door. I dug my fingers into the wall and it gave like putty.

I suppose it would have been a lot easier to pound a hole in the wall with my bare fist, but doing it that way would have been a whole lot louder than the method I did use: pulling the stones with all my considerable strength until I dislodged a piece big enough for Cathy to walk through.

It made one big wrenching noise.

A few seconds later, the piece of wall made a second noise as it hit the street.

"William," I said. "William."

Suddenly, Cathy had trouble standing up straight. "I'd given up . . . on the possibility of being rescued."

I decided to try to be charming. It worked on women, occasionally. I smiled ironically and said, "Come with me if you want to live."

She smiled back. "My hero," she said, her sense of irony fully the equal of my own.

She threw her arms around me. I wasn't quite prepared,

and the extra weight dropped me a couple of inches before I regained altitude. Meanwhile, I put my arms around hers and for a fleeting instant my opinion of the entire human race changed, or rather, became overwhelmed with a confluence of possibility, and I regretted profoundly the years of my self-imposed banishment.

"You're alive," she said happily as I carried her back toward the last tall building. "We always wondered—"

"I'm alive," I said, "But John Simon isn't."

"What?"

Quickly, I explained to her what was going on. As the implications of John Simon lying dead on a rooftop began to sink in, she also began to hyperventilate.

"What do you expect me to do?" she asked, fearfully. "We have to get out of here!"

"Listen—you bring him back and we can *all* get the hell out of here."

We were hugging the sides of ruins, staying close to the ground. Occasionally she looked to the ground and gasped and tightened her arms around my neck. A slightly longer trip and she probably would have accidentally snapped it.

As we came in for a landing and she could see John, lying like a bloody tissue, she trembled. "I'll try," she said. "I'll try to bring him back."

"What do you mean, try?" I asked. My old feelings toward the Specials began to reassert themselves. "This is the only power you've got, you mean you don't know if it'll work?"

I set her down about ten feet from John. She gasped. Flies buzzed around his wounds.

"I've never tried this on one of our own," she said. "It could have side-effects—"

"Come on, woman!" I pleaded. "It's only a matter of time, and probably not very much, before they find us!"

"Don't push me! I have to make sure I do this right. If I don't succeed the first time, the second time tends not to work, either."

"Okay, I just don't—"

Suddenly, it was too late. Two of CM's minions—a big guy in a lumberjack shirt and a flaming purple gal—swooped down from the sky.

While at the same time several heavily armed mercenaries burst through the rooftop door. The first mercenary through was clearly in a mood to ask questions later, because he fired a quick blast of bullets the moment he saw Cathy.

Most of them were way off-target.

One was not.

You know what they say about "faster than a speeding bullet"?

I discovered, running to try to get between Cathy and the bullet, that it's not true. Not for any of us. Not for them. Or for me.

Or for her.

The bullet pierced her chest as if she was made out of butter, and she fell down.

The mercenaries stood in stunned silence, then grinned at one another. The rogue Specials waited. They'd been joined by a flamehead and a malevolent babe whom I vaguely recognized. Like I said, I never paid much attention to their identities.

Least of all now, as I stared at Cathy's body—the blood flowed from her just fast enough I could suppose her heart was still beating, though just barely.

At first I could barely believe my eyes. Cathy was dying—and without her, John would stay dead.

Then, right after I could believe it, I got pissed. Really pissed off.

The mercs noticed. They let loose a sustained barrage of gunfire that ripped my clothing to shreds.

But you know what they say about the Surge—how it affected you sometimes depends on how you feel about yourself, and though under normal circumstances there was a limit as to how much lethal force my body could deflect, then I felt righteous. No, rather, I experienced profound righteousness and certitude for perhaps the first time in my life, and it was like a strengthening beacon emanating from my soul.

It was more than enough to save my life. The bullets were about as effectual as beans spat out by a bunch of schoolmarms.

Mr. Lumberjack stopped the shooting with a wave.

I was still standing.

"Leave him to us," Mr. Lumberjack said.

And they charged.

I charged back.

They started to beat the crap out me. I hadn't had the crap beaten out of me since I'd floated away from Camp Sunnydale, and you know something? I didn't like it now any more than I had then. One difference this time, though:

I kept coming back for more.

Consequently, I missed what happened next.

I can only imagine what Cathy must have been thinking as she crawled to John's corpse. I have the sneaking suspicion she was gathering what was left of her ability to concentrate, that she was fueled by her innate compassion, that she wanted to strike the blow against her captors that had been long denied her.

So much so that she would not permit her impending death to stop her.

She touched him.

She was dying, but unlike most of us—who, even during their final nanoseconds would hold onto their lifeforce with all their receding wills—she touched him and transferred to his cold, uncomprehending body what energy she could.

And then she died.

And I was still getting the crap beaten out of me.

I kept fighting back though. I was trying to get out of a headlock when I noticed the rogues not currently preoccupied with choking me to death were distracted by something. I distinctly recall one uttering that immortal phrase: "What the—?" an instant before the rooftop was inundated with a brilliant blue and white light.

Though groggy, I perceived nonetheless that the light shone at a 360-degree angle and illuminated the desolated, graveyard cityscape as if a nova had gone off just overhead.

The headlock got very loose, but I was too tired, too short of breath to break free.

I heard a single word:

"Die."

John. The word had been spoken by John.

After all these years, I still recognized his voice.

Of course, he was an adult male now. And he had been dead for a short time. But it was recognizably him, nonetheless.

The rogue trying to choke me released me and I fell to my knees and then propped myself up with my hands.

Damned if I was going to hit the ground after all this. I'd just be goddamned. I had a ringside seat and I wasn't going to miss the show, not for anything.

In retrospect, I sorta wish I had.

The zaftig rogue was the first to die. A blazing rolling ball of light, with an intensity that made it easily visible within the greater blue glow emanating from John, emerged from his body with the force of a shotgun blast and wrapped itself around her as she screamed bloody murder. Her screams were cut short when her skin melted and the insides of her body exploded, sending a cascade of blood, putrid ooze, and pieces of baked organs out through her mouth, nostrils, and otherwise empty eye sockets.

No one really had time to pay attention to her, though, because next John grabbed Mr. Lumberjack by the collar and punched him so hard the man's skull shattered like balsa wood.

More blood and guts splattered all over my nice clean, gunshot-riddled coat and tie.

Another bolt of light moved from John's body—

Over to flamehead. Putting him out like a match. The man fell, his head nothing but a charred husk that shattered like wishbone ash when it hit the rooftop.

The other Specials didn't last long after that. In fact, they didn't last ten seconds.

The glowing purple woman lasted long enough to reach the roof's edge. She'd gotten one foot off the ground and was trying for the sky—when she was struck by a beam of light that cooked her from the inside out. Her skin was already one huge red blister, and she was smoking considerably, within the three seconds it took her to fall and drop out of sight.

John grabbed two more by digging his fingers inside their shoulders the way I'd dug mine into the Cook County Jail, and he smashed them together like two rag dolls.

Rag dolls that went *crunch*.

Rag dolls that he could tear apart like straw.

I crawled away as the mercs started firing. The bullets bounced off John so hard they ricocheted around me as if they'd been fired from a cannon.

When one of them had to pause to reload, John took advantage of the three-second opportunity that provided and ran to him in a blur and smashed his fist into the man's helmet as hard as he could.

The mercenary fell like a dead ox.

John broke the neck of another mercenary before he had a chance to do more than turn, in anticipation of running, and then he ripped off the guy's head and used it to pummel another in a bleeding mass of dead meat with about six hundred rapid-fire blows delivered in approximately two minutes.

Another mercenary had fainted, while the last one had gotten on his knees and begged for mercy.

But John showed no mercy to either. Without taking his glowing blue eyes off the begging merc, he walked to the unconscious one and tore out the man's heart with the ease of a surgeon sticking in his hand in an open wound.

That woke him up.

John held the heart before the begging man and crushed it between two fingers as if it was a marshmallow.

"Please . . ." the dead man managed to articulate.

John didn't say a word. He hadn't said a single word, in fact, through any of it.

Not even at the end, when he took the begging mercenary's head between his hands and burst it like a pimple. The man's brains shot up toward the sky like a fizzled shooting flare and they shot the far side of the rooftop with a sickening splat.

"Holy moley," I said. "Thank goodness you're one of the good guys."

John still didn't say anything. He just looked at his hands, whose glow was slowly diminishing, and then he looked at what was left of the mangled corpses he'd created.

"You okay?" I asked. "I'm okay, thanks to you."

Still nothing. And here I thought I was the silent type.

"You should go," I said. "The others who came with you may be in danger. I think the rogues are setting some kind of trap. You should do something."

"We will," said John, kneeling next to Cathy and cradling her head gently. "In a minute." He gathered her into his arms and stood. He looked up toward the full moon, which could plainly be seen through the only break in the cloudy sky.

"John?" I asked.

I watched, dumbfounded, as he flew off with Cathy in his arms. I was a little confused as to what I should do next. I decided to wait for him.

For a little while.

This was the kind of visibility I didn't need.

Besides, it was beginning to smell really bad on this rooftop.

John Simon here:

As far I was concerned, as of nine years ago, there was only one true innocent left among the Specials, and that was Cathy Holmes. Yet, at the same time, she was perhaps the only genuine adult. The only one who could be a mother and yet see beyond the needs of her nest toward the common good of all. The only one who held onto a basic core of ideals and never allowed them to be compromised, even when she was on the run and adhering to those ideals would inevitably result in her being "outed." Throughout her life she'd always wondered what it would be like to be a heroine, the way she believed Randy and Matt and myself to be.

What she didn't know was that she was already a heroine. She was *my* heroine. She never allowed what she could do to interfere with her character. To augment it, to complement it, yes, but never to interfere. Never to define her. No other Special could say that.

The most regretful words are so often the ones left unsaid.

My anger had been spent once I'd extracted my revenge—no, once I'd extracted *justice* from the perpetrators of this heinous crime. Now I was filled only with remorse and grief, not only at the tactical loss of what Cathy might have been able to accomplish in the coming struggle, but at the unwarranted subtraction from my life of a valuable presence.

I wasn't even really sure where I was going, or why. I only noted—and then just barely—that I was carrying her higher and higher into the sky, to the very edges of the stratosphere, where the stars suddenly shone with additional, surreally unfamiliar clarity. This was higher than I'd ever gone before, a height I should not have achieved without an oxygen mask. I was tired, my arms were heavy, and I was short of breath, yet that did not stop me from protesting this outrage to the stars, and to the man in the moon:

"It's not fair! Why did she have to die? She never hurt anyone! She never did anything to anyone! Why? Why do all this? Why give us all these power if this is all there is? She shouldn't have had to die for me! She shouldn't— she shouldn't—not for me. Not for me."

Then again, who was I? I'd seen pictures from the Hubble telescope. They'd given me an idea, however dim and unformed, of just how vast the universe was, and of how long it had existed. In the eyes of the universe, I was less than a blink of light, less than a speck. Why should the universe care? Why should the unseen force responsible for the Flash care about the havoc it had wrought on mankind? On those it had made Special? And most especially, on poor Cathy Holmes?

The Flash answered.

It welled up inside me like a tidal wave of the spirit, and it washed over my pain and swept Cathy away in a white light.

"I'm sorry," I said, realizing where she had to go. "Starlight to starlight . . . dust to dust . . ."

And she went. Dissolved in a crucible of light that faded against the starry backdrop.

Leaving me alone, high in the sky, as lonely as I'd ever been.

As lonely, and as hurt. If ever I'd wanted to give up on the human race, both Special and mundane, and take my chances hurtling at the speed of light between the stars, it was then.

But another woman, equally as extraordinary, was depending upon my return.

Preventing me from escaping my duty, regardless of my hunger to do so.

I half-flew, half-dropped to the building in Chicago

where William waited for me. If Critical Maas had had half a brain, and had been only marginally on alert, she could have picked that moment to attack and I would have been as vulnerable as a sparrow.

A crying sparrow.

William tried to apologize as I landed. I didn't let him get a word in edgewise. "It's not your fault," I said. "You couldn't have known. You did all you could. And . . . thank you."

He looked at me with a raised eyebrow. I believe he understood words such as "thank you" didn't come easily to me.

"So now what?" he asked.

"We find the others. Warn them. Then we take it to the wall. One way or another . . . this stops. Here. Now. Forever."

William frowned. I got the impression he had his doubts.

13

THE LADY, THE LIGHT, AND THE WARDROBE

So what's your next step, John?" William asked; already I could feel him pulling away. He was a man who'd survived this long because he'd kept his head down. He'd exposed himself only because he'd felt he had no choice, and now his better judgement, as it were, was kicking in.

"We have to get to the others," I said. "Tell them they're walking into a trap. We—"

"Sorry," William said, with a dismissive wave. "There's no 'we' here. I helped you because you helped me. The rest of them . . . I never had much use for them before. Don't have much use for them now, either."

"William . . ." I said, before I trailed off. I knew he was lying, that he had been deeply affected by Cathy's death, especially since she might have lived through the coming ordeal if he hadn't moved her to another place on the chessboard. And this I knew because I could hear the quickening of his heartbeat, indicating a rise in his blood pressure, the way people generally do when they tell a lie. A walking lie detector, that's me. In that moment I seriously considered pressing William to face the truth, but I sensed his resistance would be too strong, and that even if I should have convinced him to help, it would have proved to be counter-productive.

"Sorry," he said. "I got my own life and I go my own way. At least now we're even."

"No, I owe you. What you did was far more significant than anything I ever did for you."

"Perhaps in degree," he said, rising into the air. "Perhaps in degree. You should know, though—the three who came in with you—I can get a feeling about them. That's always been one my talents. One of 'em, Randy, has been captured. Chandra is still waiting for you."

"What about Josh?"

"Which one?" he shouted from on high, disappearing behind a ruined skyscraper. I got the feeling that he'd misunderstood the question.

My first instinct was to go after Randy, to find out where they had him and break him out. But I knew Randy wouldn't want that. He'd want to make sure the others were safe first. Then we could go after him in force.

I took to the air and tried to orient myself; my sense of direction had been slightly screwed up. Probably had something to do with dying and then being resurrected. My plan was to check in with Chandra and Josh—I had only the vaguest idea of how much time had passed and though they were meant to back up one another, I wondered, somewhat belatedly, what either one could do in an emergency.

Once they were safe, I'd have to reach the others, to make sure they were sticking to the plan and holding back for the time being. Of course, they already knew not to do anything without a direct order from Randy or myself, but there were a few hotheads, metaphorical and otherwise, among them. Eli, for one. I figured chances were they were okay so long as nothing else went wrong.

I really only wished I knew where Stephanie—I mean, Critical Maas—was at that exact moment. None of us were safe until she was dealt with. Of that much I was certain.

I realized, at that moment, that the person whose safety I cared about the most was Chandra's.

Indeed, all the Specials and half the humans would have to be trapped in the very mouth of Hell before I would even consider seeing to someone else first.

Meanwhile, Chandra had been waiting, alone, for Josh to return, to give some sign, at least, that he was in the general vicinity. But although she had walked alone for most of her adult life, actually being alone was not her forte, and she resented it. She resented it until she became nervous. She walked around the buildings, never losing sight of the rendezvous point, and shouted out his name as loud as she dared. "Josh? Joshua? Where the hell are you?"

There was no answer. Several times, there was no answer. Eventually her swearing became much more colorful.

Then she saw a woman standing in the distant shadows. Chandra knew the person was a female because of her hourglass figure. Otherwise, her stance and the outlines of her clothing—a shimmering gold gown—were unfamiliar.

"Ma'am?" said Chandra. "You should not be out here—you could be seen. It's dangerous."

"I know," said the woman in a sultry voice, "but in the end, which is really more dangerous: being seen . . . or *not* being seen?"

The woman took a step back in response to the few steps Chandra had taken toward her. Obviously the shy type, Chandra decided, yet there was an aura of power and confidence about her that the mistress of pheromones almost envied.

Then the woman pointed to something behind Chandra.

Chandra turned, gasped, and stared at a wall of angry red eyes.

Eyes belonging to another wave of Critical Maas' bestial monstrosities.

Suddenly, the woman's comment seemed a little oblique.

Back in the wooded buffer zone between Chicago and what passed for the civilized world, Randy Fiske (a.k.a. Ravenshadow) was telling the other Specials the time had come to move out. They didn't know of his capture at the hands of CM's minions. They didn't know why he was so relaxed, so matter-of-fact, so humorless. Ravenshadow's normal hyper self was the stuff of tabloid headlines, had been for years. Comedians impersonated him frequently, even more so since he'd gone underground and found it more difficult to make his displeasure known.

"John and the others have got Critical Maas pinned down," Randy was saying. "A lot of her minions have deserted her, but she's getting ready to fight back with all she's got. They don't have much time, otherwise it's all going to be over before it starts! Understand what I'm saying? John's officially given the order! You're coming in!"

"Sure!" exclaimed Luigi. "Let's get going!"

"Wait!" insisted Eli. "What about John, Randy? Shouldn't we wait for him?"

"He's waiting for us at the rendezvous point. Said we should get going as fast as possible."

He's too cool, Eli thought. *I'm getting the feeling he doesn't give a shit one way or the other.* Unfortunately diplomacy wasn't exactly Eli's strong suit, so his words came out sounding more obstinate than he'd intended. "I dunno. . . . John said he'd be back."

Suddenly Randy wasn't so cool. He stuck his finger in Eli's face and gave him a look he reserved for the most reprehensible criminals. "Look, we have one chance to take Maas out, and if we wait, we'll lose it. We're running out of time."

"Get that finger out of my face," said Eli, "or I'll bite it off and shit it out blue."

The others gasped. No one had ever talked to Ravenshadow that way, not since he'd become a major superhero anyway.

"This is not a good time for macho posturing, fellows," said Susan contemptuously, stepping between them.

"If you say so, honey," said Eli, without thinking of how Randy might perceive it.

Yet Randy stood down. Indeed, he even took a bow toward Susan to show he was trying to be graceful about it. Suddenly he shook his head briskly, like an animal shaking the water from his fur, and said, "I'm picking up a telepathic signal!"

"Really?" said Eli. He felt oddly suspicious, but stranger methods of communication existed among the Specials all the time.

"Others are coming," said Randy. "They'll be here! He wants you to go ahead—and he wants me to wait to guide the others straight away to the rendezvous point the second they arrive!"

Luigi and the others nodded. As one they rose into the air.

"Right," said Randy, *sotto voce.*

Moments later, Randy was alone, at rest, with nothing to do. Normally, he was twitchy even when alone. Tonight, however, he was cool, calm, collected. Tonight, even waiting was a pleasure.

Before the Surge, the number of civil servants and law enforcement personnel slain in the line of duty during an incident involving a Special was relatively small. Only a handful of civilians whose paths crossed with Specials had been injured, died, or been murdered. The close Government monitoring all Special activities (save for matters of personal privacy) had something to do with it, of course, but the fact of the matter was that for the first three decades of the Specials' existence, they'd harmed very few, and caused remarkably little property damage, especially considering their potential.

That all changed after the Surge. So powerful were most of the rogue Specials, the concept of government monitoring was a joke; even those who were not rogues, who cooperated with the authorities most of the time, couldn't be stopped if they wanted to do something badly enough. Especially if that included stealing.

Since the Surge, there had been a lot of property damage. The deadly accidents tended to have a body count of more than one. And the number of murders was astronomical.

The possibility of dying in the line of duty was a very real thing to the mundane men and women in uniform.

The soldiers stationed at McHenry Air Force, where several dozen nuclear warheads were stored, thought about it every day. They especially thought about it while they were on guard duty, though of course in the case of an actual incident, everyone on base was expected to resist, apprehend, and if possible kill any Special who might have designs on the nuclear warheads.

But when they saw four high-powered rogues flying straight toward the base with energy streaks dragging behind them like colored contrails, the soldiers knew the time for merely considering the possibility of death had passed. Now the time had come to face it.

And face it they did, watching their buddies die via the impersonal disbursement of disintegration beams, waves of heat blasts, and crippling sound waves until they realized that fighting bravely and dying with honor wouldn't do any good one way or the other and their spirits broke and they attempted to flee.

Fleeing didn't do any good, either. The Specials dispatched with ease all personnel on the base in approximately fifteen minutes. Those who escaped the perimeter, they allowed to live. Those who were merely too injured to flee or fight back, or who were mortally wounded, they tore apart in their bare hands.

"How much time left?" asked Tommy Knofler, the human heat-generator.

"Twelve minutes," said Diana Katz, the self-styled energy queen. "Maas says we have to be exactly on time."

"We'll get there," said Tommy.

"That's for certain, dude," Diana replied, as she took to the air and melted the wall of a storage facility.

Somehow, they'd missed a few soldiers inside, either

174

hiding or deciding the best moment to sacrifice themselves. The moment had come.

Diana melted them, too.

Two minutes later, the four rogues were stepping over charred flesh inside the building.

"Tactical field," said Tommy, with the air of man stepping into a fresh strip joint.

"Beautiful," said Diana. "Where do we even start?"

"Anywhere," said Bill Lassendale. "We only need one."

"This should do the trick," said Mose Flanders, hefting the nearest warhead with ease. He carried it out holding it over his head and took to the air with equal ease.

"How much time?" asked Tommy, after they were all in the air.

"Eight minutes," said Bill with a sly smile. "The others are on the way."

My pulse quickened at the thought that Chandra might be in danger. I wasn't used to feeling anxious about anyone other than Doc, and the sense of urgency I had regarding Chandra was screwing my normally steadfast facade of stoicism. The fact that my bearings were slightly off wasn't helping matters any. Either that, or CM had knocked down a few of the local landmarks, to confuse the enemy.

I think my head would have exploded if I'd known that at the exact moment I was trying to convince myself I wasn't totally lost, Chandra was fending off a horde of CM's misshapen grotesqueries. She didn't know with certainty that these were artificial creations, but she was beginning to have her suspicions.

And though she had strength and speed since the Surge, Chandra hadn't exactly seen the point of honing those traits, given the normal state of her abilities. Nevertheless, she possessed sufficient fighting skill to make the beasts keep hesitating.

Until a large bovine pachyderm combo with wolverine claws lunged for her.

She dodged the claws—barely—and managed to dig one hand into the creature's skull deep enough to cause some damage. She threw the creature at the others as if its head was a bowling ball and then backed up quickly, panic-stricken, fearing another would take advantage of her preoccupation.

Through it all the strange woman just stood unmoving, unapproached, in the shadows.

"Get away!" Chandra shouted. "I'll cover you!"

Still the woman did not move.

"Didn't you hear me? I said I'll cover you!"

"Not necessary," the woman said, and promptly did absolutely nothing.

The beasts had Chandra surrounded. They were several yards away, but they were closing in. *That's what I get for getting caught in the middle of the street,* she thought, not feeling very sympathetic for herself at the moment. She spotted a nearby broken wooden beam and lunged for it.

Once it was in her hands, she began swinging in quick, violent arcs, attempting to keep the beasts all at bay.

This is where I came in. Alerted by the distant chorus of growls, I got my bearings and flew straight to where I'd left Chandra and Josh. From above I watched Chandra deck a wolven creature and break another's shoulder. In the next few moments she fell, rolled, and eluded capture, but it was clear I was her only salvation.

Then I noticed the woman just standing nearby, glowing with the whitest light I'd ever seen. I didn't get a good look at her—the glare was too brilliant. Forcing myself to look at it had the feel of staring at an eclipse.

I wanted to strangle her—who did she think she was, to just stand like a lump when the woman with whom I most feared a relationship was deep in the throes of a life-or-death situation?

Then I had to cover my eyes with my arms and veered off the side.

The aura around the woman flashed like a sun going nova.

I struck a ruined wall with a glancing blow and bounced off.

There were a lot of screams, yelps, and sundry other animal cries below. None of them that I could detect, thankfully, came from Chandra.

To escape the flash, she had hunkered down with her head between her knees and her arms over her head—a more vulnerable position under the circumstances I could not imagine. She surely would have been lunch were it not for the fact that the beasts didn't possess the intelligence to avert their eyes when faced with a blinding flash. Once blinded, they groped about or tried to run. Their gropings took them no where near Chandra and many ran smack into walls, poles, or dead automobiles.

"Chandra!" I called out. "Are you all right!" I tried to make my concern sound coolly professional, but judging from the way she laughed, I don't think she bought it.

"I'm okay, but what about—?"

"Hang on," I said, swooping her up. At the moment I didn't care what questions, however well meant, she had; I only cared that she had come through this latest test. "What happened?"

As she spoke, I concentrated on getting us as far away from the blind beasts as possible. "You were there," she said sarcastically, though not without humor. "I was attacked, but there was another woman. She blinded them."

"One of us?"

"I don't think so. I mean, I didn't get a good look, but I'm certain I've never seen her before. I mean, the only Special who's remained hidden has been Willie, and I know it wasn't him."

"I think I can vouch for that," I said grimly. " Listen . . ." And I told her what had happened, what had happened to Cathy.

"That's terrible," she said, with tears in her eyes. "I mean, she never liked me much, but none of the girls did, after awhile. But she went out of her way to be nice to me occasionally, even if she wasn't sure she quite meant it. I always appreciated that." Beat. "Where's Randy?"

"They've got him. I figure we'll meet up with the rest, then go in after him. At least the rest are safe for now."

Was it bloody? CM asked Mose Flanders telepathically. Mose was so startled that he almost dropped the warhead, but luckily for the current configuration of his atomic structure, he recovered just in time. He should have known, in any case, to expect CM to be chomping at the bit and willing to risk telepathic communication so she could learn more quickly if her plan was proceeding apace.

"You will be pleased!" Mose said aloud.

Excellent. I want to hear about every drop spilled. But business before pleasure.

"Okay with me," said Mose with a shrug. He was quite comfortable in life allowing CM to set her own timetable for things. Besides, when he was comfortable and she was happy, she occasionally let him make love to her, so long as he didn't take up too much of her time.

They and the others came down from the clouds to where Maas, Deedee, Hugh Dinger, and a few others were still waiting, on one of the tallest battered rooftops still remaining near where the Midwest Stock Exchange once stood. On her knees, huddled in a corner, was another prisoner, one of their former mates, a Special named Clara Day who until the Surge had been a major researcher for Sony in their electronics division.

Mose stayed on the game as he came in for a landing. He thought, rightly, it would not go well for him if he even so much as stumbled as he landed on the roof with the nuclear warhead in his hands.

Maas sashayed up to the warhead—Mose knew better than to think she was sashaying up to him—and ran her fingers across the heavy metal of the warhead as if she was inspecting a grapefruit. "Perfect. It's everything a girl could hope for: expensive, explosive, and phallic."

"Are you breathing hard?" Mose asked.

The others laughed, but CM and Clara Day pointedly did not.

CM snapped her fingers at Clara. "Get her over here," she said to Bill Lassendale and Hugh Dinger.

They did, none too gently. Dinger pushed Clara's face close to the tip of the warhead and she tried to fight back, but even though she possessed some strength beyond the capability of the ordinary human, she had the strength of a newborn babe compared to every single one of the rogues currently holding her captive.

"Activate it," CM said to Clara. "Bring it under our control."

"No—I can't." Clara's voice was stony.

"Hey, we're not asking you to swallow it," said CM.

"Though some of us here might want to try," said Dee-dee.

"Give her some space," said CM to Dinger. "Let her have some working room."

'No!" protested Clara.

"Yes," said Critical Maas. She slapped Clara once, briskly, on the back of the head. CM needed to make her point but she didn't want to damage the synapses inside the captive Special's head. "Do it. You have the power. Don't make me go inside."

Clara gasped. "You wouldn't dare!"

"Wanna bet? Christ! If I could have launched this instrument of destruction from the Air Force base, I would have gladly done so. But the job I require it for demands a certain amount of precision and flexibility."

"I can't help you. Besides, I haven't kept up with recent technological advances. I can manipulate electronics, even rewrite programs from the inside, but I don't have the skill or the knowledge anymore to do what you want me to do with this—this abomination!"

"I didn't hear you complaining when you had your security clearance."

"I only worked for Rocketdyne part time!"

"Looks like I'm going in, girl. I don't have any choice." No one detected a sense of regret in CM's words.

"No," protested Clara. She would have been better off if she'd demonstrated a minimum of defiance, but of course her fighting spirit had been defeated in days and weeks past. She'd heard the rogues talking about what happened to Cathy, and she wished with the last iota of her diminishing spirit that she had the courage to cross over with her.

"Let me in," said Critical Maas.

As if she needed Clara's permission. In she went.

Elsewhere in Chicago, the strange "woman" who rescued Chandra via a blinding flash basked in an internal glow unprecedented in her lifetime. Despite all the tragedy, disappointment, hypocrisy, mendacity, delusion, and senseless violence she'd encountered (the latter mostly vicariously, through the media), she truly believed existence was basically wonderful and good. People were basically good. It was only their ignorance and shortsightedness that caused her to take part in the game she was playing now.

Not that she minded. She felt totally fulfilled. There was no distance between who she wanted to be and who she was. There were no differences between the desires of her heart and those of her intellect. There was no chasm between her dreams and reality.

Others, she knew, were not so fortunate. The others she saw flying above her, innocently headed toward a trap they could not anticipate, would soon be needing her.

She took to the air and followed them, as discretely as a flying nimbus of bright white light could.

They seemed not to notice, though. They were too busy racing toward their doom.

"There. See? I knew you had it in you," said Critical Maas, patting Clara on the back. "Now tell it where to go and get ready to make that energy bubble."

"Yeah," said Deedee. "I'm not particularly fond of the prospect of dying instantly."

"Hey, if the explosion doesn't get you, then the radiation will," said Hugh Dinger.

"Don't worry about it," said CM. "If Clara doesn't make the energy bubble strong enough, she'll die too. And you're too afraid of death to let yourself die, aren't you?"

Clara nodded. "Yes . . ."

"Stop sniveling and make it go."

Clara did. The nuclear warhead lifted off the rooftop as if caught in a pneumatic blast, and then it disappeared in a blur, twisting and turning between the remaining buildings like a hawk swooping down on elusive prey.

"Thirty seconds," said Bill Lassendale, "and they're history."

CM waited, then said, "Twenty seconds . . ."

The media generally regarded Randy Fisk (a.k.a. Ravenshadow) as the most unpredictable Special, as the one most likely to say the rudest thing in public, to nab the most deeply buried drug lord, and to break the biggest celebrity's heart. I personally disagreed. I'd long since passed the point where nothing Randy did surprised me. All you had to do to make an accurate prediction of what he would do in any given situation was to think of the precise opposite of the most logical move. Not the most intelligent, or the dumbest, simply the most logical. Even his plan to restore the good name of Specials, legally if not historically, was logical; the fact that he would try to restore that which theoretically had been shattered forever was a vintage throw from Randy's left-field.

But seeing him standing alone in the middle of the clearing where I'd left the others definitely surprised me. I'd thought he'd still be in CM's hands, a tortured prisoner, a dead one, or worse.

Unaccustomed as I was to a speechless landing, I managed to conclude the process standing up. Chandra jumped out of my arms as quickly as possible. She had only one question:

"Where's everyone else?"

"Randy!" I said. "What the hell's going on?"

" 'Hell' is about as apt a description of what's about to happen as anything else."

I didn't like it when Randy got cryptic. It always meant something, one of the reasons why he rarely surprised me. "What are you talking about?"

"I can't stop it, John. Nobody can."

Then he caught me off-guard with an energy blast. That was about as close as he could get to stabbing me in the back without surprising me. "I can't stop it, John. Nobody can!"

I struck the trunk of a tree that was about a hundred years old. Fortunately my skin and internal organs were strong enough to withstand the impact.

The trunk, however, was not. It snapped like a twig. I caught a glimpse of a blurry Chandra running as fast as her pampered body would allow to avoid being struck by the crashing bough. It missed her by inches.

I climbed a thousand miles to my hands and knees. That really hurt. "Where are the others, Randy?" I asked, wiping the blood off my lip. It had come out of my nose and still was. I had the impression the bleeding wasn't going to stop in the near future.

"The others are dead—or are about to be," said my dear friend Randy. His hands were an iridescent green from the energy still seeping from the blow he'd landed on me. This was the kind of force he preferred not to use, because its measure was difficult to calibrate, its side-effects often unpredictable. "My job is to keep you here until they die. I have to. I must."

"Don't make me do this," I said. "Don't make me fight you."

"I have no choice."

"Listen to him!" said Chandra imploringly. "He can take you apart atom by atom!"

Randy raised an eyebrow. "Oh?"

"Trust her," I said.

"Doesn't matter," said Randy. "I still have no choice."

And he let me have it. The weird, unpredictable, annoying man who was the Special I trusted most betrayed me and all our brethren by slamming me with the strongest energy blast I'd ever felt, a brutal purging of amorphous fury that should have turned even a being as powerful as me into a flurry of aimless molecules.

It probably would have, except for the fact that I was as totally pissed off. Indeed, I'd never experienced such rage. I sensed total and utter disaster, a triumph of evil that my good friend should have helped me prevent.

Without him, I feared even my power wouldn't be enough to prevent it, another reason why I was so mad. The Specials were headed for the trash heap of history, and he was helping them go there.

Chandra screamed. I was vaguely aware she was ducking for cover. A good idea.

Randy and I radiated energy like two warring magnetic fields. Waves of sheer, unadulterated force tore apart the trees, and made the grass ripple like the ocean. Yet we could only get so close to one another. He wanted to pound me with his fists, he desired nothing more, it would be the fulfillment of his existence, yet he couldn't get within two feet of me.

I lunged and grabbed his wrists. It was how I'd always imagined grabbing glowing embers would be, if I could have been burned by such a thing.

Randy screamed. I held on.

I wanted to scream, but kept my throat contracted by biting my tongue practically off.

I opened myself to him, and forced him to open himself to me.

Beyond us, the wind howled and the earth roared, but to us it sounded like stage whispers in the dark. We were smothered in a light the Reverend Kane would have envied.

I realized that fighting Randy felt like fighting myself.

Randy managed to pull himself free of my grip and he punched me. Rather, he punched at me, but by now I was so in sync with his thought processes, I was able to duck and give him a feedback energy punch. I can't imagine it hurt him any worse than it did me, but that stopped neither of us.

A few more punches, and I noticed I was moving faster than him. Much faster. He was almost lethargic in comparison. I had time to think, so long as I didn't get too cocky.

What the hell was going on? Randy would *never* sell out to Maas. I had the distinct feeling that unless I figured out the answer to that one, I was playing directly into Maas' hands.

Suddenly I tasted Randy's power calling out to mine. I recalled Doc Welles telling me I controlled the power of the Flash at the source.

I reached for Randy's wrists again. This time I didn't release them, regardless of the pain, which, believe me, became more and more considerable the longer I held onto him.

Into his mind I went.

We were not alone.

Someone had crept in ahead of us. Someone who had rewired his gray matter.

The culprit was obvious: Maas.

Since the Surge, Critical Maas could acquire intimate access to any one of us—acquire it at will. That's how she got her minions to work for her.

At least, I assumed she had. They'd all been good people, once. I liked to think it took more than just the Surge to turn them to the dark side.

Randy and I realized it instantly. Even though he still fought me, still hated me, still wanted to prevent me from trying to save the others, a part of him remained sufficiently detached that I could communicate with him and reason with him effectively.

I was hoping you'd fight back, said Randy, telepathically.

Why hope? I asked.

I was hoping you'd fight back in kind. Using the force you possess which is similar to my own. Now I can see into you as easily as you can see into me. He paused. *Damn! You really don't know, do you?*

Know what?

The first case I ever solved, he thought, plunging me into a spiritual abyss. The last thing I needed to learn via mental osmosis was his life story. *The first case I ever solved was my own. Didn't you ever wonder why we look so much alike?*

No.

You didn't?! Doesn't matter. Ever wonder why we became instant friends?

I'm sure I must have looked as if I'd been pole-axed. *What?*

Your mom was having an affair when you were conceived. She was having an affair with my dad.

Another one? My God . . .

The point is, we're brothers, John. Half-brothers. Now use the power of the flash to cut her out of my head. Do whatever you have to do. And go save the others before it's too late.

Just one thing, I needed to know. *How did you find out?*

I asked my mother. I'm afraid she's never gotten over it. Listen—hear me—whatever—Maas is afraid Stephanie is becoming stronger. She wants to wipe out a bunch of us at once, so she can absorb enough power to make sure every scintilla of Steph remains suppressed. CM doesn't care how many innocents die in the process.

Forget about being pole-axed. I could have been knocked over with a whisper. *That's it? Cathy died so that egotistical bitch could—*

Cathy's dead? Those bastards!

The next vision he transferred to my mind was chilling. *They've got a tactical nuke, John—Dear God—they've got a nuke! You have to get out now, John! Now!*

Okay.

And I put the knife to him. I cut Critical Maas out of his mind with all the finesse of a butcher and in the process threw him fifty yards across the forest. He screamed, and I nearly fainted.

He bounced off one of the tree trunks scattered on the ground and hit the dirt like a sandbag.

"John!" It was Chandra, peeking out from a pile of charred rubble. "What did you do?"

"He's alive. But the others won't be if I can't stop them in time."

"Stop them from doing what?"

Reabsorbing the stray energy lingering about the vicinity was making me dizzy. "I have to go," I said and in an effort to rise toward the sky almost went in the opposite direction.

Chandra caught me and steadied. "You're not going anywhere yet!"

"I thought the grass was a cloud," I said, feeling giddy.

"Like I said, you're not going anywhere."

I pushed her away. "Pardon me, Chandra, I know you mean well, but I really must haul ass. There's no time to explain. Stay here. Watch him."

And I took off. I was a little jittery at first, and was mighty thankful the trees had been leveled for the first few miles I was in the air. I'd never been a fast flyer, not nearly as fast as Jason or Matthew. But I had to be fast now. I could feel the impending psychic disruption of a million deaths lingering in the air like a bad smell.

The missile had been launched.

Even as I hit the outskirts of the city, I knew I wasn't going to make it–there was no way I could intercept it before impact.

In a matter of moments the iridescent woman following the Specials flying to their doom transcended the traditional physical definitions of gender, evolving into a higher form of androgyny.

By now, she flew at a respectful distance behind them, but made no effort to conceal herself. She had hidden the

188

truth of her inner self from the world long enough, and resolved never to do so again.

She had come to terms with the fact that ultimately she had been responsible for her withdrawal from the world. She had allowed herself to be swayed by guilt, by mendacity, by the error of others, and by self-loathing. She had willingly allowed herself to be blinded to truth that lay inside her.

The price she had paid was egregious, totally out of proportion with the severity of her philosophical transgression. The price others had paid for her all-too-human frailties was equally unfair. The price she would pay might make up for some of the misery she had inadvertently caused.

The others landed on the rooftop of the abandoned building that was the rendezvous point.

"What's that?" asked Eli aloud, not knowing he was asking about a nuclear warhead. "Some kind of flare?"

"I don't know to tell you this," said Susan, "but it's coming this way."

Any other bunch of flying Specials would have been hightailing it instantly, but all these folks, though hardened by enduring years of discrimination and life underground, were rookies in the field of battle. Another reason why Randy was perhaps ill advised to enlist them in our little endeavor.

Yet the biggest rookie present recognized the flare instantly for what it really was and she acted.

"Who's that?" Rita asked, spotting the glowing woman rising from a nearby rooftop.

"What if this energy bubble doesn't work?" Hugh Dinger asked Critical Maas.

"Then we'll be dead," she answered with a smile. "Ten seconds to—What the hell's *that?*"

Chandra knelt beside Randy. The extent of her empathy surprised her. She wasn't used to caring when men were in pain. There had been no malice in her indifference, it just hadn't been a part of her personality. Until now.

"You'll be okay," she said aloud, knowing that in the final analysis, she was a poor excuse for a nurse. Hadn't even had a course in first aid. She'd always felt there'd be someone around who knew first aid better than she ever could. "I won't let anything happen to you."

His father had named him Joshua Kane, but that wasn't who he really was. Nor was he the glorious personification of the Holy Spirit, the human vessel through which the Lord spoke, that his father pretended to believe him to be.

He—the pronoun was merely a matter of convenience, of approximation—existed on a plane upon which all rationalizations withered.

It had begun with the gown, the idea for which had come to him in a dream which otherwise had been filled with a sexual content that confused and frightened him. The gown, the shiny yellow androgynous superhero costume made from fabric through which his inner light shone perfectly, was merely the catalyst. By wearing the costume he could access, however tentatively, the essence of his higher being. By having it stashed away, by keeping it a secret, he could keep his father and the world in general from harassing him. If they did not know what he was doing, what he aspired to, they could not prevent him.

The only problem, from the standpoint of keeping his

costume a secret, was that one day Jerry Montrose found his stash in the dorm. They'd been roommates, and he's noticed Joshua's tendency to be overly protective of the box under the bed. One day, Jerry melted the lock and looked inside. Joshua tearfully begged him never to tell a soul, and though Jerry could not for the life of him comprehend why anyone would care that Joshua liked to dress up like a girl when no one was looking, he agreed.

And he had kept his word, which had been one reason why Joshua had trusted him when he and Jason came to them with the knowledge of the Specials' so-called plot against the US Government. Despite all the angst he'd endured as a result of being under his father's thumb, Joshua realized he'd had a lot be grateful for. He could be grateful for the time alone in hotels, when he could wear his preferred clothing and transcend barriers. He was grateful for those days when he was truly himself, when he could accept all his glorious power, all the beauty that he could never accept in his other life. He thought he might have experienced orgasms upon those occasions, but he couldn't be sure.

He realized now, though, that it had been wrong for him to keep his true inner nature and outer physicality secret. He should have revealed himself before, when it might have made a difference.

No matter. He could make a difference now. When he came to Chicago, intending to rehabilitate the Specials in the eyes of the world, a goal definitely in opposition to those of his father, he realized for the first time in his life, he could go all the way. He could transcend his nature. He could transcend his light. He could transcend his energy.

And in so doing, he will be that which he had never

been, that which he had never had the courage to be:

A hero.

In an instant, an irresistible force met an indestructible phenomenon.

I saw it. Racing toward the warhead with only the vaguest plan—I thought I might grab it and try to throw it toward the moon—I watched in astonishment as someone I'd never seen before, someone who glowed like a white star, enveloped the missile in an illuminating embrace.

The missile was stopped cold.

I heard the person stopping it say: "My father said I was worthless—nothing but a glowing ball of light. But what is energy but light? What are we all but creatures of light, and hope, and love, so rarely given the chance to shine?"

And with those words, I knew exactly who the person was. Only Joshua Kane, of all the people on the planet, possessed the unique ability to so inappropriately and yet so glibly draw the connection between the metaphor and the aphorism.

Now, somehow, he was halting the progress of a nuclear device. The process should have turned the planet into a tiny star for about four minutes, before its molecules were sent flying off into the fifth dimension somewhere. But somehow he contained the warhead's unleashed power, and transmuted it into a harmless though temporarily blinding flash.

Reducing the potential atomic blast to an effect vaguely analogous to that of a light bulb when it conks out.

And then Joshua and the missile were gone, just like

that, their atoms dissipating, I presumed, upon some higher plane of existence.

Another innocent had died, protecting the others and me. And I had failed, again.

On the rooftop, Susan asked the question that was on everyone else's mind:

"Does anybody know *who* that was?"

14

TWO-FISTED MEN OF ACTION

I think it was the earthquakes we caused that alerted the media. Not fifteen minutes after the first, I detected the planes and satellites taking photos of the battle from above. Part of the photos undoubtedly were being taken by mundane intelligence services, trying to get a good handle on what was happening down here.

I wished them luck.

I do have to say that the first twenty-four hours of the battle were the easiest. At the time it seemed nothing could be harder. I began to understand how the Russians must have felt when the Germans overran the city of Stalingrad during the Second World War. They weren't thinking of how much was at stake or how their bravery might be written up in future history books, they were simply refusing to back down, surrender or retreat. They dug in, and made the Germans fight for every inch of ground.

And they did it simply for what it was worth.

The difference between those Specials opposing the minions of Critical Maas and the Russians was that we were good guys led by good guys, whereas the only good

194

thing you can say about Stalin is that he was a more competent monster than Hitler.

Otherwise, both matches were pretty even. For every punch we gave the minions, they punched back. Every energy bolt we threw at them, they deflected. Every fireball we hurled, they dodged or extinguished. We were crippled by our reluctance to harm innocent mundanes while the minions accepted no such limitation.

The innocents were huddled in the fractured skyscrapers CM had forced them to hole up in during the occupation, and occasionally a few would scurry down the streets in the hopes they could go unnoticed in the confusion. That rarely happened: the bad guys would invariably endanger them or use them as a shield. Every time we got an edge, fate would conspire against us by giving them the pawns they needed.

Randy and I fought as a team most of the time. We watched one another's back and fired energy bolts at the opponents of our inexperienced recruits, usually—but not always—before they did some serious damage.

Randy and I tried not to kill any one because by now we both realized that most if not all were operating under CM's telepathic control. We had come to Chicago to drive her out, to liberate the city, and wound up facing something a lot bigger than we could handle.

In retrospect, it was like going to war with a sovereign nation without having a game plan or exit strategy when things got complicated. Which is what the current President of the U.S.A. did with a country in the Middle East whenever he felt people were paying too much attention to the perpetual (from his point of view) Specials debacle.

Seemed like Critical had had more of a game plan than we'd ever given her credit for. She certainly improvised better. She wanted us to kill one another, knowing all the residual power that would have been allotted to the newly deceased individual during his lifetime would now be evenly distributed to the others.

I could imagine her watching. Smiling. Sensing victory in her existential quest to accrue enough Flash power to ensure that Stephanie remained buried in *her* subconscious for the rest of her days. Clearly, she didn't care how many people—Special or otherwise—died in the process.

"We still don't know what the hell's going on in Chicago," said Senator McClellan, hefting his great round belly to the side so he could get out from behind his desk to shake the hands of his two brightly costumed visitors. "We got satellite photos but we can't see who's doing what to whom. And the President's getting reports about mass devastation and loss of life. The loss of life is probably conjecture, but the mass devastation is certainly real.

"Furthermore, Satcom has picked up indications that a tactical nuke was used, though for some reason it apparently didn't do any harm."

"You think it's possible one of the Specials stopped it?" asked Matthew Bright, NYPD.

"It went off!" McClellan exclaimed.

"But *it apparently didn't do any harm!*" Matt pointed out. "Sounds like we still have a few angels on our side."

"I fail to see what that has to do to anything," said Jason Miller, wrapping his American flag-themed cape tightly around his shoulder, instinctively striking the pose he'd once used for public appearances.

"Either way," said McClellan, "we can't let this go on. We have to intervene. Mr. Miller—" he cleared his throat "—Jason, Nexus Corp has agreed to loan you to us because as I understand it, it is the corporation's position that you should serve when and if your country needs you."

"First clause of my contract," said Jason grimly.

"And Officer Bright, you're the only Special who's ever been granted legal authority to make arrests."

'True," said Matt.

"Gentlemen, today your country needs you. I understand you two are the strongest Specials, by far, even after the Surge."

"That's right, Senator," said Jason.

"Officer Bright," said the Senator with a nod in his direction, "I'm expanding your authority to include this whole situation."

"You mean to include Chicago?"

"No, I mean to include this whole damn hemisphere, if necessary."

"What do you want us to do, Senator?" Bright asked, his eyes narrowing suspiciously. Although he'd spent most of his life as a paradigm of virtue, he was getting tired of those powerful old men who thought they had him perfectly under their control.

"Find out what's going on, and stop it if you can. You're authorized to take whatever steps you feel are necessary to resolve the situation. Allow me to be redundant on that last point. Do *anything* you feel is necessary. But stop it."

"Are you telling us to do *anything* with extreme prejudice?" asked Jason with a smile.

"Wait a minute!" Matt said. "Sir, I understand that some of the Specials in this fight went in because they promised immunity from all prosecution if they cooperated."

"Yes," said the Senator gravely. "Some of the boys in

197

Justice got a little ahead of themselves. Made a deal they shouldn't have."

"Oh, come on!" exclaimed Matt. "You can't tell me the President himself didn't approve the deal personally!"

"Now, Matt," said Jason, "you can't go around questioning your country."

"Maybe the President did," replied the Senator. "Maybe he didn't. Personally, I have no idea. Either way, he has plausible deniability. The Specials don't. If things had worked out, well, maybe the boys in Justice wouldn't have been so wrong after all. But the situation has gone from bad to worse. We don't know how many civilian lives have been lost as a direct result of this conflict. If things keep going as they are, there won't be a Chicago left to liberate. So the offer has been revoked."

"Just like that!" exclaimed Matt.

"Just like that," the Senator replied. "The President doesn't care any more how this gets handled, as long as it stops. That's your job. Stop this. By any and every means necessary."

"Be glad to," said Jason, shaking the Senator's hand.

The Senator reached out for Officer Bright's hand, but Matt was already moving away from him, flying toward the balcony with his eyes fixed in the direction of Chicago. Jason was right behind him. The Senator watched with a heavy heart as they disappeared toward the horizon. He found it sad that so much depended on two men who, in the final analysis, he could not entirely trust. Who knew, who could ever really know, which side they would ultimately take?

Meanwhile, Matt and Jason found that they had time for a few words before they broke the sound barrier.

"Haven't seen you around much lately," said Matt.

"Nexus Corp's had me keep a low profile during this whole Chicago business. They still need me, but at times I've been bad for the image. Depends on what's going on." Jason looked at Matt from the corner of his eye and smiled. "Haven't seen much of you either. Docs fix you up okay after your dust-up with John?"

"Well, it has been ten years," Matt snapped back. "Yeah . . . I'm fine now . . . fine."

Further conversation became impossible when a sonic boom signaled that Jason had accelerated. Matt cursed to himself and caught up. He never cared for Jason's posturing. He also remembered—and Jason had conveniently forgotten—that John could have easily killed him. But he hadn't. He had beaten Matt to a pulp, but only with apparent great reluctance.

Furthermore, John had claimed Jason was behind the murders that had started this damn civil war in the first place. But John didn't have any evidence then, he'd wanted Matt to take his word for it.

On the other hand, as arrogant as Jason was, Matt didn't think him capable of committing murder. He was definitely one of the good guys.

Or was he? For the past decade Matt had kept his mouth closed and his eyes open, waiting for the evidence to point one way or the other. At the moment, he still didn't know whom to trust.

But he probably would by the time it was over.

Chandra had watched in horror as the slab of concrete from the crumbling building had fallen on top of the man. He had sneaked out of an office building, probably in search of water or food, when one of the evil Specials had knocked me into a building and I'd ricocheted into another on a wobbly foundation. I didn't see what had happened immediately afterward; Chandra told me about it later.

The block of concrete had fallen at an angle, supported by other large pieces of the wall. Otherwise the man would have been crushed to death instantly. As it was, the man screamed in agony. Chandra wouldn't have been surprised if every bone in his chest had been broken, if his lungs had been punctured. Still, she had to try to save him.

"Try not to move," said the most beautiful woman in the world. "I'll try to get this off you."

Adrenaline surged through her. She lifted the slab over her head and hurled it across the street.

It landed, hard. Luckily, no one had been standing there.

She knelt beside the injured man. His face was as pale as a sheet, and blood flowed freely from his nose and mouth.

"I'm sorry," she said, afraid to touch him. "We'll get you to a doctor and—"

"Too late," the man gasped. "Why did this happen? We never did anything to you."

Maybe not you personally, Chandra thought, but said, "I know. You got caught in the middle of something that's just out of control. I'm sorry—"

The man smiled blissfully. "How can you be sorry? You're the most beautiful thing I've ever . . ." He gasped, coughed a huge amount of blood, and then without warning stared glassily toward the sky.

The man was surely dead, but Chandra couldn't help hoping. "Mister. Mister!" she said, shaking him gently.

Of course, he did not respond. Chandra touched his

eyes, hesitated, then closed his eyelids. She wondered what his name was.

Had been.

She fought back tears. She didn't know how much more of this death and destruction she could stand before she went absolutely bug-crazy.

Poor Chandra, said a voice in her head.

"Critical!" exclaimed Chandra, looking around. "Where are you?"

But the streets were empty. Any person who might have seen Chandra try to save the man had fled, and the Specials were currently fighting elsewhere.

You wanted him to see you suffering for him, but all he saw what they all see—the most beautiful woman in the world. Even if she's the angel of death.

"Now. that's not fair!" Chandra snarled. *"Where* are you? I want to kick your—"

I am nowhere you can find me. With every one of us who dies, the rest get stronger. Especially me. As well as controlling my group, now I can touch your thoughts— everyone's thoughts.

"You're insane!"

Then you should be worried. What's it like, having a crazy person inside your head, Chandra?

"It feels like a mosquito's buzzing in there."

That's because there's so much room. Poor little baby— grieving for a normal. You're making it too easy, all of you. Hey, look! Even more of us who've seen what's happening on the news, coming to help your side. More willing batteries come to make a donation.

Chandra's heart didn't know whether to sink or soar as she saw a flock of Specials speeding across the decimated Chicago sky.

There's Ted Kramer. Dear, sweet Ted. He's thinking about his wife and kids. About how he doesn't want to be here. He doesn't want to be a hero. But he feels he has to carry his weight. Oh, look, there's Ed Massie. You know that mouse Stephanie actually had a crush on him once? He's scared, so very scared. He doesn't want to die. He doesn't want to kill anybody. But he doesn't know how to get out of this.

They're going to make it so very easy. Because there's not one of you with the balls to do what needs to be done. Except me.

"What . . . what are you going to do?"

I'm going to get everyone who's not on my side . . . on my side. By making sure you've got nowhere else to go.

"I will *never* join you!" shouted Chandra to the unheeding sky. "Never! Ever!"

You won't have a chance to kill yourself first, honey, said Critical Maas.

Most of the fighting occurred in a place that was once a ritzy park area, surrounded by the best condos. Most of the condos were rubble, the park resembled a desert haunted by images of the oasis it had once been. By now Ravenshadow and I had worked out a system, wherein he or one of the other "enlisted" Specials would bring an unconscious rogue and lay him or her out on the ground. Then when one came to, it would be my job to knock him unconscious again before he could do any damage. Usually I used an energy bolt, but every time I had an opportunity to get physical with a rogue who'd participated in killing me earlier, I took a little extra pleasure in my work.

I was getting tired. Didn't know how much longer I

could sustain this level of power drain. I felt as if I was wasting years of my life knocking out these louts. Tempted as I was to do the world a favor and erase them, I knew that to kill would only be doing exactly what CM wanted.

Some of us had gotten hurt in the action. Rita Young had a broken shoulder and Luigi had almost had his head torn off. Eli and Susan had gotten beaten up pretty badly. They were all nursing their wounds at the edge of the park. I had to keep an eye on them all the time too; if ever there was a crew ripe for ambush, it was they.

Critical Maas, meanwhile, felt a peculiar trembling in the recesses of her twisted consciousness. Stephanie Maas was stirring, downstairs. The sensation was like a whimpering in the soul, a plea for someone to open the mental windows and let the air in.

"It's not going to happen, Stephanie," said Critical Maas, taking a last drag of her cigarette. "Are you watching from inside? I hope you're seeing it all. Because you're going to love this!"

She sent out a blast of energy to the rogues I'd laid out in the park. They all began to stir at once. I walked up behind Bart and struck his temple with a two-fisted energy punch. His eyes rolled up and he fell over like a wooden dummy.

My spirits sank like a golfer in a quicksand trap. There was no way I could keep knocking them all out fast enough to prevent several from ganging up on me. Then the others would have plenty of time to wake up.

And at my feet, Bart stirred.

No doubt about it, my current tactic had outlived its usefulness.

I know you can all hear me now. I've been thinking.

You know all those mundanes who've been hiding during this, watching, sometimes dying? All those potential witnesses who can tell the outside world who the bad guys and who the good guys were?

Randy glided to a landing beside me.

"What's she doing?" I asked him.

"I don't know."

We both feared we'd made the ultimate tactical error in battle: Assuming our foe would not respond to our actions.

Well, I've had the most wonderful idea:

Kill them. Kill them all. *Kill them* ALL!

With Randy and the wounded, I watched in horror as the rogue Specials rose as one and made toward a group of mundanes. Diana Katz, having shifted her aura to a purple color I instinctively knew would be deadly hot to the touch, was the closest to the mundanes, and she laughed joyously as the beginnings of an energy bolt started to ignite from her clenched hands.

"NO!" I screamed.

I could feel though of course I couldn't take the time out to see Randy's jaw drop in amazement as I unleashed a wall of force before Diana and knocked her on her keister.

"Damn you, John!" she exclaimed. "I'm getting freeling tired of you interfering with my mission!"

"Get used to it!" I said, shooting toward her like a rocket and connecting my fist to her chin with cosmic force.

She went flying into a wall. Chunks flew out with such speed that they made it across the street in nanoseconds and almost struck a bunch of cowering onlookers.

Randy kicked Bart in the crotch, while the other "enlisted" Specials did their best to keep the rogues too busy to go off in search of innocents. I found myself going man to man against Hugh Dinger—maybe if I hadn't been so weak he wouldn't have been able to fight me to a stand-still, but the fact remained that was what he was doing, and I knew if I couldn't beat him, I wouldn't be able to beat anyone. My reflexes were slowing down, my vision becoming blurry. I feared I was on the way to an even bigger letdown.

The others were in the same situation. We couldn't hold back any longer—not with innocent mundane lives at stake. And CM knew it.

I heard Mose Flander scream. Randy was tearing out his heart.

I immediately felt stronger. All it took was the death of a Special.

Only problem was, Critical Maas felt an equal surge.

Hugh brought me back to reality with a sledge hammer blow. I hit back. He laughed. I struck him again and he fell to the ground. I didn't have an opportunity to gloat, however much I wanted to, because Diana was flying to-ward me with the clear intention of locking me in a hot and deadly embrace.

I steeled myself for the worst. Maybe I could turn her energy against her—

Suddenly, a blue streak of wind and power separated us. She was thrown into a building, while it was all I could do to stand my ground.

The same streak swept around the park several times, knocking apart dueling Specials time and time again until they all got the picture: stay still. Stop fighting.

"John! Look out!" Randy shouted, and I whirled just in time to see Hugh Dinger coming toward me with a sharp-edged piece of wood that he wielded like a knife. I got ready—

But the blue streak knocked him on his ass. Knocked him clean out. Then it proceded to knock down Bill Lassendale.

At first, I couldn't believe it. It was Matthew. Matthew Bright.

And he was fighting on my side. On our side! For the first time, I allowed myself to nurture the serious hope that we might actually win this doomed game.

Then I saw a second trail cutting its way through the sky.

It smashed directly into the force that was Matt and sent him spinning into a building, right through the upper story of the deserted skyscraper and into a wall. He lay dazed and confused, asking aloud what the hell had hit him.

"It was just me, Matthew," said Jason Miller (a.k.a. Patriot), looming over his fallen rival for Special supremacy. Dust and debris swirled from the fresh hole in the wall. "It was always just me."

Just the two of us, said Critical Maas. It was her, speaking through Jason. Her thoughts resonated in the minds of all the Specials still duking it out below. She wanted us to hear, and to know what she had done, so that her gloating during this, the time of her victory, would be sweeter.

Jason was the first one I infected. Back when I was still mostly trapped inside Stephanie. She always liked him, wanted him. So one day when he came back to Pederson to visit his family, well, it only took a little nudging from inside for her to make the first move. And you know men. They only have enough blood to fuel either their brains or their penises. Get one working, and the other's willing.

Randy, Chandra, myself and the other "enlisted" ones were stuck below on the ground, still trying to keep CM's minions from slaughtering innocent civilians. We tried, even though we—good guy and bad—were distracted by the images flashing into our minds from Critical's tortured consciousness. I'm certain Matt and Jason had the same vision: The sight of Stephanie and Jason in bed in mutual ecstasy, while Critical was feeling bored.

I'm sure that up above, that assessment made Jason fight Matt harder. A man has his pride after all, and CM was an expert at exploiting people's weaknesses to help her get them to do what she wanted. And in this instance, she wanted Jason to fight Matt to the death.

Those of us below felt that, too.

I was still weak, so I took him, infected him, in the one moment of his own weakness. Typical male blindness. He thought he was inside me, which was true as far as it went. But I went even further inside him. And we got to work. I sent Jason out to kill the expendables, the low-powers first, starting the process. With every death I got stronger and could come out more. And kill more—and get stronger—and stronger—

And we saw images. Images of Jason smothering Peter Dawson with a plastic bag. Of pounding Clarence Mack's face into mush. Of throwing Darcy Krell's semi-comatose body from a third story window.

The images sent Matt into a fury. As a professional policeman he knew that a certain amount of objectivity could mean the difference between achieving your goal and being frustrated, between life and death—it wasn't his job to dispense justice, after all—but the images of seeing his childhood friends being systematically slain by another childhood friend made any feelings of neutrality or impartiality impossible.

He hurled himself at Jason. But Jason was ready and threw a roundhouse right at Matt that connected square on his jaw and threw him back into the wall. Shock waves rumbled throughout the building. Those of us on the ground fighting to protect the mundanes felt them also.

"We have to get up there!" Randy said.

"We can't! If any one of us leaves, these people die. God help Matt. He's on his own."

They say the worst things in the world are the regrets a person has, and to this day I wonder if I made the correct decision. Randy and the others acquiesced. They did as they were told. They trusted me.

In the building, Matt charged at Jason like a rhino. Jason, knowing that throwing a punch would put him off balance, stood his ground. Matt collided with Jason, and the shock waves of the impact blew out what was left of the walls on all four sides of the building.

The roof collapsed around them.

They shrugged off the debris and continued fighting. Chunks of concrete and steel flew from the ruined roof and landed on the street below. The rogues were content to dodge the debris, but the enlisted ones and myself had to watch out for the mundanes as well.

Matt and Jason, meanwhile, were trying to knock the white off one another. Never had they fought so savagely; never had they encountered an opponent who would not buckle down beneath the onslaught of their power and wrath. The vehemence of their fighting was caused by more than the simple knowledge that the fate of the world rested on the outcome of their battle. For in some ways their fight was the culmination of years of speculation and resentment. Who was the better man? The stronger man? And why did it have to be him?

So intent was Jason on pounding Matt into dirt, and so angry was he that Matt was refusing to be compliant, that he barely noticed the quiet whisper that reverberated in one of the few places of his cranium that was still capable of rational thought.

Jason, said the voice. *Can you hear me, Jason? You've got to fight her, Jason. I know you can do it. I know you can do it . . .*

The voice was soft, soothing, strangely familiar. Wholesome. So unlike the voice that had spurred Jason on to commit his acts of atrocity. He answered it by delivering the strongest, most brutal blow to Matt yet.

Matt went flying against one of the few walls yet standing in the upper portions of this wrecked building. Jason stood with his hands on his hips and gloated, his cape billowing in the breeze, as Matt staggered to his hands and knees and then realized he was too fractured to move. Not physically, though he hurt all over. It was his spirit. He was afraid his spirit was about to be broken. It was his greatest fear.

He was barely aware of Jason punching him square in the face and of his subsequent struggle not to lose his balance completely and fall off the roof. His mind was square on his memory of his uncle's funeral, a few years before that of his father, when he had asked his father why Uncle Alex had to die.

"Because your Uncle Alex was a police officer, Matthew. When you put on that badge, it means you put the lives of other people before your own."

"Couldn't he have run away?" asked little Matthew,

touching the cold wood of his uncle's coffin.

"Yes, he could have run away, but he knew if he did, other people would die."

"So he stayed?"

"Yes, Matthew. He stayed."

"He was a hero, Daddy?"

"Yes," said Matt's father, tears streaming from his eyes. "Yes. He was a hero."

Two years later, Matthew and his mother would again be attending a funeral. A funeral for his father, who had, true to his badge, put the lives of others before his own and died a hero.

Died a hero. That being the operative phrase here. Through the haze of his pain, Matt saw the humor in it. His fate was obviously the result of a genetic predisposition.

Jason kicked him in the balls. So great was the trauma already inflicted on his body that he barely felt it.

"Hope you don't mind me butting in," said Critical Mass, "but I couldn't miss the end of this one." She floated toward the demolished roof like a malevolent angel, then hovered above them with an air of anticipation. Obviously she wanted the show to go on. "We always used to wonder who'd win if Jason and Matthew fought."

But Matt was no longer interested in fighting Jason. He lunged toward her.

"Not so fast," she said, and sent out a mental command.

Jason grabbed Matt by the foot and threw him to the roof. Hard. Matt screamed. Every muscle in his body trembled, his every nerve felt seared with agony, and yet he still struggled to stand. He did not want to die having given up.

"Okay, this is taking way too long," said CM. "Finish him. Finish him."

And Jason moved in to do the job.

But in that moment a hundred things happened inside Critical Maas' mind. A hundred things that changed everything.

Looking back, I can see now it had to do with the woman and her children who had been crossing the street earlier in the day. They'd stayed put throughout the entire melee, for what reason I never did know. Perhaps they were simply frozen in fear, or could not decide which direction would be a safe one. In any case—call it typical human stubbornness or the capriciousness of fate—they caught CM's eye just as she was about to taunt Jason/ Patriot with the suggestion that he was afraid to slay Matt.

Afraid. It was the continuing presence of fear that had created the personality known as Critical Maas deep in the bowels of Stephanie's subconscious, and it was Stephanie's innate compassion for others caught in a similar morass of fear that allowed her to crack CM's mental resolve and remember . . .

Remember that she had been a lonely frightened child, beaten regularly by a drunken father.

"I'll give you something to be afraid of!" he'd invariably said. "You hear me? I'll give you something to be afraid of!"

Then the belt would come down. Again and again. And again.

No one had ever helped Stephanie at the camp, or during her tenure at high school. She had never confided in any one. She managed to hide her welts and bruises from everyone. And it had never occurred to the myriad doctors, nurses, teachers, scientists that a parent, even a

211

drunken one, would be so stupid as to brutally whip a daughter who at any moment could suddenly gain the ability to turn him into a disgusting little lump.

The only place Stephanie had to hide in was the secret garden inside her mind. A place where she was powerful and could do what she wanted. A country where everyone did as she bid and a world where her slightest whim carried the weight of constitutional law. This was the universe of Critical Maas, a radically different one than the one Stephanie endured. This was the universe where Critical permitted Stephanie to hide. A place where her father could never hurt her. A place where she did not have to be afraid.

For, as Critical was fond of pointing out, it's not right to be that afraid.

But the girl below, with her mother and her little brother, *was that* afraid. Just because she was a poor, pathetic normal did not mean her fear was any less an affront against the ethics and ideals of a moral universe.

Critical knew that. And for the several hundred times she'd been a poor whimpering normal girl, she hadn't given a damn. But unbeknownst to her, Stephanie had spent the last decade attempting to reassert herself. And the sight of that girl, even filtered through an alternate consciousness, gave her the strength and determination to achieve the supremacy which had hitherto eluded her.

"They're afraid," Critical said, somewhat in surprise.

And that's when it really happened. From below, I spied the visual cue, as CM's hair color went from black to brown. The style changed too, back to the more modest straight style Stephanie had preferred. Her body was suddenly less voluptuous, less muscled. Stephanie was back, back in control of her own body.

212

The battle below suddenly ceased. As did the battle on the roof. A gas main erupted with a roar, and huge flames spread through the lower floors and began licking through the cracks in the roof, but believe me, that was a secondary concern to all of us compared to seeing Stephanie emerging so suddenly after all these years.

At the exact moment of Stephanie's emergence, Critical's control and influence over the minds of the others disappeared. The effect dazed them somewhat. I realized I had been holding Hugh by the head and was about to twist his head 360 degrees. He was too dumbfounded by the new waves of perception to put up resistance.

But no one, I think, was more dazed and confused than Jason. He looked at the broken, bleeding Special crawling through the rubble and the flames before him and gradually, over a period of about ten seconds that formed a subjective eternity, grokked the extent of his transgressions against not only Matt, but the whole of humanity.

"Matt? Matthew?" he stammered. "What was I—? Oh, my God, I didn't—I didn't want to—"

Stephanie tried to speak to him, but his anguish and shame were too great. He howled the word "no" like a rabid banshee and took to the clouds. The *whoosh* of his leaving caused the flames to flicker up in the draft. The time it took for him to disappear in the stratosphere was but a few moments.

"What happened?" Randy asked me, as he took one last half-hearted punch at a semi-conscious Diana Katz.

"I don't know," I said, dropping Hugh. "I don't feel Critical inside them anymore. My God—look!"

The fire had begun to melt the already weakened steel

213

beams. Soon there was going to be one less standing sky-scraper in Chicago. Very soon.

"Come on!" I shouted, and grabbed the first mundane I came to. I took him far from the vicinity, what I presumed to be a safe distance, and began doubling back. Randy had already started organizing the others, and they were carrying mundanes away.

Though some of the innocents, I noticed, resisted being held in the arms of rogues—*former* rogues who, just a few moments ago, had been trying to kill them.

Meanwhile, up on the roof, Stephanie struggled mightily—not physically, because she was so weighed down by the massive guilt inspired by her alter ego's litany of evil deeds that she could barely stand—but mentally. With all her untested will she strove to erect and maintain a mental barrier between her higher self and the subterranean id that had once usurped her.

"Matthew, please, you have to help them. Before Critical comes back. I can feel her fighting to get back out again. Please. *Please!*"

"Help? Help *who?*"

"That woman and her kids down there."

He could barely see. *"What's* happening to them?"

"The building is collapsing. They're too scared to move. They don't know which direction to move in."

He could barely stand upright as the roof shifted beneath their feet.

"What do you want me to do?"

"Rescue them!"

"Right!"

And he took off. Flew directly toward the woman and the children though his mind was barely coherent and his body was awash in a sea of pain. Matthew Bright was a man who, for himself, had not an iota of reserve energy left, and yet for this woman and her children, he did.

The wall was coming down on them. With a single punch he knocked part of it into pieces and then he got under a slab about to fall directly on top of them and he caught it. He held it. His knees wobbled and his arms threatened to crumple, but he held it. "Run," he told them. "I don't know how long I can—"

A mental flash: of himself standing next to his Uncle Alex's coffin, saying goodbye. Or was he standing next to his father's?

Either way, he was standing with them both again. He was worthy of them both. He was a Bright.

Goodbye, world, he thought. *And hello.*

The building collapsed around him. With that last conscious thought, he hoped the woman and her children had made it to safety.

Flying above the building where Stephanie stood on top of its one remaining wall, I got the distinct—and I do mean *distinct* feeling the fire had become psychic in origin.

"Stephanie?" I asked—despite everything, I still couldn't believe my eyes.

"I'm sorry, John, I'm so sorry, and I'm so scared. I didn't know what Critical could do, what she had already done!"

I reached out for her. "Come with me! We can get you the help you need to control her."

The flames whipped around her like dancing solar flares and yet she did not move. "No, I can feel her, don't you understand? Fighting to get back out. If she comes back again, it'll start all over. And this time, none of you will be able to stop her!"

"Yes, we will! I'll—"

"You'll what? Kill her?"

She had me on that one.

"Funny," she said. "Critical had all the abilities I never had. She could fly. Can you imagine that, Johnny? She could fly. I've always wanted to fly."

She rose up into the air.

"Stephanie!" I shouted. "No!"

But in vain.

The flames rose up to meet her. They enveloped her and she imploded instantly. Just like that, she was gone.

It was a spectacular immolation. The shock waves sent me flying three blocks away, where I landed on another skyscraper.

A cloud of dust spread between the various rows of ruined buildings like the tentacles of a ghostly octopus.

Staggering to my feet on the roof of the skyscraper where I'd landed, I watched the dust cloud in horror. And I, who was not a religious man at all, prayed with all my heart both normal and Special survivors of the battle had survived. I'd seen more than enough death. Seen too many brave people volunteer to meet their maker in the name of the common good. Stephanie had made the ultimate sacrifice. We could only be grateful.

I flew to the others as soon as I had the strength. "Did we get everybody out?" I asked Chandra as I landed.

"I—I think so," she said.

"Where's Randy?"

"Here," said a voice behind me.

And he walked out of a dust cloud, carrying Matt in

his arms. Randy was hardly slight of stature, but Matt's bulk made him stagger.

Randy laid him down. I moved to take off my coat and throw it over Matt's face, but Randy raised his hand. "I think there's still a pulse. Barely there, but—"

"Then I'll take him," I said grimly. "I think I know the best hospital to take him to. Maybe the staff there can help him."

Hoping Matt didn't have a broken neck or spine, I picked him up, hefted him a couple of times to make sure my hold was comfortable. I didn't want to drop him from two thousand feet. But although I was anxious to start my journey, I hesitated. The other Specials were looking at him, they wanted to touch him, as if to transfer part of their life-giving energy to him. This was especially true of the former rogues. I realized then that none of them had willingly joined Critical Maas; they had all been manipulated. Granted, the evil in which they had indulged themselves so thoroughly might have already existed within, but that is true of everyone.

"What do we do about them?" Chandra asked. She nodded to the mundanes, who were standing about, waiting, I presumed, to learn if they were free.

We had just saved their lives—even those who'd been making them miserable for the past decade had contributed to their survival—but when I looked into their eyes, there was no gratitude. There was only fear.

I was momentarily angry. Ungrateful louts. But then I reconsidered. Why should they think otherwise of the Specials? We had given them no reason to think our kind meant them anything other than harm. No reason at all.

"The thing to do," I said, "the *best* thing we can do, is

to get the hell out of their town. Randy, get our people out of here. Find a safe place."

"I got one. But safe for how long, I don't know."

"Then just do the best you can. I'll catch up with you later."

"Will do. Come on." And he swept Chandra up his arms and rose into the air.

The rest followed. Nearly all could fly, but those who could not were taken by those stronger.

Flying Matt to Pederson, I contemplated the terrible price that had been paid in Chicago. By us. By the mundanes. All our powers, all our gifts—had we squandered it all?

Or was there still something left for the surviving Specials to do? Perhaps something we were always meant to do with our powers. I wondered if, at the last, Matt had finally shown us the way.

I prayed there was still time. For Matt.

And for the world.

I can't say the lights of Pederson were beckoning when I finally saw them on the horizon. But this was as close to going home again as I would ever get.

15

THINGS CHANGE

I have it on good authority that it was a quiet night at the Oakhurst General Hospital in Brooklyn. It was especially quiet at the E.R. No accident or heart attack victims had come in, and the gangbangers must have been glued to the news, along with the rest of the country, because there hadn't been any drive-bys or overdoses.

Like I said, quiet. Though I have it on good authority that the two nurses shooting the breeze at the admittance window weren't so quiet. Their conversation reportedly went something like this:

Tara: "And the man could *not* keep his hands to himself the whole night."

Donna: * snicker! *

Tara: "He kept telling me 'the hands of a surgeon are the eyes of God.' I told him I'd already had one hysterectomy and that if he didn't keep those hands where I could see them, God was going to get a black eye."

Donna: * snicker! *

Tara: " I mean, c'mon, it was a first date, for crying out loud. What does he think this is, the '70s, when every-

219

body went to bed with everybody because, well, that's just what you did?"

Donna: "Oops. I think I must have been a victim of nostalgia last week."

Tara: "Oh, Donna, you're such a tease. I don't where nurses got this reputation for being easy, I really don't."

Donna had been about to make a joke about how she'd once known a town whore—the town being New York City—but she was totally distracted by the sight of none other than me carrying the wounded, comatose Matthew Bright through the doors. I vaguely recall her whispering aloud: "Oh, my God . . ."

"Help him," I said. "Please help him."

Every drop of his blood that fell to the floor made a noise that my super-acute hearing perceived as a loud, sickening plop. Because Matthew had worked for the NYPD, and there was always a chance he could be badly hurt, Doc Welles had given all his medical information on Matt to this particular hospital. I suppose he felt the surgeons and directors could be trusted to keep it confidential, even if they did occasionally have trouble keeping their hands to themselves. Doc had always assumed Matt would get hurt in a terrorist bombing, or a big accident, something massive enough to have an effect on someone as powerful as him.

Obviously, being beaten up by Jason *before* having a building fall down on him was enough to do the job.

I watched from the window in the doorway as the trauma specialists tried to repair Matt in the operating room. Fortunately, someone in the bureaucracy had listened to Doc Welles and the hospital was prepared. The doctors had to use tungsten steel syringes to get the I.V.s going, and high-intensity dermal lasers to soften the tis-

sue underneath before they could even try to sew any of
him back together.

That which made us strong also made us very, very
hard to help, or to fix once the damage was done. 113
Humpty Dumpties. Now, less than sixty. And for what?
Why? Why had fate singled us out for "special" treat-
ment? When clearly most of us would have been much
better off growing up as mundanes in a world where
everybody was a mundane. (I say most of us because I
was reluctant to include myself in that category. Even
after all we'd been through, I couldn't imagine myself a
normal person with artistic ambitions living in a suburb
with a wife, 2.3 kids, a dog, and probably too many cats.)

"John Simon?" someone asked officiously.

Clearly my ruminations as well as my waiting were
over. I turned to face three police officers, all pointing
their weapons at me, all trembling, nervous, itching for
me to give them an excuse to make a mistake.

"We have orders to place you under arrest and hold
you for questioning in relation to the events in Chicago
over the last few days. Turn around and put your hands
behind your—"

I cleared my throat. He stopped talking.

"I don't think you should do this," I said. "I'm not in a
very good mood right now."

"I'm not going warn you twice. We have you covered."

"Do you?"

I confess I might have been a mite too enthusiastic.
The white light I unleashed to blind them could have
blinded the doctors in the operating room. I read in newspaper reports that it seeped through the walls and through
the ceiling into the second floor.

The energy, fortunately, went only in the direction I'd

intended it to, at the policemen. The impact threw them off their feet and they dropped their guns before landing.

Two were knocked out immediately. The third groaned and tried to get up. I grabbed him by the rear collar of his uniform and slammed his head once against the wall. That still didn't put him out, but he was in no condition to fight me anymore.

"Anybody else?" I shouted to the doctors, patients, and orderlies. "Anybody else want a birds-eye view of all nine circles of Hell at once?"

The policemen waiting outside the hospital all froze or stood between the civilians and me. Who were running away.

Except for a woman trying to protect her children beside an ambulance. "Please!" she said. "Please don't hurt us!"

I looked down at the unconscious policeman I was still holding by the collar. I realized that their fear wasn't anything I was interested in. It wasn't what I'd wanted. Or what I'd come here for.

I dropped the policeman. Eliciting fear from mundanes, I realized, wasn't what *any* of us were here for.

"I'm sorry," I said to the woman. "I'm just . . . sorry."

I rose into the air. I had already done what I'd come to do. I had gotten Matt to a friendly hospital as quickly as I could. The rest was up to fate. Staying was the natural thing to do, but I shouldn't have. I should have remembered I wasn't entirely natural.

Besides, I had other places to go.

I had to check up on Doc Welles. Things didn't look good for him. I sent away the nurses Randy had contracted to look after him for the duration of the battle of Chicago and like a goddamn selfish fool, sat beside a dying man and told him my problems. I know that's what he wanted to hear, because my problems were, in the final analysis, the Specials' problems, but looking back on it, I feel that I could have been a tad more spiritual.

And considerate. After I gave him the lowdown, which included the latest death count, I said:

"I blew it, Doc. We all did. We had all these powers, all these abilities ... and I look back on it now ... and what was it for? It's all been lost ... squandered away. That issue of *Time* was right. When the history of the Specials is finally written, it'll be a catalogue of missed opportunities."

"Ah, but opportunities missed by whom, John?" Doc replied, hoarsely. I could tell that every breath cost him vast reserves of energy, but he wasn't going to let that stop him. "If a mistake was made, it was mine."

"Don't be ridic—"

He cut me off with the tiniest gesture. For him it must have required considerable will. "I'm not. I've had a long time to lay here and think about it. Now, listen to me. I wanted to keep all of you safe. Keep you out of trouble. Watch over you. I made you afraid of the outside world. Even as you moved around it as young men and women and some of you conquered various spheres of influence, you were still afraid of it. Always afraid."

"The outside world has given us plenty of reasons to be afraid all by itself."

"It always does, no matter who you are. The trick is not to be afraid in return. Listen: I made one final mistake with you personally, John. I knew you could kill any of the others, and I made the mistake of telling you that— telling you that you the responsibility to stop them if they

223

ever got out of control. I made you the one who had to live with the burden of being their potential executioner, when I should have guided you into being their . . . their guide. I should have taught you to lead them into the world in relative safety."

He paused, and I should have said something. Damn it, I should have said something. But I was too busy crying. I could feel his essence slipping away.

"This is important, John," he said. "Every damned one of us come to a day when we say, 'What could I have done? What opportunities did I miss? How could I have made a difference?' We all have powers of our own. We all have abilities, and we have an obligation to use them. The fact that most people don't is no excuse. Your obligation—you and the rest—was a little greater than that of the mundanes, but it was the same in principle. You still have time, John. You know what you have to do. Free yourself from the burden of my fear, from the concerns of an old man. Look at the world anew, John. Make me proud."

"Doc? Doc?"

But he didn't hear me. He was gone, just like that.

I threw myself across his body and cried. That struck me as odd, because I hadn't cried when my own father died.

Instead of class reunions, the Specials held funerals.

We had an entire slate of funerals and memorial services to attend, but the one for Doc Welles was the first. We knew it was going to be difficult. So many of us had been forced to betray the others, and had been given free reign to do things that anyone with half a conscience would refrain from doing. But that had been exactly the problem: Critical Maas had suppressed the conscience of those she'd influenced. And those who had survived her reign of terror now had to look their former schoolmates in the eye and say, "I did not mean to try to kill you. I did not mean to kill our friends whom we'd known since childhood. I did not mean to kill your friends, family members or just average innocent mundanes. I never would have done so, had I been acting of my own volition."

Murder hadn't been the only crime committed by CM's minions—torture, rape, robbery, verbal abuse, and having unprotected, nonconsensual sex were just a few of the other social transgressions associated with their regime. Not to mention the traitorous takeover of an American city. They weren't likely to be forgiven by the general public any time soon.

The authorities knew the time and location of the funeral, of course. I'm certain they watched from a safe distance. And I think they knew they'd better keep it safe for the time being. I'm sure I wasn't the only Special seething inside, knowing that the tragedy and travail of the last decade had been essentially caused by a single Special whose dark side knew how to exploit our character flaws and weaknesses. And I am equally sure the authorities knew better than to piss off any of us when we were all in such a foul mood to begin with.

We were all here. All the survivors. Three days after the end of Chicago. Eli and his wife Susan were gone, and so was Ted Kramer. I had been so preoccupied with Matt, I hadn't even known they were dead until hours after it happened. So many were gone—in addition to Joshua, Stephanie, Clarence, Cathy, Peter, and all the others. Our numbers had dwindled severely. But not our pain.

CM's former minions had a tendency to avert their eyes whenever anyone looked at them. They clung together, ashamed, fearful, certain that redemption was impossible. But they were here, former foes, traitors to all that was decent and good in Specialkind, because the Doc was our collective father figure.

All here, except for Jason. So far I'd been unable to sense his presence. My ideas concerning his relative guilt or innocence in this whole sordid affair were somewhat ambivalent. My mind was filled with so many ifs, the main one being that maybe Critical Maas never would have been able to get her mental claws into his lizard brain if he hadn't been so prone to mistaking his pecker for a dowsing rod. (Of course, Jason wasn't the only male Special with that problem; she would have gotten to someone powerful eventually.)

The service was brief. The few mundanes who did attend left with the preacher (who was *not* Reverend Kane), leaving me to be the first to say a few last words.

I began simply, telling what Doc had meant to me. What he had said to me about it being my responsibility to one day kill the others if things got out of hand. About how I should have realized that Stephanie, through no fault of her own, was secretly the most dangerous of us all. And I told them what Doc had said to me on his deathbed.

"The last thing he'd said," I told them, "was 'make me proud'. I think that's the whole reason he held on as long as he did . . . to point the way. As Matthew pointed the way. I think that everything that's happened has made us realize that however strong we may be, we are finite in number and duration. The power does not cross to our children. When we are gone, we are gone.

226

"We must do more than we have done, because it's right. Because we have an obligation to do so. And because I believe that's what the power was meant for. The power that came out of the sky over Pederson that day had a purpose. And I think I've finally figured it out.

"Even as kids, the foundation for our future was in front of us. We just didn't see it. Some of us could fly. We were aerial scouts. Some of us were invulnerable. Ground scouts. Some of us were strong, to handle the heavy lifting. A few controlled fire, necessary to life in difficult conditions, while another brought light. One could bring us back to life if reached in time. Another could seek information from the past, and still another from the dead. To learn from others' mistakes.

"Stephanie Maas—Critical Maas—was able to communicate with all of us over long distance, direct and control us. Yes, her power became twisted and perverted by the multiple personalities that afflicted her. But the intent was always clear: a command and control center.

"Energy. Earth. Air. Water. Fire. We had control over all the things anyone would need to build a perfect world. The power was conscious. The power was directed. The power had a purpose. I know that. I can feel it inside me now. When Matthew saved those people in Chicago, I felt the power inside me say, *Yes. Yes.* Followed by: *What took you so long to get here?*"

By now, the rain was torrential; I was amazed the others could hear me over the machine gun staccato of the rain hitting the ground and umbrellas, turning the grassy knoll into a sea of mud. Yet I sensed they had no desire to leave, that they were hanging onto my every word.

"That's why each of us gets stronger when one of us dies. Because the job before us would become harder as there are fewer of us to deal with it. The job is still there, waiting to be done. We have the power. We have the obligation. We should do it now, while we still can."

I paused, waiting. Hoping for a reaction. They all just stared at me as if I'd decided that, from now on, all Specials had to wear their underwear on the outside of their trousers.

Finally, Jerry Montrose asked the question they all must have been thinking: "Do what?"

"Change the world." It seemed obvious to me. Indeed, the rain let up slightly as I spoke. "We step outside the rules. We turn our eyes to the future and we never look back, no matter what it costs us. And we change the world.

"After the ceremony, I'll be by the hill. Whoever wants to join me is welcome to do so. Anybody who doesn't, I'll understand. Because I don't know if we'll succeed. I only know we have to try."

I walked. The longest twenty-five yards of my life.

I waited. The longest wait of my life.

The rain kept coming down. Even from twenty-five yards away, I heard the drops strike the pool in the Doc's open grave and the soft conversations of my friends and former enemies. I caught some of the phrases: *I have kids. I have lawyer's bills. I need to find some other way to rehabilitate myself. Utopias never work; remember Communism?*

I waited.

Who are we to say what's right for the world? Doc said—

Doc's gone.

I waited.

We have to do what's right for ourselves.

228

We have an obligation.

To whom? Why?

Is redemption even possible anymore?

I don't want redemption. I'm just tired of them hunting us.

I waited.

I was beginning to think I was going to be alone in this endeavor. I closed my eyes, leaned against the tree I was standing under so as not to be completely soaked six times over, and tried to imagine myself in a universe where all 113 of us had been just normal folks. Would we have been friends? Would we have even known very many of the group? I couldn't believe that mundanes had such intense connections to so many of their contemporaries. I was so lost in my musings that I didn't realize what was happening until later.

Chandra asked Jerry Montrose what he thought about my proposition.

Jerry said nothing, but apparently he'd been thinking pretty hard, which as much as I've liked Jerry upon occasion, I must say was still quite a stretch for him. Finally, he said:

"I've been a screw up all my life, Chandra. About time I did something about it."

And he walked toward me.

Chandra and Randy exchanged glances. Actually, I never doubted either of them for a moment, they just didn't want to be the first. So they were just a few steps behind Jerry.

Beyond that, I had no idea what was happening.

Until Jerry said, "John, we're with you," and I looked up:

To see all of them, standing with me. I couldn't believe

it. Everyone intended to join in the good fight.

Everyone, I noted, except Jason.

Chandra saw him first. Lightning struck behind him and this huge monolithic individual stood silhouetted in the momentary flash of light. It seemed the thunder rolled around him.

Jason had changed. I knew that—we all knew that immediately because he wasn't wearing his costume. (We'd used to joke that Jason wore his costume in public, or he wore nothing at all.) Tonight he wore jeans, boots, and a brown leather jacket. Gone was the flamboyant superhero hype. He resembled a big bruiser working-stiff, nothing more.

With faltering footsteps he came closer to us, and with uncharacteristic timid tones, he said, "I—I'm sorry. I didn't want to do it, to do any of it. She had me totally under her control. I wanted to tell you, but every time I tried, she *slammed* into my brain. There was nothing I could do except hide behind my arrogance. But even that was lie, because I hated myself. All the justifications in the world couldn't help me hate myself any less. My God, I have children. How can I tell them their father is a murderer? I'm sorry. Dear God in Heaven, I'm sorry . . . I'm sorry."

I realized then, perhaps belatedly, that if there was one Special whom I detested more than Critical Maas, it had been Jason Miller, a.k.a. Patriot. I'd hated him not only because of his arrogance, but for his hypocrisy, his holier-than-thou-while-he-killed-you attitude. But I had been mistaken about him for the last decade. Every theory, every observation, every conclusion I'd ever entertained about him had been based on the supposition that he cared more about his personal power than for others, and that meant that every theory, every observation, and every conclusion had been in error. And I had been very comfortable, existing in my erroneous zone. Granted, as an adolescent, Jason had been arrogant, full of himself, a cocksman extraordinairé in his own eyes, and a materialistic superman the likes of which no comic book page had ever seen, but drawing the straight line from his youth to the conclusion that he was a sociopath was my intellectual failing. The bottom line: I should have known better. I should have realized the truth. Instead of detesting him, I should have helped him.

I went to him and we looked one another in the eye. He wasn't sure what I was going to do—I believe I detected the momentary fear that I might try to harm him—and in fact, I wasn't sure what I was going to do myself, only that I had no intention of harming him.

I reached for his hand. I intended to merely shake it, but instead we embraced. The chasm which had once been so wide was thus easily crossed.

"You must forgive me," I said. I realized I was crying.

"Forgive you?" he said, crying as well. "What for?"

"Because I should have forgiven you a long time ago. If I had, things might have been different."

Jason looked me in the eye and laughed. "John. John. You have to catch the bad guys before you can forgive them." Then he grimaced. The tears were still streaming from his eyes. "I just could never accept that I could be one of the bad guys."

"Well, you aren't any more. We can't change the world, if we do not begin with ourselves. And I think you've taken a bigger step than any of us."

One week later, in Columbia, South America, two drug lords looked upon the bountiful fields of coca about to be harvested and pronounced it wondrous.

"How does it feel, Carlos," said the tall one, "to be at the top of one's profession? To know that few indeed could dare to dream—and dare to reap such profit—on a scale comparable to your own?"

Carlos shrugged and put his hand on his friend's shoulder. "It feels much as it did last year at this time, and the year before that, and the year before that. Yet I confess I feel inner peace this evening. This starry night. It is a thing of beauty, is it not, Salvador?"

They stood on a balcony of a great hacienda overlooking those fields. Gone were the days when they had to hide their crop in the high mountains, or in the jungle. Gone were the days when they had to process it underground. They had become bold, thanks to the Yankees' preoccupation with their internal disorder. The drug lords were practically legitimate businessmen in their homeland, and they were wealthy beyond the dreams of Avarice.

"It is beautiful," agreed Salvador. "Money, as far as the eye can see."

"We have expanded the coca fields almost twenty percent over last year," said Carlos, sipping his drink. "Our plantation, friend, is the biggest in the country. Tomorrow, we begin the harvest, agreed?"

"A thing of beauty, indeed," Salvador said. He made it a habit to always agree with his friend. "It—"

His next words died stillborn as a hungry red fire suddenly ran a ring around the coca fields. The light was so bright the stars dimmed, and within moments plumes of smoke began turning the sky into a dark haze. Straight lines of fire shot from the edges of the ring and converged in the center of the fields with such determination they almost seemed conscious.

The hearts of Carlos and Salvador became heavy with dread. A crop wasted and the possibility of arrest imminent—those misfortunes were humiliating enough. But they'd paid for protection not only from the Colombian military, but from American moles in command and in the field, as it were—and they'd paid good money too. This onslaught meant they'd been ripped off by their most dependable crooked officials.

"This is not an ordinary fire!" exclaimed Salvador. "It's heading for those men in a straight line!"

Carlos saw that his friend was not exaggerating. "They say Peru is very nice this time of year."

"Meet you there."

And they promptly left, taking separate cars and heading in separate directions, along prearranged escape routes. By now the humiliation of having been ripped off and lost so much money had given way to sheer, undiluted panic, motivated by fear of imprisonment in the U.S. After all, hadn't Noriega met an abrupt end soon after he'd been ousted from power in Panama, and he'd merely been a facilitator. They had no reason to believe they'd survive long in Yankee custody.

Meanwhile, men on foot fled the fire. The braver ones fled through the ring and made it to the other side, but that didn't always mean the fire would leave them alone. Straight lines chased a few of the men, and one line of fire led directly to the hacienda.

One man carried a sack of grain intended for the kitchen. He fell as the flame swept under his feet. He leaped up only to fall back again. A great and terrible light had blinded him.

"*Madre de dios,*" he said.

A man of fire hovered before him.

A man who was naked, whose body was white hot in places, and who radiated the heat of a thousand plus stoves.

He looked like he was very, very angry at the entire enterprise.

Soldiers and mercenaries fired automatic weapons on the man.

A barrage of bullets flew toward him with the intensity of a hailstorm.

He should have been ripped to shreds, but he wasn't.

Instead, the bullets melted nanoseconds before they could penetrate his fiery shell, and he simply absorbed them and let the molten metal drip from his feet to the ground.

"Let's party," said the flaming man. He waved his arms.

And a gigantic fireball the size of a city block of tall buildings suddenly illuminated the countryside for miles around.

The drug lords Carlos and Salvador interrupted their journeys down separate roads and had their drivers stop their cars so they could get out and watch their fortunes burn away. They both had the feeling business was headed for a double dip recession of the worst sort.

Night once again, but on the other side of the world. In the port of Athens in Greece, in an otherwise deserted warehouse, a terrorist cell formed of three radical Muslims was making the final preparations for a strike against the infidel.

"We have made all the arrangements," said their leader. "The American destroyer will dock tomorrow between nine and ten in the morning. By then we should be ready."

"Very good, el Fahid," said one of the men, a young firebrand who until now had harbored the secret (or so he thought) notion that their leader was too slow and cautious. "When do we move the explosives?"

"In a few hours," said the leader. "Just before dawn. According to the Weather Channel, the fog shouldn't burn off until after eleven, and should be thick enough to provide the fishing boat with more than enough cover to get to this point." And he tapped the rear of the rough sketch of the destroyer on the spreadsheet lying on the table. The sheet's battered corners were held down by mugs and coffee cups purchased from a leading chain of coffeehouses. "It is the most vulnerable point. We anticipate the blast will result in nearly twice as many dead Americans as we achieved with the bombing of the *U.S.S. Cole.*"

"Excellent," said the firebrand. "More coffee?"

The leader nodded.

"Then we should—"

A terrorist standing guard at a barred window gasped. A blue glow had suddenly permeated one of the bars. He opened his mouth to speak, to warn the others, but before he could do so, the blue glow, at the behest of none other than yours truly, had spread from the barred window to the light fixtures and throughout the warehouse's entire wiring.

"What in the name of Allah?" exclaimed one terrorist.

"Get out! Get out! Before it—!" the leader managed to say, as the blue glow reached the explosives they had been planning to use.

The blast happened a few moments later. Actually, as I flew away, I hoped the terrorists had all managed to evacuate the warehouse before its walls were blown out. Although my regret at their demise, if it happened, would be minimal, I wanted to save lives, not end them. As I knew all too well, everyone deserved a chance at redemption.

I flew high above in the Athens sky. The sound of the explosion was nevertheless quite loud and vivid. Still, I did not look back. My mind was already turning to the next job.

And the power, meanwhile, was pleased. I could feel it. And I know the others felt it, even as we had all felt the pleasure of the power when Jerry had embarked upon his coca eradication plan.

In a certain hospital in the Bronx, Jason Miller climbed through an open window on the top floor, looked upon his comatose friend, and wept quietly for several minutes. After he composed himself, he spoke softly, so the nurses and the police officer standing guard outside would not hear. This was not the first time he'd visited Matt, but he had no desire for the authorities to know he was making a habit of it.

"It's begun," he said. "Maybe we'll do it right. Maybe we'll screw it up—won't be the first time, obviously ... But John's right. We have to try. It's the only way we can make it right. The only way I can try to make up for what I did to you. I still feel I should have fought harder. I should have. I really am sorry, but I will make up for it. I'm going to make up for *all* of it.

"And I'm going to come back here every night, until you're back with us again. I'll make sure you're okay, and I'll tell you what we've done and what we're doing.

"We're going to change the world, Matt."

Jason rose through the window and flew across the city. The lights in the buildings and in the streets illuminated it beautifully; it glittered like a jewel of civilization. But he knew all too well the slime and the grime that crawled along the streets with the stink of a sewer.

Oh, well, it wouldn't be long before the streets were cleansed of all that filth and muck. Nor would it be long before there would be profound limits to the damage nations could do to one another. Jason would see to that. Personally.

We're going to change the world, Matt. Even if it kills us. . . .

16

POWER

There's only a margin of difference between not reading books and not knowing how to read. It's the same with not having a power and not knowing what to do with it, exactly, once you do have it. And that was exactly the same situation Jason Miller found himself in. All his life others had paid him to allow them to do his thinking for him, and now through no fault of his own, the circumstances of his life had changed so irrevocably that he would never be able to return to that comfortable position in the world he had so easily won twenty years ago.

I must confess straightaway that much of Jason's conundrum—what to do? what to do?—was probably my fault. I'd laid out a general direction for the Specials to follow—change the world, change the world—but I'd offered them no specifics for that, and furthermore had no intention of doing so. Leading them—*trying* to lead would have been the worst decision I could have possibly made. Leaders made other men and women jealous, and tempted them into vying for power for its own sake. Each and every one of us had already learned the hard way that jealous Specials, greedy Specials, or Specials answering the call to all remaining deadly sins were counterproductive.

We had to go our own way. Each and every one. We could work together if we chose, but I wasn't going to organize this affair. I wasn't even going to make a judgement so far as the loss of life, innocent or otherwise, was concerned. What a Special did to make the world a better place was his business.

And no one else's.

So what Jason did was entirely up to Jason, so far as I and all the others were concerned. The only thing we would do to help him was simply trust him. We wouldn't supervise, second-guess, or criticize unless he got wrapped up in unintended consequences. That was the same way we were going to treat everyone else and we weren't going to change that for him or any of the others who'd been taken over by Critical Maas.

Even those who hadn't required much, or *any* pushing in that direction. We had decided to write a new page in history. For the first time we weren't going to allow the mundanes to control our history.

I think Jason first began to grasp the full implications of that idea the morning he'd read on a newspaper webpage that Patriot was going to give a speech that afternoon at the NexusCorp HQ in the small city of Erie, Indiana. Erie had been just a small town until the Reagan Era, when five or six people decided it would be the perfect location—isolated, but reasonably close to centers of power—for a global entity's headquarters. Today Erie was *the* center of power.

As was so often the case, before the speech there was a press conference. It was being held at the HQ square, which at SRO was 1,000. Today the square hosted 700, about one quarter of which were reporters. At least three TV crews were televising the event live, not to mention C-Span, which planned to repeat the conference/speech in its entirety several times over the weekend.

Word had it that certain unspecified Nexus South American investments had been hit hard lately, and Vice-President Gabriel Andrews, in change of Global Communication, was eager to put a stop to certain unseemly, but not altogether inaccurate, rumors.

Andrews was a dark-haired officious man, who wore glasses and affected an imperious tone whenever he was outside his office or the boardroom. He would have preferred not to be sharing the stage with Patriot, but he had things he had to say, things the public needed to hear, and the public would pay a lot more attention if Patriot were around.

He would have preferred not to be answering question put forth by suspicious and hostile reporters, but that seemed to be the only kind there were these days. Andrews was making a routine statement about how NexusCorp's real contribution to the well-being of several third world countries came in the form of creating jobs and encouraging investment when an ABC reporter asked:

"But isn't it true that most of those jobs were created at the expense of firing thousands of American workers? And isn't it also true that the workers you're talking about are working for less than a dollar an hour, without any kind of benefits?"

That did it. Andrews was tired of talking to these bozos. But standing at this podium wrapped in an American flag, against the backdrop of a flag-themed curtain, standing beside a man dressed in a costume based on the American flag, Andrews figured that at the very least, the stockholders deserved to hear a few quick words of defense of their interests before he could wash his hands of this charade.

"Whatever limited adjustments have been made to the workforce of our American offices are very much in line with what we've done before, and with what other companies are doing to maximize revenue for our shareholders. And now, to make the case for how we're helping these people—and helping the workforce of the entire world rise up in the process—I want to introduce the man who is the personification of our corporate spirit: Patriot!"

A few wind machines discreetly switched on, and Patriot's cape billowed heroically as the man himself stepped up to the podium. "Thank you very much." His voice was deep, booming. It hardly needed the microphone. "I just want to say—"

Whatever it was, the man who called himself Patriot didn't get to say it.

Andrews was able to say one word—*"Earthquake!"*—before his stomach rushed up to meet his face, while the rest of his world turned upside down.

The stage began to tilt. The reporters and the audience braced themselves and tried to ward off the strange sensation that the earth was moving beneath their feet. Their reaction was strictly visceral.

Patriot and Andrews had a somewhat different perspective, as the stage fell through a tremendous plate glass window (equipped with safety glass, thank goodness!), taking them and all the props along with it.

Andrews' landing broke his ankle. Patriot landed on

his padded behind. He was shaken up, but otherwise un-harmed.

"The padding in this costume is terrific!" said Patriot, his enthusiasm quite genuine. "I almost feel like a super-hero!"

"Take that off!"

Patriot looked up to see the massive finger of Jason Miller pointing directly at his face. Patriot gasped. He'd never been close to Jason before, and though he'd heard people speak of how Jason's anger sometimes radiated from every muscle of the man's iron body, he'd never imagined that it would extend to his forefinger. Patriot gulped. That forefinger looked like it could penetrate steel as though it was tissue.

Patriot moved faster than he ever had in his life, and took off his mask. He handed it to Jason. Gladly. Eagerly. "Here! Take it! I—I was just hired, not three weeks ago. They hired me to stand in, to impersonate you. I didn't mean anything personal by it! It was just a job."

Jason nodded. "Uh-huh." He took the mask.

Behind them, Andrews grimaced in pain and said to a few staffers who'd rushed in to assist, "Security! Get se-curity!"

But it was already too late. The reporters and camera-men were arriving faster than both the security and the medics. "Wait a minute!" shouted out someone. "You mean there's more than one Patriot?"

Jason laughed contemptuously; he could still be arro-gant. "You think there's only one Santa Claus?"

Some of the reporters abruptly ceased talking; the question had caught all of them by surprise. Only Jason's wide territorial aura prevented them from pressing around him.

"At last count," said Jason, "they had about four or five different guys playing Patriot, usually at social functions and photo ops where no powers were necessary. Behind the mask, Patriot could be anybody."

"Anyone who was a man, of course!" shouted one of the ladies.

Jason smiled. He wasn't as angry as he'd been earlier, but there was still an air of unpredictability around him. "But this is just me. And I have an announcement to make. Effective today, I'm resigning as the corporate symbol of NexusCorp. A corporation that, I should add, has been operating sweat shops in six states through a number of subsidiary companies, has illegally dumped substantial amounts of toxic waste, and has been engaged in unauthorized medical experiments using unwitting human test subjects. You know what they say—it's in the water; that's why it's yellow!"

By now, the flash bulbs were popping and every cable news network had switched to a live feed. Andrews staggered to a stand and with a pronounced limp tried to get between Jason and the reporters. By now, the stand-in Patriot was nowhere to be seen.

"He'll never prove it!" exclaimed Andrews, with all the desperation of a man denying a court room revelation in a black and white movie. "He'll *never* prove it! It's our word against his! He's a nut case, a disgruntled employee."

"Needless to say," responded Jason, "I've just obtained documents from the CEO's office that will corroborate what I've said here. I've just had some friends fax copies to all your editorial offices."

"Shit," whispered Andrews. He promptly slinked off. No one would pay attention to where he went or what he was doing until later; by then he'd already slipped town.

The reporters peppered Jason with questions: "So what's the reason for your resignation?" and "Was there a better offer from another company?" being the two loudest.

"No," said Jason. "No to both questions. It's just I've realized I have a finite number of years to live. We all do. For me the years before today have been wasted chasing celebrity, squandering it on stupid jobs like this. Now I want something a little more profound out of life. It may sound naive, but I want to do something valuable with my powers I have, in the time I'm given." He nodded.

It was a cue for the reporters to start shouting questions.

No one said anything.

Finally, a woman asked in a meek voice, "So. You're saying you're not sure yet which company you're going to be working for?"

Jason sighed. These people were even less practiced in using their God-given intelligence than he. "Just write this down: 'Be ashamed to die, until you have won some victory for humanity.' Horace Mann. He said it better than I could. Of course, I don't have much time for reading, so I heard it quoted from a friend of mine. Matthew Bright. You may have heard of him.

"Now, goodbye."

Like a whiff of smoke in a dream he rose through the shattered window.

The reporters shouted a flurry of questions after him: Could they have another picture? What's his new nickname? Would he like to pose for *Playgirl*? They'd grown hoarse by the time someone finally noticed he'd left his Patriot mask behind.

Jason rather pointedly did not look back as he flew away from Erie, Indiana. Just the thought of returning someday brought back the shoulder-weight and the tension that had evaporated since he'd made his decision to leave. He had said what he'd come to say and that was it, though he doubted the media pundits and commentators would understand it or believe it.

There was no reason why they should either, given his previous record. His speech used to rail on about how America was once a true land of the free. While today it was the land of the hustle, land of the hype. Everybody had an angle and nobody told the truth. He'd said it many times while working for NexusCorp, but deep down inside, he never believed the words nor did any of the "few morally and ethically superior" audience. His speech was a form of kabuki theatre, that everyone understood was ritual but which no one commented on.

And now he knew that when he'd said those words, he had been talking about NexusCorp and himself. There was no reason why the reporters would believe he had had an epiphany. He'd never given them a reason to before.

High above the clouds, he knew the time for words was over. It was time to make a difference. Time to go to work.

Only one question remained.

That night, Jason Miller carried his wife Wendy and their six-month-old son Jace to a remote cabin in the Rockies. He'd taken Wendy flying lots of times, but never his son, and he couldn't recall ever having held her so tenderly, with such love, not even when they were making Jace.

Jason loved Wendy, as much as he loved anyone—he realized now much of his behavior, even the most extroverted, resulted from a fear of intimacy—and he had been more faithful to her by far than he had been to any other woman, but tonight the extent of his love filled him with trepidation. What good would it do him, he wondered, if he saved the world but lost them in the process?

Maybe that was point. Maybe loving her wasn't supposed to do *him* any good, only her. Her and little Jace.

"You're sure we'll be safe here?" Wendy asked, as they descended to the driveway of dirt and gravel.

"I think so." The very thought that something might happen to them tied his stomach up in knots. He tried not to show it as he showed her in.

"I paid for this with cash, out of money stashed away in a private account. Fake name, fake social security number, but with enough money, nobody asks questions. I hope you like it here. I wanted this cabin to be a surprise for our next anniversary, a place where we could get away, just the two of us."

"The *three* of us!"

"Of course! Actually, I was thinking of hiring a nanny so we really could be alone." He pinched her on the behind.

"I know what your idea of a nanny would be. And don't pinch me while I'm holding Jace. I can't pinch back."

"That was the idea." He opened the front door for her.

"Oh, Jason!" she exclaimed. "It's beautiful."

Actually, she was simply being polite—the place had strictly the essentials without being Spartan—but he loved her all the more for it. "I went shopping before I got you. The larder's full. Enough to last for months. And there's a line of pre-paid credit at the local store."

"Jason—"

"Enough to feed a small South American village for a

year. The longer you can avoid using the credit cards, the harder it will be for the Feds to track you."

"Ja—son!"

"There's a transistor radio, and the satellite feed is rigged so anyone tracing the signal will think it's from Peoria. I've arranged it so you can rent videos and DVDs at the local rental joint, and check books out of the library, without having to sign in and out. Like I said, with enough money nobody asks questions."

"Jason!"

"Yes." The moment he'd dreaded had arrived. She was going to respond.

"From the way you're talking, either you're expecting not to come back here very soon, or very often, or both. Is that true?"

"I—"

"I have a right to know."

Jason cleared his throat. "I don't know. I wish I did. I do know that everybody knows what the matter is with the world. The only problem is changing it. We Specials are going to change the world, whether or not the world likes it. It isn't going to be easy. We're going to make a lot of enemies.

"Jerry's taken out half the cocaine plantations in Columbia; Deedee's doing likewise with the poppy farms in Afghanistan. Some of the others are demolishing oilrigs in environmentally sensitive areas and others are putting the kibosh on unsafe nuclear plants. This is the sort of activity that can make you unpopular. Jerry's getting the most attention though. Last I heard the bounty on his life had hit over a billion dollars. I think he enjoys the danger. I personally don't mind it, but I don't want to put you at risk. I can't do that and still do what I have to do. I can't."

Dinner that night was a somber affair. The baby slept quietly while his parents ate in silence. Wendy had the feeling she'd better get used to pasta and rice. Jason had meant well, but he'd been rather unimaginative while stocking provisions. They only shared a few sentences during the meal; Wendy inquired how Jason had known how to set up a secure secret location.

"Doc," answered Jason. "Doc Welles taught us never to unequivocally trust any mundane, not even those who permitted us to live a life of luxury. He taught us certain modern survival skills too, even if some of us took to the lessons better than the others."

Wendy grunted and finished the meal. Jason had never confided *that* to her before. After she finished washing and putting away the dishes, she joined Jason on the balcony. The sky was crystal clear, she couldn't recall having seen so many stars before, and in such detail. For a few moments she could almost imagine she, Jason, and Jace were the only people in the world.

"So, you're ready to start?" she asked.

"Yes, except for one small significant detail."

"Except what?"

"What do I do? Where do I start?"

"Well, you could, I mean ... You mean, you don't know what you want to do?"

"If you had the powers I have what would you do?"

"Well, I'd go into Iraq and take out Saddam Hussein, bring him to trial at the Hague."

"It'll just lead to more terrorism in the area. He's wrapped himself in the Islamic religion, and you know how the Arab in the street views the Specials as the infidel personified."

"Then I'd stop the fighting in the Mideast."

"How? Disarm one side and the other will exploit it. Disarm both sides and they'll go at it with sticks and stones and knives."

"It's true. Both sides do act like they've got nothing better to do than hate one another. Why don't you go after criminals?"

"Randy's got that covered. He knows where the criminals are and he's already got a team to help him. Believe me, they don't need me. Remember, he's been doing this stuff a long time. I just went where NexusCorp told me to go. They always had the info. Otherwise, I wouldn't have known where to start.

"It's funny. I can crack mountains open with my bare hands. I can fly just under Mach 2. But I can't help a kid to read. I can't rebuild barrios or ghettos. If I drive muggers out of one area, they'll just move to another. I can't stop people from drinking and driving. I can't stop domestic abuse. If there's a comet heading for Earth, and you need somebody to take a shot at it, I'm your man. But most of the problems out there can't be solved by smashing them. It's just not that easy."

"Well, this is silly, *silly*. There has to be *some*thing."

Jason's only answer was a shrug.

"I can't believe you went through all this preparation without having an idea of what you were going to do!" She looked away from him. He did know what he was going to do. He had already decided that his course of action, whatever it was, should be on such a scale that the governments of the world would be distressed. And she knew all too well what lengths distressed governments were willing to go to.

"What are you looking for?" Jason asked.

"A comet. Just hoping."

"The thing is, I've been pretending to be a big hero for so long, and now that the chance is here to be the real thing, I don't know how to do it."

"There is!" Wendy had had an inspiration, and she hated herself for it. But of course Jason had told her everything that had transpired during the last ten years, he had held nothing back, and she knew his shame would eventually kill him if he didn't find a way to redeem himself in his own eyes. Forget the rest of the world. It was his self-respect that mattered. "There is one thing. Something only you can do, as the strongest of the Specials. It's just, if you do this, I may never see you again."

"You will," he said, looking deep into her eyes as he had never before. "I promise. It's okay. Just tell me what it is."

"In the morning," she said. And she kissed him.

Somewhere in the Ukraine, two men—Ivor and Feyodor—were having a drunken conversation. Their office had a single ceiling lamp, a table, a battered stove for heat, and several empty lockers. Once the office had been part of a thriving military base. Now it was a decrepit military base.

"Tell me something, Feyodor," said Ivor, watching the few drops of vodka remaining in his bottle gradually evaporate. "What did we get paid last week?"

"Nothing, Ivor."

"As I thought. And the week before?"

"Also nothing."

"Ah, so, then the week before that. That would have been—"

"Nothing," said Feyodor, wondering what his point was.

"Ah. And the going price for one of those warheads in the bunker. It is—"

"Ten million dollars."

"Canadian or American dollars?"

"American."

"American," said Ivor, lost in his distorted reflection in the empty bottle. "We are paid nothing. To guard that which would make us rich. And why do we do this? Because we are patriots. Because it is our job. And because we are idiots."

"You have certainly summed up our problem," said Feyodor. "Do you have a solution?"

Ivor shook his head and returned his full attention to his distorted reflection in the bottle. Feyodor shrugged and turned his attention to the cigarette he'd half smoked. As bored as they were at the moment, they knew they would be even more bored two hours from now, when it was their turn to take a shift at a guard station outside.

Time stood still, as they became enmeshed in their boredom. It became a weight upon their shoulders that—

Dissipated in a flash. A tremendous magnesium bomb sent a white flash that even through the bunker's dirty windows temporarily disoriented them.

"That can't be good," said Ivor, rubbing his eyes.

Feyodor nodded. He was thinking that if the explosion disoriented them, it must have confused the comrades outside quite a bit.

That's when the shooting started.

Ivor and Feyodor grabbed their weapons and stumbled outside. What they saw dumbfounded them.

Their comrades were firing—half-blindly—at a man who was in the process of ripping the lid off the storage compartment of the massive weapons conveyance tank where the nuclear warheads were currently being stored. Although most of the bullets missed him, several scored direct hits—the main evidence of that being the holes torn in his clothing and the ricochets that came back wounded some of the soldiers.

"He's after the warhead!" said one of the commanding officers.

More bullets fired. A normal man would have been cut to hamburger by now, but this individual did not appear to be scratched.

Ivor and Feyodor were among the few who realized this, who lowered their weapons because they knew bullets would be more of a danger to their fellow soldiers than they would be to this man. If you could call him a man.

Obviously he was one of the American Specials, but what he was doing here, why he was attacking the sovereignty of Mother Russia was beyond them.

He picked up one of the warheads; it appeared he'd driven his fingers through the metal casing and made a handhold as easily one might make a hole by piercing the corrugated folds of a six-pack.

"There we go," he was overheard saying in a booming voice. "That's one down, four more to go here."

By now the soldiers had regain enough of their mental bearings to aim more accurately, and the Special was being inundated with a hailstorm of bullets. Forget the hamburger, he should have been sliced down to his component molecular parts by this point. Yet he was standing, strong, and quite capable of flying to the ground, setting down the warhead, and flying up for the next one. Those bullets might as well have been gnats, as far as he was concerned.

"Are you insane?" shouted the commanding officer,

dashing from man to man until the entire force began to get the message. "Stop shooting! If we puncture the warhead, we will be exposed to the plutonium and we all die!"

"Then how do we stop him?" asked Ivor indignantly.

So intent was the Special on his work that he did not notice the armored tank, equipped with a flamethrower, moving his way. Two soldiers with automatic weapons tried to distract him long enough for the flamethrower to gear up.

The flamethrower shot a burst of fire.

The Special was inundated with flame. He should have burnt to a crisp in about forty seconds, but actually all the flame-thrower did was make him mad.

He leaped from the weapons conveyance vehicle, grabbed one end of the tank, and lifted it above his head as easily as a mundane might lift a large bag of Styrofoam peanuts.

Men inside the tank screamed, but unfortunately lacked the wherewithal to switch off the flamethrower. The fire swept over the men like a tidal wave from Hell, scorching several, and setting a few totally ablaze.

The Special was oblivious to their suffering. He tossed the tank high in the air. It went long. It landed on a fuel dump and exploded with volcanic proportions.

The Russian soldiers fell back. Not only were they doomed to fail in their efforts to stop this man, but merely to try would sentence them to doom—period.

The site was engulfed in fire while the Special calmly retrieved the five warheads he sought and tied them together with chain.

Then he picked them up and flew away. He regretted the loss of life—he'd seen too much of that recently—but they should have known better than to fire at him. They should have known better. Maybe next time.

In a remote area in the Rocky Mountains:

A radio technician working at his station in an underground bunker at a nuclear missile silo said to General Reed, "Sir, we're getting reports that a missile silo in the Ukraine was hit by one of the Specials, who extracted all its warheads."

"Hmmm. The Specials have been threatening to make this a better world lately," said General Reed thoughtfully. "Hmmm. The Ruskies aren't blaming us, are they?

"I don't think so," said the technician. He smiled. "Not yet anyway."

"Well, I'm sure the State Department will make sure they understand we had nothing to do with this. Everybody knows what loose cannons the Specials are. Though I certainly don't mind a few less nuclear warheads floating around what's left of the Soviet Union. I'm sure that if we think about it long enough, we can find some way to convince them that we aren't . . ."

Alarms sounded. They echoed through the metallic chambers like Gabriel's horn gone mad on a wah-wah pedal.

General Reed's initial exclamation was succinct: "What the hell?"

Once he and the technician ran outside, their guns drawn, his second exclamation was even more to the point: "Jesus!"

After all, it wasn't every day you saw a Special carrying a nuclear-armed missile into the sky.

*　　*　　*

Jason Miller flew over the North Pole. He was thinking ahead of himself, way ahead, which for him was very unusual. For most of his adult life he had let the NexusCorp do his heavy thinking for him, and the majority of evil deeds he had performed were done (and rationalized) because Critical Maas had usurped his natural benevolent personality. Jason Miller had always wanted to do the right thing in his life. It wasn't his fault he wasn't an intellectual, that he did most of his thinking with his gut.

Today (actually, it was the long afternoon of summer here in the North Pole), his gut was telling him that this was the most profound, courageous thing he had ever done, and he was okay with the fact that he probably wouldn't be receiving much social approbation because of it.

So far, he had collected 900 warheads. So far he had alternated between the United States and Russia, but soon he was going to Israel, Pakistan, India, and Iraq.

Nine hundred. Out of how many? Twenty thousand? Thirty thousand?

He didn't care if the answer was a million; he was going to take care of them all.

He believed that if any Special could do it, it would be him. He wasn't sensitive to radiation poison, but he was able to detect its presence quite easily. He always believed he could smell a nuke at five miles, through as much lead shielding as the governments in question wanted to use. Sooner or later, he'd find them all.

Figuring out what to do with the warheads once he had them was the hardest part. He couldn't just dump them in the ocean, or hide them.

Carving out the fissure in the North Pole was the second hardest part.

Two miles beneath the surface, down a shaft so delicately balanced that the only safe way down was to fly. Touch one of the sides and the whole thing would collapse.

And at the bottom of the shaft, the nuclear warheads. That far beneath the surface, away from water tables and population centers, the warheads might as well be on the surface of the moon. They'd never be dug out.

He dropped off his latest load and flew up the shaft, toward the eternal light of the northern summer. He imagined a world free of the threat of nuclear war or terrorism—at least until the nuclear powers could rebuild them.

Then Jason would just find them again, and take them.

But the current job would take him a while.

Maybe a long while.

He knew it was a fight worth fighting.

Jason remained true to his resolve. He discovered it was not only a fight worth fighting, it was the most difficult fight he'd ever set out for himself. He systematically stole the nuclear warheads stockpiled in Pakistan, India, Great Britain, China, Israel, and Iraq. He even found the ones that had been smuggled into Syria and Brazil.

Jason did not eat during this time of extreme effort. He did not sleep. He did not find a change of clothing when what he had been wearing was in complete tatters. And when the clothing fell off, and he was naked, he found he did not care. For some reason it was ennobling to steal every nuclear warhead on the planet while in the nude. It was like taking part in a pagan ritual, a ritual designed to elevate the whole of civilization rather than the spirits of a few mere men.

The nuclear caretakers tried to hide the warheads between lead, steel, behind concrete. None of it worked.

Jason was rapidly coming to the opinion that within a few more years, he might actually be able to pull the thing off.

But he knew he would have to remind himself what he was really fighting for: the safety of the little ones. One night he returned to the lonely cabin, where he found his wife standing on the balcony, staring at the stars while she held young Jace—the future—in her arms.

"Did you hear?" he asked as he came in for a landing.

She turned and gasped. He was naked! Not that she minded that on principle, but he was flying around the world naked!

"Jason Miller!" she exclaimed.

"Next time I'll bring a towel. Sorry, honey—my clothes got shredded. I didn't see the point of picking up any more. They'd just get shredded too.

"I don't care if you have to carry a duffel bag!"

"Did you hear?" he asked, insistently. Which was his way of deflecting the conversation away from a subject he found unpleasant, or embarrassing.

"I heard, all right," she said. "It's been on the news all week. Half the people on TV say it's the most important positive development in world affairs for over half a century."

"And the other half?" he asked as he gathered his wife and child in his powerful, exhausted arms.

"They're not here," she said, "and I don't care."

* * *

The last few years had been unkind to Special Agent Paulson. Years of botched efforts to rein in the Specials had eaten up his political capital, to the point that he merely drew a salary, and was little more than a figurehead for the effort to deal with the Specials problem. His health had deteriorated severely, to the point that he was constantly cold and he had to use a wheelchair half the time. Plus, his personal life had gone to Hell. The less he thought about that, the better.

He suspected he had been poisoned. Perhaps poisoned telepathically, by some irate Special.

Either way, he detested being such a shadow of his former self as he was wheeled into the meeting of the secret Specials Surveillance Committee that had been established in the wake of the Chicago takeover. The Committee was composed of powerful men who put pragmatism above principle, and who met in a nondescript office in the Supreme Court Building. The men were important judges, generals, elected officials.

There were guests today, representatives of Russia, Britain, and China.

Paulson knew these people felt not the slightest iota of pity or compassion for the toll his life-long crusade to protect humanity had taken on his body. The only reason why they cared if he lived or died was that they occasionally needed him for answers.

He knew he'd better have answers today, or they would never ask him again. He would be put on a pension, and there would be nothing left for him to do.

The first topic on the agenda, as Paulson knew it must be, was the Special Jason Miller, and his one-man campaign to rid the world of nuclear weapons.

"This individual poses a significant threat to the sovereign rights of our respective governments," said General Fast.

General Francis lit a cigar—these meetings were exempt from workplace environmental regulations. "The question is, what do we do about him? What can we do about any of them?"

"We are not without options," General Fast replied. "We have been preparing for just such an eventuality ever since we became aware of the potential threat posed by the Specials. To that end, I have requested the presence of an expert on the Specials. Gentleman, Special Agent Paulson."

Paulson nodded.

"Mr. Paulson, thank you for coming," said Fast, not meaning a word of it. "I know you haven't been feeling well. I believe you know, or at least know of, the rest of us."

"Yes . . ."

"Do you have any initial thoughts?"

"As the Specials were growing up, we collected files on their abilities—their strengths and weaknesses. Their powers and associated weaknesses have changed as they have grown, and they have accumulated more energy with the death of other Specials. But my people and I believe certain principles still remain. Principles that we have been reluctant to exploit until now."

"I understand," said the General. "But the point of my question is very simple: Can we kill them?"

"Yes, I believe we can. The dynamic may need reinterpretation, the principles may need to be studied and re-examined and adjusted. It's going to take a while to be sure it works, and we have to be sure because we won't get a second chance.

259

"But yes, I do believe that in time, we can eliminate any that are a threat to national security."

"Even Jason Miller?"

"Oh, yes, *especially* Jason Miller."

Night in the woods, far from the obvious travails of modern civilization, contained within its starlight the illusion of eternity. Lying in bed next to his wife, who was snuggled with their baby son, Jason Miller relished the illusion.

It gave him strength. Made it easy to believe that regardless of what might happen to him in the future, his family would be safe. His wife would grow old and his son would grow straight and strong. Both would be secure.

Whether or not he was by their side.

He did not want to leave them, he wanted to maintain the illusion at least until the dawn. But there was something he had to do.

He got up, dressed, and flew out of the cabin, through a window.

He did not break the sound barrier until he'd flown for at least an hour, to give those who might be tracking him as slight a clue as possible to the whereabouts of his sanctum.

By now he knew exactly when to slow down when he spotted New York City.

The chances of anyone seeing him entering Matt's room late at night were slim.

Besides, there was the combination of fear and respect he inspired to help give potential witnesses the motivation to be quiet. He might be a more modest man than he once was, but he still couldn't help using his position to his advantage occasionally.

He sat down near Matt and whispered. Of course, he could not be certain Matt could hear him, but he had to try, he had to keep stimulating Matt's brain cells because right now it was the only thing he could do to help him.

"I think we've made a good beginning, Matt," said Jason. "It's the right thing to do. I don't know if you would've approved. You're such a straight arrow about national sovereignty. But, well, I guess the only thing for you to do is wake up out of the coma, drag your sorry ass out of bed, and straighten me out, right?

"It's okay, take your time. I'll keep coming here to report in, tell you all the good news. I mean, Jerry up against the Colombian coke cartel, can you imagine?

"You've got to get back into the game, Matt. Or it'll all be done and we'll be living in a perfect world and then what're you gonna do?"

There was no answer. There was never any answer in the darkness, though time and time again Jason could almost imagine a flicker of movement. But it was only the fan rustling Matt's hair, or a trick of the light.

"Well, anyway, I'll keep coming by as often as I can. Keep you informed about how it's going. For as long as I can.

"So . . . heard any good jokes lately?"

17

SELAH

Death is a capricious presence in the world. Usually it is a force to resist, to rage against until one has no choice but to be pulled into the dark, dark night, but occasionally it can be a friend, a partner, a force for good in this world.

And without death, there can be no birth/rebirth cycle.

We Specials were trying to resurrect ourselves from the spiritual death we had inflicted upon ourselves, we were trying to rise like a flock of phoenixes from the ashes of our earlier, narcissistic incarnations. We were not trying to create a paradise for ourselves, or even to bring about a utopia for mundane mankind; our goal was instead much more modest. We simply wanted to leave the world a better place than it had been when we had entered it.

Considering the damage we'd done over the past few decades, that was a tall enough order.

But we were up for it. Take Randy Fisk, for instance. Ravenshadow. It took him a little while to get his operation up and running, but once he got going, he inspired more media coverage than we'd seen (or endured) since the Surge.

I concede he was a little blunt, but I couldn't fault his intentions.

CNN ran a characteristic story:

For seven days, Randy Fisk—or Ravenshadow, as he is more commonly known—has been tearing through crack houses and street gang enclaves across the eastern seaboard, from Albany to Miami.

And on the screen appears a nondescript Boston brownstone with the sound of gunfire emanating from inside. Then a cut to a shot taken by some brave soul, a view through a busted window of Randy in full Ravenshadow regalia, busting up a coke lab by yanking a gas stove from the wall.

All while three gangbangers fired automatic weapons at him. The bullets bounced off his steel-mesh costume. Of course, they couldn't have hurt him anyway, but Randy always did like to look good while fighting crime.

During those seven days, he has not slept, has not eaten. He has been only a figure of destruction, tearing out hidden caches of weapons, heroin, and other drugs with the aid of ordinary citizens, using his 1-800-Be-A-Hero hotline.

He tossed the stove directly at the gangbangers. From the looks of things, they avoided the stove, but not the gas fire that immediately sparked and engulfed the entire room. The camera moved to show the gangbangers, their clothes and hair burning, fleeing out the building, down the front steps and, in at least two cases, jumping through windows, but when it moved back to Randy, he was just calmly walking through the fires.

And outside. When he passed a gangbanger who'd just put out the fire in his clothing, Randy casually socked him on the back of the head and sent him sprawling.

It appeared that no one died this time. Randy didn't go out of his way to do physical harm to the bad guys during this operation, but he wasn't exactly careful either.

And on the soundtrack, a replay of his phone message:

"Hi, this is Randy. If you know where the pushers and the gangbangers are hiding, let me know and I give you my word, they won't be a problem anymore." BEEP!

Next, an announcer cuts in:

Residents who previously would never supply this information to the police have come forward in large numbers to help in this extraordinary campaign.

And a long shot of Randy walking down the street, surrounded by admirers and representatives of the media, all wanting a word with him, while in the background a tremendous fire rages throughout the building. A fire engine arrives and the firemen bring out a net to catch an old lady trapped on the roof.

CUT TO: One man, who enthusiastically proclaims:

"Randy is the Man! You tell the police about the shit goin' down, they don't do a damned thing about these guys. We been complaining for months, and they ain't done nothing. Now we can walk on our own streets again."

Even for a Special, said the announcer, *the question becomes, how long can he continue this assault? With police and other government agencies powerless to stop him from going wherever he wants, any reasonable person has to ask, where does it end? When asked that question, Randy Fisk had only one answer.*

PUSH TO: A close-up of Randy's profile. Perhaps his eyes narrow, and he looks sideways toward the camera—

but perhaps not. He remains face-forward, and you cannot see his eyes for his mask. And he says:

"When it's done."

CUT TO: Stock footage of heavily armed military men using cranes to move crates from storage facilities to truck beds.

In an effort to prevent the further destruction of the domestic nuclear weapons, the Pentagon has issued directives to make every effort to move the ICBMs or their warheads from their silos to unmarked flatbed trucks or railroad cars, believing that this makes them harder for the Special Jason Miller, formerly known as Flagg, formerly known as Patriot, to locate and destroy.

CUT TO: A smashed flatbed truck.

Efforts that have so far proved less than successful.

Pentagon officials have declined to comment on the status of strategic nuclear assets on submarines. Sources close to the Joint Chiefs indicate that they are awaiting an internal study of the situation.

They expect to have an answer to this question very soon.

CUT TO: A scene with the phrase "Animated Dramatization" on the bottom of the screen. A nuclear submarine glides just under the surface of the ocean water.

PUSH IN: To just beneath the submarine. We see the face of a man. A man who puts his hands on the bottom of the sub and pushes.

The man rises. The sub rises.

CUT TO: The surface. The sub is rising from the water. The man is still below the sub. The man is carrying it. He carries it along the surface for a while, then he rises up toward the sky.

In addition to stealing and concealing somewhere the world stockpile of nuclear warheads, Jason Miller has been confiscating the world's fleet of nuclear submarines. He gives the crew time to radio their location and jump over-board—usually about twenty minutes—and then when their time is up, he lifts the submarine to the upper stratosphere and tosses it into space.

So far, none of the submarines have been detected in orbit. Most appear headed directly toward the sun, so un-less they are caught by the gravitational pull of a large object, such as Venus or Mercury, they will eventually cease to exist.

But not every action taken by the Specials has proven to be violent or destructive.

CUT TO: A helicopter shot of Specials, including an angelic Deedee Noonan dressed in a red-and-white cos-tume, building an apartment complex in an inner city. They move fast, so fast they are but a blur.

Some Specials have taken on the task of rebuilding pub-lic tenements and public housing in dangerous conditions—

CUT TO: Another group of Specials putting together the steel skeleton of an assembly plant in an industrial dis-trict, while mundane hardhats look on, scratching their heads and sipping a couple of brews.

—Renovating abandoned factories in the Midwestern communities like Flint, Michigan, offering these state-of-the-art facilities for minimal fees to overseas investors in order to eliminate local unemployment—

CUT TO: A group of flying Specials carrying boxes, landing on the front lawn of an old folks' home.

—Or using that money to bring medicines to elderly cit-izens from sources overseas, where a wider range of pre-

scriptions can be obtained for a fraction of the cost paid here for the same prescription.

CUT TO: The Specials dispensing the drugs to grateful senior citizens. Prominent among them is a clean cut Hugh Dinger.

This has led to several lawsuits filed by the FDA and the AMA against every known Special for circumventing trade agreements and price setting protocols maintained by the major drug companies. To which one of the Specials had this to say:

"Screw 'em!"

CUT TO: Hugh giving the finger.

The Specials fly away.

And this doesn't include other activities undertaken by the Specials overseas, which have provoked great concern on Capitol Hill and the White House.

Well, let's see: Those activities would include, but are not exclusive to, the destruction of Japanese whaling vessels, the decimation of the cattle ranches encroaching upon the rain forests, stealing and leaking to the press all the secret documents of the Catholic Church in Rome, installing wind-generators throughout the Third World, providing birth control information to women whether or not the Mullahs or the United States Government wants them to have it, busting African poaching rings in the most definitive way possible, and being instrumental in a slew of "regime changes." It's gotten a little bloody occasionally, but all in all, I'd say we've handled ourselves pretty well.

So far.

Of course, so far one could justly say we've begun handling the easy, the obvious conflicts between men, and attempted to correct the obvious things men and women

267

were/are doing wrong in their management of the planet. But there is one conflict that seems to be the most intractable of all, one which is easily the most politically divisive in modern history, one whose solution has eluded the grasp of the greatest thinkers, politicians, and peaceniks of both the 20th and the 21st centuries. No conflict has cost more lives or inspired more suicide bombings since the Algerian campaign to rid itself of French rule. No conflict has been allowed to remain such a potential powder keg, or has inspired such hate-filled propaganda, or has continued despite the obvious advantages that compromise and peace would bring to both sides.

I'm talking of course about the Israeli-Palestinian conflict. There was a time when, like all sane men, I would have nailed my own head to a coffee table to prevent becoming involved in the affairs of this torturous, tortured land. And at times I would have believed my own intestines would have burst out of my body and choked me to death before I could utter an opinion on how I thought a just peace might be achieved.

But just as there can be no peace without war, there can be no utopia without a solution to this most unyielding of struggles.

That was what brought me here: Latitude 31 degrees, 47 minutes north. Longitude 31 degrees, 13 minutes east.

Jerusalem.

The dry air is heavy with the psychic residue of 6000 years of history and struggle.

Mostly in the name of religion and peace.

This was the air breathed by Solomon when he had to decide between two mothers vying for the same child. You know the story: he offered to split the child in two so each could have half. One mother agreed, but one did not—she would rather give up the child than see it dead. So Solomon decided she must be the real mother, and gave the child to her.

I suppose the real owners, the true heirs of this land have yet to show up, because neither side of the Israeli-Palestinian conflict is willing to give up the land so that it might live.

Names lingered in its air nonetheless. I sat beneath an olive tree on a rise overlooking the city, watched the sun set, and the crescent moon rise.

The wind whispered those names. Solomon and Shishak and Nebuchadnezzar and Isaac and Ezekiel. Sedars and Suppers and Salaams. Alexander and Elohim and Allah and Pilate. This was the ground where Lazarus got a second chance at life—though I always wondered if he or the Son of Man himself were the first vampires—and the ground where Mohammed ascended. The land of the eastern stars and the crescent moon, who broke apart one day and declared themselves forever at war—failing eternally to understand that they are both part of the same sky.

And that if the sky itself should war and fall, what hope is there for those of us below?

A figure approached.

A lean, strong woman, with short black hair and sharp ears. She was dressed in black—a sleeveless shirt, baggy jeans, walking boots. I couldn't see her face but I knew at once who she was, and I tried not to be too nervous.

For after Critical Maas, Jason and Matthew, and everything else that happened on that day in Chicago, I swore I'd never lift a hand against one of our own again.

I didn't want to break that promise, not after having broken so many others.

Not with her.

Not with Laurel Darkhaven.

The only Special who could scare even me.

I knew my first words of greeting should be fraught with significance. I think I can rest assured I failed in that regard. Because the only thing I said was, "Hey."

She grinned slyly and nodded. "John. It's been a lifetime."

I relaxed. As long as she was relaxed, I was going to be relaxed. "So, how you been?"

"Okay. Spent the last twenty years killing troublemakers for the government. Stayed out of Chicago because I made it clear that if my handlers sent me after a Special, I'd kill them first. It discouraged them somewhat. Otherwise, I haven't been up to much. How are things by you?"

She was much more laconic than I'd remembered, but I could only surmise that being a master spy could have that kind of effect on your character.

"Sold a poem to *The New Yorker*," I said. "Rescued a boatload of Haitians."

"That's good," she replied. "About the poem, I mean. And the Haitians, too."

"Thanks."

"So, how did you know I would be here?"

"I have my sources of intelligence and information. You should know that better than anyone."

"Yeah, I suppose I do," she said, her expression darkening. "Even so, how did you know?"

"I detected residue of an electromagnetic pulse indicative of the Flash. Similar to the one you find in Pederson, but much weaker. About 113 percent weaker. This one obviously has been lingering here over a long period, though, just like the one in Pederson. I suspected this is a place where you hang out occasionally."

"I come here to be alone."

"I can appreciate that."

Which was a diplomatic way of saying I couldn't blame her. Many Specials have had essentially crappy experiences with the human race, but Laurel had drifted into doing those dirty thankless jobs which no one should have had to do in the first place. Within a month of graduating from high school, she had been grabbed up by the CIA, the NSA, and just about every other intelligence agency beginning in darkness and ending with the letter A.

She had one power: the ability to affect small objects, the smaller the better. During grade school we figured her power wasn't worth much, though the boys did ban her from games of marbles. During middle school we banned her from Ping-Pong, and during high school we banned her from playing pool because she kept distorting the lay of the cloth. We still didn't get it.

Soon after graduating, I overheard Eli and Bart discussing her unique abilities at providing sexual pleasures. She could excite a man's nerve endings, and bring him to climax, without even touching him.

We still didn't get it. I mean, who needs a power to affect something so tiny? Eli and Bart figured Laurel had a career awaiting her in sexual therapy. None of us realized that the carotid artery, for instance, is a tiny vessel. One little pinch from her thoughts, and the blood dries up on its way to the brain, and voila! You have the perfect assassination. One that appears to be existential doom from natural causes.

I don't think Laurel began her espionage career believing she would be an assassin. I'm sure she was thinking of the more glamorous aspects of the 007 fantasy: exotic locales, sophisticated partners and foes, maybe some great sex thrown in on the side, perhaps even using her own body rather than just her power. I'm sure the CIA, NSA, etc. gradually seduced her into becoming a killer.

And who is to say those she assassinated didn't need killing? Since the job could never be traced back to her or anyone, the wetworks boys sent her after the worst of the worst: terrorists, bombers, you name it.

She'd begun life as such as sweet girl. I used to wonder how she was able to do it. But how is less the question than why, and where does it stop?

"If you knew I was coming," she said, "then you must know what I'm going to do."

"Not in so many words. Sometimes I can get a feeling from the psychic residue, some insight into the individual who's left it behind and her motivations. Sometimes. I must confess, yours are a little vague. Why don't you tell me?"

"When I was recruited, I was proud that I could be of service. We were all under suspicion all the time, and to have a place where I could fit in, serve my country, I thought would make things easier for the government to accept us.

"Of course, it changed nothing. But I was young, naive, and stupid. I used to keep track of the people I killed. Then the numbers just got too big. I killed them here, in Jerusalem, in Syria, in Lebanon, Egypt, Iraq, Iran. I took comfort in the fact that they were terrorists, suicide bombers who were sure their actions would propel them to heaven on the ashes of their enemies. Men who organized the bombings of shopping malls and boats, and embassies, or who sheltered and trained those who did.

"It changed nothing. The fighting continued. The dying continued. And I began to wonder if either side was truly right or truly wrong. If God spoke for them, or if they spoke for God, or if in his shame God had turned his back on the whole region, waiting for them to stop fighting. They're fighting for control of the icons of their beliefs, as if to say, 'If I control this, I am right and you are wrong.'

"So you take away what they're fighting over. Take away the symbols. Level the theological playing field. The Dome of the Rock, where they say Mohammed ascended into heaven, and the Wailing Wall, the remaining vestige of the Temple compound, last legacy of Solomon—I'm going to tear them down. I'm going to reach into the very molecules of the stones themselves and explode them from the inside out.

"Then the warring factions will be united in their loss. They will be forced to rebuild together, side by side. If children won't play nice with their toys, you take them away. It'll give these children something to hate besides each other, and a common loss they can mourn together."

"Seems a little extreme," I replied. "You really think this will help?"

"In all these years, I've learned only one thing. People like these respect only strength, only force. I have the strength. I have the force. And I'm going to use them. Furthermore, neither you nor Jason are going to stop me."

Jason, responding to my telepathic call, had landed silently behind us. He'd traveled across the Atlantic in approximately five minutes.

"Howdy, Laurel. Long time, no see," he said, in his patented straight-ahead, all-American tone, as if they'd bumped into one another at the supermarket.

"You may be invulnerable on the outside, Jason," she said, without so much as how-do-you-do, "but on the inside, the carotid artery is as vulnerable in you as it is in mundanes. Do you really want to take that chance?"

Jason looked at me and shrugged. He would take the chance if I wanted him to, and there was a chance that his speed was quicker than Laurel's thoughts.

"Suppose I said there was another way," I said.

"There isn't," she replied.

"But suppose there is. My grandfather used to read to me from Psalms, and Proverbs. In Psalms there's this word he loved a lot: 'Selah.' It means 'pause and consider.' The word's used as a break in a song or a psalm. A pause to think, to absorb what was just said before continuing. A call for reflection.

"Selah, Laurel. Selah."

"Humph," she replied. Immediately. Turning her back and folding her arms in a petulant gesture of defiance. "There's nothing to consider."

"The radical mundanes will hunt you down. They'll kill you."

"I'm not proud of what I've done over these last few years, Jason. I'm tired of living, tired of fighting. This way, at least, my life will have meaning."

"Will it?" I asked. "I said there was another way."

"John—"

"Just hear me out. It's easy to hate when there's no food on your plate, when you suffer from dawn to dusk straight through to the dawn again, when you scrape at the soil, and the ground mocks you. Stop and ease the suffering, and you may achieve the same results. No guarantees, but it's possible."

"And how do we do that?" she asked.

I rose in the air. "Come with me," I said. "They fight for every scrap of land because so little here is livable."

"They fight for more than that. There's religious and—"

"But that's the largest part of it. If there was green, arable land as far as the eye could see, do you think they'd be fighting for a few square miles of land here and there?"

Jason and Laurel followed me, high above the urban sprawl illuminating the desert night.

"Your control over the smallest objects is absolute, Laurel," I said. "Marbles and molecules, a mustard seed or a grain of dirt. Far below the desert, below the sand, maybe a quarter of mile down, maybe further, there is fertile soil. And in the stone desert there is water below ground. Neither does anybody any good because no one can get to it.

"But you can."

"How?" she asked.

"Liquefaction. During an earthquake, loosely compacted soil becomes almost liquid, and anything on top of that soil drops straight through. You could raise the good soil up, grain by grain, and make the dry sand pass it on the way down. Substitute the one for the other. You could do it without disturbing the buildings. You could turn this whole region from a desert into a fertile land."

"Hmmm. Never thought of that," she said. "You'd have to do it for the whole region. Not just Israel. You'd have to do it for Syria, and Lebanon, and Iraq, and Iran and the West Bank and . . ."

"I know."

"Do I have enough power to do that?"

"Yes. I see it in you. You have just that much. But no more. At all." Beat. "Selah."

She flew off. Obviously, I had to leave her alone for a while.

"I think it's safe for you to go now, Jason."

"You sure?" he asked.

"Pretty sure, yeah."

"What did you mean about 'no more at all'?"

I considered telling him. After all, was there a difference between lifting my hand against a fellow Special and letting Laurel go through with the plan I'd planted in her head? I could perceive the deep conflicts inside her, and perceived she might one day go mad, reacting to the guilt she felt over what she had done. Perhaps she would become even more dangerous than Stephanie had been. On one hand, the possible reality of her potential madness was too great a risk to take. But on the other, was a mere possibility a good enough reason? Good enough to justify a pre-emptive psychological strike?

"It's okay, Jason. Leave her to me. It'll be fine."

"All right, if you're sure."

"I am. One thing though. I'm feeling something strange in your energy. Are you all right?"

Jason laughed. "Fine, John. I'm just—I'm just fine. Little head cold, that's all."

"But our kind doesn't *get* colds."

"Yeah. Funny that." He waved, and then disappeared, fading out against the backdrop of stars.

I rejoined Laurel, at her favorite seclusion spot.

"John?"

"Yeah?"

"Do you ever have any regrets? About what you've done, the road you took, the way things went?"

"Some days they're all I have."

"Same here. And you know what? I'm tired of them. Hang onto your socks."

* * *

At that moment, everyone in the Middle East was going about his business. Husbands and wives were cooking dinner, watching satellite TV, praying, and enjoying the company of their families. Some were having intense political discussions. Israeli and Palestinian Cabinet members were having typically unsuccessful, dead-end talks. Soldiers patrolled empty streets, enforcing curfews, while enemies who believed themselves to be freedom fighters were plotting, scheming, building bombs, indoctrinating their youth. The construction of the latest Israeli settlement in the West Bank had halted for the evening. Palestinian civilians were having a hard time relaxing in the calm—the Israeli Prime Minister had threatened to occupy a few different villages, and the Israeli armed forces were always on red alert, ready to spring into action.

A desire for peace might be in the hearts of men, but they could as yet find no way to translate that desire into action. Quite the opposite.

A group of Palestinian freedom fighters threw a bunch of Molotov cocktails at an Israeli army transport vehicle and shouted, "Get them! Israeli, go home! Israeli go home!"

The freedom fighters were unarmed, so they scattered into various alleys and side streets as the Israeli soldiers jumped out of the burning transport vehicle. A few were burned or burning, but their comrades were more interested in firing on their attackers.

"Break left!" shouted an officer. "We'll take the terrorists from both sides!"

It was going to be blood bath, one way or the other. The freedom fighters/terrorists had laid a trap—a couple of bombs waiting to be detonated—deep in one of the alleys. All the fighters had to do was live long enough to lure the soldiers into the trap.

But it happened before anyone else could die. By *it* I mean the earthquake. It was like no earthquake that had ever previously been scientifically recorded. It did not originate miles below the surface. Its rumbling was not a deep, severe sound; it was instead a contralto version of the typical earthquake sound. Furthermore, its force originated near the surface.

The soldiers and the freedom fighters struggled to stay on their feet. The ground was constantly shifting under them. Even the dirt between the cobblestones forming the sidewalks shifted. Liquefied.

All the ground in the village was liquefying.

The process began in a circle and spread out in the fashion of pinwheel. Stones large enough for the combatants to stand on did not remain still, and they had to support one another, lest their feet sank into the ground. The wheels of the burning transport vehicle began sinking as well. Not far, because the ground just below the road was solid enough (though it was fracturing), but far enough for the wounded to panic and scramble.

To where? It wasn't long before these combatants—as well as people everywhere throughout the region—realized there was no place to flee to, nowhere to hide. But their worst fear—that the ground would turn to quicksand under their feet and they would smother to death—was never realized.

Laurel had too much control for that to happen.

Tapping into her inner strength as never before, motivated not only by her tremendous guilt but by the love for all mankind she had never been able to declare, Laurel manipulated millions of tons of earth, moving, sliding dark, rich soil from below, passing the dust of ages on its way down. Alluvial layers of soil, the dust of prophets, mingled with the echo of saurian giants.

Throughout the Middle East, men, women and children watched in wonder as the color of their earth deepened and darkened. Where once there had been only sand that when scooped, fell from the fingers like flour, now there was a moist, slightly malodorous soil that clung to the fingers like mud.

And I wondered: was this what creation was like?

And was it always accompanied by so much pain?

For kneeling in her favorite place of seclusion, Laurel reached deep in her soul and unleashed an unsuspected power that frightened and humbled me. It radiated from her like the heat of a red hot metal coil.

Light and blood seeped from her pores like water flowing from a squeezed sponge. "John . . . John . . . Help me," she pleaded in a hoarse whisper.

"You can stop now, Laurel," I pleaded, for I had come to regret my ploy to push her to sacrifice herself for the good of all mankind. Besides: "You've done it. Look around! You've done it!"

"I can't. I have to finish!" she said. She reached, no, she groped for my hand. "Help me. I can't see. I can't feel anything any more."

Steeling myself against the heat, I took her by the hand. "I'm here! I'm with you! I will always be with you!"

Blood burst from her eyes and nostrils.

Her pain became my pain. I did not suffer physically, but I felt everything she did, and I could not imagine an individual enduring so much and still being able to live. I felt her heart give out inside her, yet still she fought.

She still managed to find a way to give, and to atone. Would that my motives had been as pure.

"Houston," said Colonel Janis Andrews, high above the Earth in the space shuttle Enterprise II, "you would not believe what we're seeing up here. Get a camera going, because it looks like God's sending somebody a special delivery package."

NASA TV was the first to broadcast it, though of course the networks and cable news services picked up on the footage immediately.

For what Laurel was doing was visible even above the Earth: the enriching, the movement of the soil. The creation of a new land.

A miracle, said the farmers on the kibbutz.

A miracle, said the rabbi.

A miracle, said the cleric standing outside the mosque.

A miracle, said John Simon, a.k.a. Poet, as he held the blood-splattered yet bloodless corpse of Laurel Darkraven in his arms.

At that point, I could only wonder if she had succeeded, and if I was the good, moral man I presumed myself to be.

The newscast from CNN that I picked up at dawn gave me some small degree of hope.

The reporter said, "I'm standing in Jerusalem, Wolf, where geologists are still arriving on the scene, trying to unravel this astonishing geological event. Explanations range from a new kind of earthquake to, well, an act of God. It is a blessing beyond all blessing. The land is fertile and rich. It will feed everyone here and their children, and their children's children, for generations to come. It is as if God looked down and chose to give us a symbol that

we are in need of his care, that we all his children. That
the event is a miracle is beyond doubt. That it came to
the Israelis and to the Arabs in equal measure says that
if God acted for both, and if God can act for both, care
for both, then perhaps we can care for one another."

Well, that was what Laurel wanted them to think, but
for once I wished the reporters would give credit where
credit was due. What occurred was indeed a miracle, but
it was a miracle wrought entirely by a daughter of man.

That morning I mourned for Laurel as she lay at the
top of a hill, in a sepulcher upon which I had written, in
Hebrew, the word SELAH.

She had, but I knew now I had not.

The world was changed. The human race had made a
mess of the last 6000 years. Maybe the next 6000 would
be better, because of what she had done.

I laid some flowers on the sepulcher, and then sat down
to watch the dawn.

Jerusalem. The light of a new day was dawning, and I
could only hope the denizens of that ancient city would
recognize it for what it was. After all, it's one thing to
espouse peace as the result of a temporary epiphany, another thing altogether to commit one's self to peace over
the long haul.

Jerusalem. City of a thousand lights and a thousand
swords. A divided city in a divided world. Brought together in an act of sacrifice.

Not the first such act, not the last.

Prophets and wise men and first-born children and
messiahs and tyrants and Romans and Crusaders—blood
spilled across millions of acres for thousands of years.

No wonder the soil turned dry. How many tears, how

much blood, can the land absorb without finally turning away in shame and sorrow?

There will still be tears, and still be blood, because this was Jerusalem.

But now there was a new soil, new hope, and a new start. A miracle to share, not to argue over—a newly minted covenant written in a billion grains of soil.

Purchased this time with Laurel's blood, Laurel's tears, Laurel's heart.

Their miracle.

Selah. I prayed the people of this land would consider the implications of that heart, and take it into their own hearts.

And then I walked away. My job here, for better or for worse, was done.

Selah.

TO BE CONCLUDED . . .